Garden of Hope

Jo Piazza O'Mara

REDEMPTION
PRESS

Published by Redemption Press, PO Box 427, Enumclaw, WA 98022
Toll Free (844) 2REDEEM (273-3336)

Redemption Press is honored to present this title in partnership with the author. The views expressed or implied in this work are those of the author. Redemption Press provides our imprint seal representing design excellence, creative content and high quality production.

Scripture quotations marked ESV are taken from *The Holy Bible: English Standard Version*, copyright © 2001, Wheaton: Good News Publishers. Used by permission. All rights reserved.

Scripture quotations marked NLT are taken from the *Holy Bible, New Living Translation*, copyright 1996. Used by permission of Tyndale House Publishers, Inc., Wheaton, Illinois 60189. All rights reserved.

ISBN 13: 978-1-63232-838-0 (Print)
         978-1-63232-839-7 (ePub)
         978-1-63232-840-3 (Mobi)

Library of Congress Catalog Card Number: 2014950238

Chapter 1

"Come on, come on, answer the phone," I impatiently commanded my brother. "Just pick up the stinking phone!" My frustration level, not to mention anger, was becoming more difficult to control with every failed attempt to connect with my older brother.

Suddenly, like a cat stalking its prey, my husband appeared out of nowhere; verbally pouncing on me. *Caught in the act!*

"Trina!" he reprimanded me, "exactly how many times have you dialed Joey's number today, huh?"

I found myself responding to him with my Cheshire cat grin and a weak shrug of my shoulders.

"Sweetheart, did it ever occur to you they may be out of town?" Sal asked, now a bit mellower.

Bah, now he's attempting to placate me; that's so annoying, I thought to myself.

"Sal, I just don't understand why he won't respond to me on Christmas of all days. I never would have predicted he'd grow to be such a knucklehead!" Sarcastically, I complied, "Okay, okay, watch me. See … I'm putting down the phone. Are you satisfied? And … furthermore … I promise not pick it up again. Well, at least not today," I sweetly smiled.

"That's my girl," Sal chuckled.

Slinking away, my grey matter was running a marathon. *So, that's that? Big brother Joey doesn't give two hoots about me?* Settling into my favorite fireside chair, I wrestled with the reality of that concept. No, I could not, would not, swallow that bitter pill. I refused to wrap my brain around the ugly fact that we had grown apart.

But then, it's not just me; he's shunning our entire family.

Gazing out my frosty windows, I was immediately mesmerized by my frequent visitor, a beautiful male cardinal. There he sat: vibrant red feathers, black mask, and distinctive head crest lending a certain mystique to this my favorite of all birds. He was proudly perched on a low, snow covered branch, oblivious to the fresh swirling snow.

Oh to be similarly impervious to issues swirling around me! Never going to happen; that is just not who I am.

After a few calming moments, I promised myself it was time to enjoy this special day and put aside the whole "Joey business."

My daydreaming was rudely interrupted by the sounds of Sal opening and closing doors. He was already loading gifts into the car, which was my cue to get ready. *What to wear? What to wear?*

Catching my dresser mirror reflection jolted me out of my pity party. My childlike image hopping around my bedroom, one shoe on and one shoe off, sparked a giggle. That same reflected image was so familiar and reminiscent of my childhood days. Even back then, an elusive shoe or sock pitted me against my enemy, the ever ticking clock. Hopping around my bedroom, feverishly racing against either my church or school clock, was an all too common occurrence. Some habits die hard.

Silently upbraiding myself, I questioned for the gazillionth time why the heck I continue to be late. I'm a grown woman—a professional grown woman for goodness sake.

The answer is simple: Trina, you're late because you can never find your other shoe, and it is definitely not cool to run out the door shoeless. Humph!

The missing shoe can often be found keeping company with the dust bunnies under a bed. Then again, it could be growing mold somewhere in the depths of the laundry basket … last week's laundry.

Okay, New Year's Resolution #1: get organized!

The sobering truth is I'd never be late if my shoes were organized in an orderly system like Angie's. Visualizing her closet, I estimate seventy-five pair of shoes, lined up uniformly like little soldiers just waiting for orders from her dainty feet.

Ah well, guess my sister got the *neat gene.*

A while later, my husband pleaded from the front foyer, "Trina, are you ever going to be ready?"

"Okay, okay, I'm ready," I shouted as I hurried down the steps. "See, both shoes on, makeup on." I am so ready for our Christmas Day celebration with my family and friends. "Sal, how do I look?"

"Trina, you look like a Christmas angel, and I will admit you're worth the wait," he said as he good naturedly nuzzled my neck.

"Thank you. You always know the right thing to say … well most of the time," I offered with a smile.

"You'd better trade those pretty shoes for your boots; it's really coming down out there."

At forty-three, Sal is still the handsome, loving guy I married fresh out of college. He's as steady as a rock, and I cherish every precious minute we've shared together. Admittedly, it hasn't been a bed of roses for us. Yes, we have a committed love, but even that love has been sorely tested when so many new lives began with such excitement and hope. Yet each one ended with my heartbreak and empty arms. From the day he tenderly placed that ring on my finger, we dreamed and planned for a house full of children.

It seems that just wasn't to be. But we have each other and we have Buddy, our vivacious golden retriever. He is the best companion and truest four-legged friend a girl could have.

"By the way, did you let Buddy out?" I asked.

"Yup, he's ready for a cozy day on the heating vent," Sal smiled that easy smile, as we scooted out the door and into the blowing snow.

The familiar drive to my mama and daddy's home is somehow therapeutic for me, maybe even soothing. The snow and wind are wildly gusting around us, and I cannot help but compare it to a giant pillow fight, stuffing everywhere. What's new, after all it is Christmas Day in New England? So far this year, the snowfall has been extremely heavy; more than a few times I pretend we're living in a snow globe. *Beautiful!*

The never-ending display of festive lights and decorated homes is nothing short of dazzling; no other place on earth could ever satisfy me. Every street Sal turned into boasted another beautifully quaint Norman Rockwell scene.

Living in New England is not for the faint of heart, but its beauty grows more breathtaking with each changing season. I have never minded the blizzards or the nor'easters that blow in causing so many folks to grumble. It's not like moaning or groaning will change it. *Just enjoy its beauty and stay off the roads and out of the path of those monster plows.*

As children, Angie, Joey, and I would be glued to the local radio stations on any given snowy morning, waiting to hear the no-school announcement. Within seconds of hearing our school name, we'd spontaneously break into a happy dance. Mama laughed and laughed, watching us scramble to get into our snow suits. We had important business to tend to on those very snowy days. After all, there were snow angels to be made and snowmen to be artistically created. Once outside, no power on earth could drag us back inside, save Mama's promise of hot cocoa and cinnamon toast or freshly baked cookies.

Gazing through snow crystals on the car window, my mind transported me back to the time Joey and I made a humongous snowman, and that snowman desperately needed clothing. Poor

Angie, being the youngest, always got a raw deal because she was so easily manipulated into doing our dirty deeds. At our sober urging, we convinced her to secretly confiscate Daddy's scarf, jacket, and hat. *How could we possibly know she would steal his Sunday best overcoat, new scarf, and hat?*

Remembering brings a smile to my face, but we paid dearly for that one.

What winter time fun we had, breathlessly giggling as we chased and pelted one another with snow balls. Life was so carefree then. Never did we Agosti children guess how the complexities of our lives would evolve.

Shortly after Sal and I married, we found a modest split-level in the suburbs. I loved my hometown, Lawrence, Massachusetts, yet those newer houses in the suburbs held such appeal. Many other younger families flooded the suburbs during those years as well; the area was growing.

I am still proud to have been reared in Lawrence especially knowing its rich history. In the early 1900s Lawrence and sister city Lowell were known around the world for their sprawling textile mills that were built along the banks of the Merrimac River. In those days, immigrants poured into the city seeking work and the American dream. It was truly a melting pot of ethnicity. The Irish, Polish, German, as well as my Italian ancestors were just a few who came and worked in filthy, dangerous conditions hoping against hope to feed their families and succeed in this new country.

As a youngster and voracious reader, I learned about those poor, yet determined mill town inhabitants. I often reminded myself then and now, we are blessed and in reality have no inkling how hard our ancestors worked; back breaking labor and dangerous work took many lives prematurely.

One particular story of a young girl who worked in one of those mills will stay in my memory until my final days. For weeks after hearing her plight, I had nightmares. Apparently her long hair was somehow caught and pulled into one of those monster weaving machines, in essence scalping her. I still shiver thinking about her; she was just a child.

Even tragedy couldn't best these brave immigrants. Their pioneering spirit laid the foundation that became the platform for so many others to build upon, including many of my own loved ones. I'm proud to be of their heritage.

Immigrant City, as it was called, could not have flourished if not for those courageous immigrants. They were the key to its success!

Neither Sal nor I ever had the desire to geographically separate ourselves from family, so fortunately our drive is relatively short. I cannot hide my smile as we pull into my parents' driveway. Daddy has not changed a single Christmas decoration in over ten years and since he handles each piece with loving care, I anticipate seeing them for another ten years. Even after all my teasing to add something fresh and new, I have to agree with his style. It is simple and tastefully decorated, and Daddy continues to make this home warm and inviting.

"Sal and Trina are here!" my sister excitedly yelled to the whole family as we made our grand entrance through the mud room. Today, however, it could more accurately be described as a snow cave; boots, hats, and coats were piled high against the windows, blocking any natural light. Stepping into Mama's kitchen is like stepping into the pages of my treasured old story books. Christmas music is softly playing in the background, and the tantalizing aroma of simmering spaghetti sauce tickles my salivary glands. Most importantly, the family I love is gathered in this place called home, almost all of them.

Our parents' home has always been an oasis for their children and anyone else I might add. At Christmastime, however, they go over and above, never failing to create special and enduring memories for each one of us.

Everyone descended upon us offering to help carry those mysterious Christmas packages and my specialty—antipasto. My contribution to our family feasts is almost always antipasto. Lawrence has no shortage of Italian markets, and I need no coaxing to roam the old world shops. My self-imposed mission is to gather up the best quality provolone cheese, Genoa salami, capicola ham, roasted red peppers, and a selection of every imaginable cured olive I can find. A mouth-watering antipasto is the happy result of my in-town excursions. Experience has taught me well. I must guard this mouthwatering masterpiece as one would an endangered species, at least until dinner, or this gang will pick it down to the romaine lettuce long before it's placed on Mama's pretty Christmas table.

Hugging, kissing, laughing, and teasing are the everyday norm with this crew, but this magical season brings extra joy and levity to the Agosti household, if that is even possible.

"Oh Mama, you made braciole and raviolis!" I exclaimed hugging my dear Mama. "You know I could have carved out a chunk of time to help you," I firmly stated as she dismissively brushed me off. We're all keenly aware that she enjoys the prep as much as the serving and the eating of these delicacies for which she's well known. She would never dream of parting from Christmas Day tradition by preparing anything other than her delicious cheese raviolis. Christmas Eve may boast the tradition of serving seven fishes, but these wonderful pillows are strictly reserved for Christmas Day. She learned the art of pasta making at her mother's side and as an adult, has lovingly perfected that skill.

My niece, Mia, wrapped me in a hug and whispered, "She made cannolis that are to die for."

Who makes cannolis when there are so many wonderful Italian bakeries in the neighborhood? Mama! And none of us would be foolish enough to dissuade her from using her skills to create these scrumptious delights.

New Year's Resolution #2: lose ten pounds.

But I would not think about calories today, not with this amazing selection of once a year succulent dishes.

A sweet, joyful spirit permeated our gathering as we girls set the table and puttered in the kitchen. It didn't take us long to settle into our normal groove, inquiring about jobs and family life. Well, that is to say, when *they* talk about jobs. I never get much beyond a vague overview of one or two of my cases. Rehashing what I purpose to leave behind every day at five o'clock is just too emotionally painful.

Since childhood my career path was crystal clear to me. I was unwavering, never wanting to be anything but a social worker. While my work usually gave me immense gratification, there were countless cases that clawed at my insides. Witnessing abuse or neglect of small children, when Sal and I ached for one of our own, was almost unbearable. Sadly, my biological clock reminds me that at forty-three, it's just not in my cards. Four miscarriages accompanied by buckets of tears have closed that chapter of my life. Now, I pray for grace and strength with every difficult case that comes across my desk.

More and more frequently however, I am suppressing an urge to scream at the top of my lungs, there are so many parents out there who have proven themselves unfit. Marching across my mind's eye is an endless parade of endangered babies and toddlers. The stories of those children will generate mounds and mounds of paperwork; files too numerous to count will require many home visits. Yet, the sad reality is that many eventually were or will be returned to those unstable homes. And so, I share little of my job.

As usual, my sister steps into the spotlight, everyone listening with rapt attention. "Some days I'm oh so tempted to do bodily harm to those little rug rats," Angie joked. But truly she is the best of the best teachers and is adored by her students. Who wouldn't love her? She's beautiful, has an amazing sense of humor, and simply loves life and everyone in it.

Angie is only two years younger than I, so I have enjoyed a front row seat, watching her as she's floated through life. We look a lot alike, olive skin and dark, thick hair, although she is shorter and still quite athletically built. Our temperaments, however, are polar opposites. She is the eternal optimist, never seeming to have one problem or care in her world. I liken her world to a well-constructed cocoon, protecting her from everything harmful or ugly. I truly have never met anyone so kind, thoughtful, or just plain happy.

I, on the other hand, worry and brood over any and every tiny little thing. It's been said by my family that I will create a worry event if there is no authentic worry event with which to struggle.

Humph, with friends like that ...

I don't have an excessive display of grey hair yet, but I'm convinced what I do have, I have worried into existence.

Angie continued to ramble on ...

She should have been in the theatre.

She reenacted her most recent parent-teacher conference and mimicked an unidentified parent's response to their child's progress. Laughing, she described one mother sporting the familiar "deer in the headlights glazed-over look" when she was offered a few simple suggestions for improvements that could easily be accomplished at home.

Indignantly, mommy responded, "Why would you say that? My child needs no improvement in that area," Ange chortled, "Yup. I have nothing but perfect students! Not one has the slightest need for improvement whatsoever! Just like with me, right Mama!" she laughed turning her attention to our mom, whose nod was almost imperceptible.

Mia, Angie's sixteen-year-old daughter, then took the spotlight, ranting on and on in unending chatter about her ex-boyfriend. "Jerk!" she firmly ended. Sal and I smiled, but couldn't begin to imagine what that poor boy did to earn that title. We have a well-guarded secret theory about our niece. Simply put, that girl loves the hunt; once caught she drops the boy like a cat drops a dead mouse. The unspoken message being, fun is over—I'm moving on. Her cheeks flushed as she described, ad nauseam, a new possibility. I don't know this boy's name, but I have a distinct feeling he is her new mouse.

An often replayed scene caught my attention; I smiled at the guys holding their drinks while roasting their backsides by the fireplace. Sal and Angie's husband, Jake, refrain from anything remotely resembling personal dialogue. No touchy-feely stuff for these macho men. For them the sacred and I might add only topics, are limited to the Red Sox, the Celtics, and the Patriots.

Is there anything else on God's green earth (or white today) to talk about?

They have become the best of buddies over the years and would do anything to help each other out, unless it interferes with a sacred game.

My Sal has been an accountant since college graduation and somehow still loves the numbers game. Jake, a high school history teacher, is motivated a whole lot more by the after school coaching than the classroom. "Hey, I'm still trying to get tickets for the Celtics game next month. You still in?" Jake excitedly blurted out.

"Are ya kidding? Of course. Just give me a yell," Sal responded. They are two happy campers, grinning at each other like dunderheads.

Kevin, Angie's Boston College-bound eighteen-year-old son, wandered into the living room, munching on a stalk of fennel (Italian celery). *Stolen from my antipasto platter no doubt.*

This kid is also a sports fanatic but for today, he seemed content to simply listen. Kevin is smart as a whip and has always impressed me as a rather deep thinker given his youth. On occasion, his inability to solve the world's problems causes him to become somewhat sullen. He's so the opposite of Angie. He has grown to be quite a handsome young man, and I seriously doubt he has any shortage of female admirers. For a brief period of time, Sal and I had our doubts that Kevin would find his own way. He had a very brief brush with the local police, but thank God it was only kid stuff, and he quickly got his act together. He obviously caught hold of a vision for his future—a vision that did not include striped pajamas! His determination to earn a degree is admirable, and he certainly has what it takes to succeed, although he's yet to decide on a major.

Jake continues to reassure his son he has plenty of time to make that decision. No pressure.

"Hey, I'm starving here," Kevin tried to interject into the buzz of conversation, thinking dinner had been forgotten. Smiling, we all responded in unison, "What's new?"

"Hang in there," I reassured Kevin, "dinner is almost ready, so don't order out for pizza just yet."

"Funny, Aunt Trina. Very funny!"

The proverbial elephant in the room unexpectedly reared its ugly head. My husband innocently and all too loudly asked, "So, what was Joey's reason for not joining our Christmas dinner this year?"

Oh no! I didn't want to hear that!

Everyone momentarily froze, and I sensed the immediate change that just occurred; the thermometer plummeted. Mama's head quickly went down as she busied herself with folding napkins. Daddy made a fifty-yard dash toward the mud room, God only knows for what reason. No one attempted to answer Sal's question as it fell like an anvil in the middle of the kitchen.

"Sorry," Sal sheepishly whispered, "I did it again! I wasn't thinking." We have no clue why Joey has chosen to avoid the family gatherings he once relished. Heck, he just plain avoids the entire family, despite our individual efforts to approach the subject. There is a gaping hole in our family, and I would forfeit a million bucks (if I had it) to know why my only brother has turned his back on our family.

Everyone, including the youngsters, remained silent; the atmosphere had certainly soured.

I refuse to let my absent brother hijack our Christmas celebration.

In an effort coax the Christmas spirit back into our gathering, I awkwardly changed the subject, asking, "So Mama, how was the Christmas Eve service at your church?" Haltingly, she answered that it was quite lovely.

Okay, she's talking so we're back on track, I think.

Jumping in with both feet, I added, "Our service was just wonderful, and I am thankful our leadership decided not to go ahead with a live nativity," I stated. "We had enough trouble with the live kids in the play let alone any contrarian donkeys!" Mama gave an obligatory grin.

A few minutes passed, and I looked up to see Daddy reentering the dining room. *Serious face, but at least he is back with the family. All is well for now. Crisis averted!*

"Hey Daddy, I was talking to Donna the other day, and she said she saw you at the post office last Monday," I casually mentioned, attempting to keep things light.

"Huh, Donna who?" he stammered.

"What do you mean Donna who? Did you two talk?" I inquired.

"I don't remember talking to her, but yes I think I saw her."

I sent a curious glance to my sister.

Yup, that was odd if not rather elusive. Either he saw her or he didn't see her.

Daddy has known Donna for more years than I can count; she has spent as much time at our house as her own home. She's been my best, best friend since grade school. Suddenly, Daddy bolted in the direction of the cellar, calling over his shoulder, "I'll get some nice wine for dinner."

I was perplexed and even a bit concerned at his response as well as his evasive move away from the family gathering. But I decided to let it drop, for the time being.

For the most part, Daddy is a passive guy, but on a few rare occasions I have witnessed his hot Sicilian temper. Joey used to joke, "When you see the steam coming out of his ears … run for cover." But in reality, those explosions were uncommon in our home. He is the typical Italian husband and father; he loves his family with-out question and is respected as the head of the household. His authority was never questioned, always honored.

Over the years, our dad endured lots of good-natured teasing. He was labeled the "odd man out" of the family. The reason being, every single one of us has olive complexion, dark hair, and dark eyes. Joey's eyes are almost black as coal.

Oh, but not Daddy! He has the most arresting eyes. Once you look into those emerald green eyes, I guarantee you will never forget them. They are green, green, green and so beautifully distinctive that it's possible to get lost in them with just a casual glance.

To this day, Mama finds great satisfaction in tormenting him by divulging to us stories of their youth. Apparently, much to his embarrassment, love-sick girls followed him everywhere attempting to capture his attention. She said he was continually being stalked by dreamy-eyed girls and harassed with statements like, "It's not fair that a man should possess such beautiful eyes and eyelashes when most girls would kill for those green eyes."

Time after time he endured her cajoling, always seeming un-comfortable and then finally ending it with, "Ah, you can tease all you want, but this man only has eyes for your mama."

While waiting for Christmas dinner to be served, I found my-self studying Mama as she moved about her kitchen. She is still a beautiful, graceful woman, and no one would disagree that she possesses a much envied gentle and quiet spirit.

She never maintained a career outside the home after marriage, but her hands were never idle. As a teenager, I was completely and utterly spellbound watching her sew our beautiful prom gowns. What a gift she had for creating stunning and stylish dresses for Angie and me. My friends, especially Donna, were actually jealous of my wardrobe. Sadly, like many children I didn't see the value right before my eyes. I took the love each stitch represented for granted.

My mother, tall for a Sicilian, was just beginning to show her sixty-six years. Her striking features, a silky smooth face and just a little silver streaking through her dark, thick hair, displayed outwardly an elegance and grace she possessed inwardly.

This woman, Maria Fantino became the bride of Vincent Agosti in 1952. She was twenty-one at the time, fairly old for her old world tradition. She had only one sibling, Connie, who was four years younger and constantly craved my mother's time and attention. As a social worker, I would describe Connie as … just plain needy and a bit self-absorbed. She was only thirty years old when she lost a long battle with pneumonia. My mother often mentions how she yearns for her only sister's company. Despite the fact that I truly loved my aunt, her passing brought me great relief for which I am secretly niggled with guilt to this very day.

I resented how Aunt Connie sucked the life out of Mama. Not surprisingly, my mother never once complained to her family or anyone else for that matter. It was as natural as breathing to unselfishly yield to Aunt Connie's demands. It's just what she did, no reservations.

Daddy reluctantly agreed to postpone their wedding for eighteen months; once again Mama accepted the responsibility of caring for her ailing sister. Connie, though beautiful, was frail and sickly; a myriad of childhood diseases compromised her immune system. Mama recounts with gratitude that her sister regained some physical strength, enough that wedding plans could resume, and Aunt Connie was able to stand with Mama as maid of honor.

She rarely dated and never married, but she did become assimilated into our family unit. Regardless of the fact that Mama now had three demanding children, undercurrents of competition could not be ignored. She wanted Mama all for herself. Despite her self-centered personality, Aunt Connie was good to her nieces and nephew, showering us with goodies and trinkets our parents couldn't afford.

Despite all of that, sweet memories of Mama and Aunt Connie strolling arm in arm through downtown Lawrence suddenly washed over me, and it warmed me. As a child, walking on Essex Street was an adventure, and neither Angie nor I ever turned down the opportunity to accompany them. A wonderful family five and dime store, as they were called, prized itself as one of the few remaining soda fountains. Of course Angie and I nagged until they consented to suspend their shopping for the day to treat us at that ice cream counter. Without fail, I ordered a strawberry ice cream soda and if I closed my eyes right now, I could still taste those luscious strawberries floating in their icy cold liquid. Angie was just as predictable, but her weakness was hot fudge sundaes, a particular preference that remains to this day. One of our long-standing traditions was being treated at the soda fountain on the last day of school (if we were promoted to the next grade, which we always were). Joey dug in his heels, refusing to go with us since the allure of the baseball field was much stronger.

My wanderings down memory lane continued as my thoughts turned to summer days spent at the common, a New England term for the local park. The common held an irresistible magnetic pull for every kid in town as we daily gathered for endless fun. The bandstand, which proudly graced the center of the park, was brightly painted in primary colors. High school band concerts, summer youth camps, and numerous other community events found their niche there. Fourth of July celebrations, which also took place in the common, were eagerly anticipated and talked about for weeks in advance. All these years later, I'm still unsure how parents managed to retrieve their children during those chaotic picnics. Kids could be seen running with wild abandon all over the park as though orphaned. As we grew to be teenagers, yes, we paired off, sneaking away toward the overgrown bushes for stolen kisses.

As I think back, it was not uncommon for younger children to continue riding their bikes until dusk and occasionally after dark.

Parents' level of trust had not yet been violated by horrific headlines. We played until we dropped from hunger or exhaustion, whichever came first. Every kid on the block heard the familiar mantra from their parents again and again, "You'd better get home when the street lights come on." Then and only then did we surrender to the end of that particular summer day. The next morning promised its own mystery and adventure; we awoke ready and willing to grab hold of that new day and squeeze out every fun filled minute.

The city of Lawrence was so different in the days of my youth, "before dinosaurs roamed the earth" as my nephews so often joked. The truth of the matter is, for the most part, it was safe to walk all over town, day and night, without encountering any problems. It saddens me to think of such innocence lost over these past decades. People seemed … nicer and definitely demonstrated concern for their neighbors' welfare. Over the past few years the crime rate has steadily soared.

My home town has changed, and I don't think it's for the better.

Angie's shrill voice snapped me out of my private meandering down memory lane, yelling "Dinner is served!"

"All right!" Kevin shouted back at her with gusto.

You would think from the way we rushed to our seats that gold was being thrown down from a balcony. But it's always been that way—the Agosti signature. This family loves to make and eat food, but it's so much more than that. We genuinely enjoy getting together around the table simply to share our lives with one another.

Someone, probably Leah, Angie's youngest daughter, had made adorable place cards with snowmen and snowflakes drawn on each corner. There is no denying she has an artistic bent and never fails to show off her latest creation.

Daddy happily whistled while pouring wine for the adults. Mia clumsily poured soda for the younger set. My antipasto had already been showcased in the center of the dining table. Several delectable pieces had gone missing, but miracle of miracles, it is mostly intact.

Chairs scraped the floor and a melodic hum filled the room as we blended together on another beautiful Christmas Day.

At eleven years old, Leah is Angie and Jake's most precocious child. She could not stop giggling as she jabbed and tormented Mia. Although she is absolutely adorable, her perpetual motion can be really hard to take at times. Judging from Mia's demeanor, I'd say she's had just about enough of her younger sister.

"Cut it out Leah," Mia shrieked. "You're being a pain again!"

"Settle down girls," Mama firmly commanded, "it is time for the blessing."

All eyes turned toward Daddy and as though perfectly choreographed, heads bowed while he gave thanks. He praised our Lord for the gift of His Son, Jesus and for another Christmas together.

Everyone agreed with the prayer and the sense of missing Joey's brood with a slightly melancholy, amen. *I just wish Joey and his family were here to be part of the joy.*

My brother and his family faded into the rear view and as we raised our heads from prayer, it was a near free-for-all! First, the antipasto was passed along with my special vinaigrette, which is my secret recipe. Angie joked that I would only reveal it if and only if I was to be slowly and methodically tortured.

She's probably right.

Next, warm, yeasty bread from my favorite Italian bakery gets passed along. *Yum, I could park right here and feel like I'd died and gone to heaven, it is so luscious! Is there anything better than warm Italian bread with Italian dipping oil?*

I have descended from a lineage of serious eaters, and we all know how to pace ourselves. After the familiar symphony of "umms" is heard from around the table, the braciole and raviolis move into the spotlight. They look perfect enough to have jumped from the cover of an Italian cookbook. Suddenly, the dining room goes just about silent as we simultaneously begin to eat, or maybe devour would be a more accurate description.

A few minutes into the raviolis, my husband, brother-in-law, and nephew in practiced unison, stood to attention and rendered a dramatic salute to Mama for her culinary accomplishments. She laughed bashfully and brushed them away with a hand gesture as though doing a backward wave. Laughter filled that dining room once again, as it has on so many Christmases past.

I hesitate to insinuate the Agosti family lacks table manners, but at meals like this one, it is every man for himself. Another appropriate saying would be, those who hesitate are lost (and won't get a full plate). We ate until our hearts and tummies were content.

Our family gatherings usually generate light-hearted conversation, but occasionally it can become politically charged, and today is no exception. The emotional temperatures rise around the dining room table as we become animated, if not somewhat opinionated. Yet, it all ends as it began. No one has been convinced of the others' point of view, and so we cease and desist.

When finished, we gals cleared away the dishes and happily headed for the kitchen to make room for the next onslaught of goodies. Bowls filled with fruit, nuts, and torrone candy were placed on the dining room table to "hold" us until dessert. Torrone has always been one of my weaknesses, and I somehow always find room for several pieces of the rich nougat candy!

"Mama, I invited Donna and her family to stop by later for dessert," I casually announced. No surprise there since Donna's crew and my family have been sharing Christmas for years.

"It will be good to see her," Angie responded. "I think it was early autumn since we last visited. Do her kids still demolish a twenty-by-twenty path wherever they go?"

"Slight exaggeration Ange, but I agree they can be rather rambunctious, especially Suzanne."

"Ya think?" Angie joked back then whispered, "Maybe we can clarify the mystery encounter, or whatever that was."

It didn't take very long before the kitchen was cleaned up and back into some semblance of order. I snickered to myself, noticing that more than one of us was fumbling to loosen their belt, as we collectively slipped into our familiar food coma. Too much of a good thing prevented us from shoveling in dessert just yet.

Until then, we headed to various parts of the old homestead for a brief reprieve. This old Cape Cod-style home affords lots of nooks and crannies in which to nestle. I loved growing up in this house. It is just as charming and cozy as a home can be, especially when a roaring fire is lulling us into la la land.

I claimed my favorite spot, the window seat, and wasted no time curling up, purring like a kitten. I mentally began reminiscing over just a few of the many wonderful memories created in this place. I recalled more than one attempt to slide down the full length of the banister, which didn't end well for me or Joey; the local hospital's emergency room workers were soon on a first name basis with my mother.

I will never forget the variety of hidden treasures all three of us kids secretly stashed in the bookcases under the dormers in Joey's bedroom. Most were fine, harmless in fact. But, not one member of this family will ever forget that foul, and I mean foul, odor that couldn't help but give away one of Joey's treasures. Fresh frogs legs are indeed wonderful in a fancy French restaurant, but dead ones … oh no … not good … not good at all. I felt somewhat vindicated when I caught Mama and Daddy attempting to hide their snickering behind pseudo-stern faces, all the while making Joey and me scrub the entire bookcase with some strong-smelling disinfectant. Even today, if I catch a whiff of that same detergent, I instantly imagine myself crouched before that bookcase, scrubbing my little hands to the bone.

Then there was the year when Mom and Dad apparently hit a financial rough spot, which prompted them to put our beloved house on the market. We, of course had no clue they were in such dire straits; they kept those things to themselves. Our only focus, selfish as it was, was that our world would implode if forced to leave behind our friends and neighborhood.

Oh what little imps we were and what evil plans we devised! Whenever we'd become aware of an upcoming tour by a prospective buyer we'd put our devilish scheme into action. Unsuspecting prospective buyers were greeted by a snake or some kind of rodent in our basement or crawl space. Joey kept a stash of wiggly creatures hidden behind the garage, feeding and tending to them until just the right moment.

Needless to say, we got through that rough spot, never having to pack a box or suitcase. We never 'fessed up to it, but to this day I wonder if Mama or Daddy knew what wicked pranks we pulled. Thankfully, the house did not stay on the market for long, and our family survived our temporary crisis.

Yes … it's been a wonderful homestead, filled with laughter and love.

The harmony of soft snoring was abruptly interrupted by Mama's gentle voice, "What do you all think about exchanging gifts before the LeBlancs get here?" We sleepily agreed and fought to clear the cob webs and shake loose from our individual food comas.

"Yeah, yeah," Leah shouted, jumping up and down, exhibiting more energy than any one person should be allowed to possess.

And so, we robotically assumed our gift-opening positions. Over the years each person had fallen into claiming their favorite place to sit where they witnessed our exchange of gifts. It reminds me of Sunday morning church service and the imaginary reserved signs on each chair. God forbid a newcomer doesn't recognize the warning, invisible as it may be, and has the audacity to claim one of those reserved chairs.

Ecstatically giggling, Leah began handing out each treasure to the appropriate recipient. Her excitement was palpable. Another one of our unwritten traditions dictates we open one gift at a time, youngest to oldest, slow and painful as it may be. More than once, this tradition nearly bit the dust, yet somehow it has survived another year. I guess it's because deep down, every person is anxious to see the expression on their recipient's face. Seeing the smiles and hearing, "It's just what I wanted" makes it worth the wait.

Some gifts are that special something that took forever to find. Other gifts lack imagination, such as ties or cash, but all are given with love and received with appreciation.

After bagging all the discarded wrappings and setting the living room back in order, I wandered to the front window to watch the swirling snow. The snow was still falling heavily, and I began to wonder if Donna and her family would venture out on the roads.

Ah! She was raised in New England. A little snow is just another bump in her day. If anyone has the pioneer spirit, it's Donna.

"Hey, which of you strong, hardy men would like to shovel the sidewalk before company arrives?" I inquired, clearly appealing to their manliness. "You can work off the raviolis while making room for desserts at the same time."

"Honey, you sure have a way with words," Sal laughed.

"Yeah, the power of persuasion is more like it," Jake said. But then Jake and Kevin stood and began a slow shuffle toward the front door.

"You guys are *all right* in my book, and I am only too happy to sweep the front steps," I loudly teased. "I could use some fresh air not to mention some exercise."

Kevin gave me that sarcastic grin of his and said, "You'll need a lot more than a broom, Aunt Trina. Have you looked outside lately?"

"Okay then, hand me one of those shovels when you guys are done. I'd be happy to shovel the steps."

While the boys were in the process of clearing the driveway (and the steps, I might add) in marched Donna and her family looking like Eskimos, living proof that the LeBlanc family are no wimps.

"What did you bring, what did you bring?" Leah excitedly shouted as she yanked the bakery shop dessert boxes from Donna. Another round of hugging, laughing, and teasing erupted before we all settled back into the dining room. I watched Donna pinching Leah and whispering that she brought tiramisu and lemon tarts.

"What's a teeny masue?" she whispered back.

"No honey, it's tiramisu. Just wait and see, you'll love it," Donna replied. By now the whispering had grown so loud everyone easily overheard, triggering another volley of laughter.

Donna's husband, Pete, settled in with the guys, and of course Suzanne and Frankie were looking for something to do other than be with the boring grownups. Donna and her husband waited to start a family, but now Donna often laments that her more "mature" energy levels are just not keeping pace with her children. Yup, it was easy to see they were still energetic and overly rambunctious, but it's a short visit so our family would gut it out as usual. As a couple, however, they are totally oblivious that they are responsible for two very busy children. They sort of abandon those parental responsibilities, leaving the rug rats to whoever is unlucky enough to occupy the same room.

Donna and I tried to catch up with the happenings in each other's lives as we sat together in the middle of a whirlwind of perpetual activity. I inquired how their house construction and remodeling was going, but the cross-current of conversation made it almost impossible to follow any train of thought.

"I give up!" I said, throwing my hands up in surrender. These crazy people left us no choice but to abandon our conversation until later. "Is anyone ready for coffee?" I yelled in frustration, to the oblivious gang.

"Finally!" Kevin yelled. "I'm ready to scarf down those desserts sitting out there."

"What's new?" We all responded, yet again in unison. Normally, he takes our jabs good naturedly but surprisingly this time, we were met with a scowl.

As each of us filled our plates with generous samples of every dessert, which has also become tradition, Donna addressed my dad, "Hey Mr. Agosti, it was nice to see you the other day. I could not believe how busy that post office was, could you?" Angie and I shot glances at my dad waiting for his response. None!

"Daddy, did you hear Donna?" I gently chided. "She asked you a question."

"Yes, yes it was busy, but I just had to mail something; I wasn't there very long. Can I get anyone a glass of amaretto? It's nice with dessert," he said, then quickly scurried to the kitchen. He successfully changed the subject, yet again.

What was that interaction all about? I looked up to my sister in time to catch her raise that expressive eyebrow. We have always communicated in that way, with just that certain look. For the time being neither of us pressed. Everyone's attention was captured by the variety of decadent desserts and mellow conversation.

Now's not the time or the place.

The kids were glued to the television, laughing hysterically as *A Christmas Story* once again numbed their brains. *How many times can anyone watch poor little Ralphie lusting for that 200 shot, range model air rifle? "You'll shoot your eye out! You'll shoot your eye out!" Enough already! At least they're not trashing the living room.*

My best friend was wise enough to talk around the obvious missing sibling. Donna is like a sister to me and has helped me survive every crisis in my life, from sibling rivalry to multiple miscarriages. With her youthful freckled face and never ending positive attitude, she repeatedly encourages me to be patient with Joey, knowing him as well as her own family. All throughout our early teen years, Donna had a wild crush on Joey. He, however, seemed oblivious to her flirting. But for now, this day, we were all talked out on that subject.

After scraping and shoveling out their cars, Donna and her family headed home, leaving the rest of us to begin the process of retrieving our dishes and gifts. It's not hard to read the signs: the kids were getting restless and Mama looked exhausted. The guys' conversation had declined into a series of grunts and monosyllabic comments. It was clearly getting close to putting the final bow on another Christmas Day and a fine one at that.

But as always, the women ended the day chatting at the kitchen table. "Mama, you look exceptionally tired tonight," I said. "Are you okay?" I know my mom, and the silence that hung between us told me that she was *not* okay. "I hope these gatherings are not getting to be too much for you," I seriously asked. "Next year, let's celebrate Christmas at my house, Mama." Of course, I already knew she would have none of that. Still silence.

"Mama, what is going on?" Angie pressed.

"I really don't want your dad or anyone else to know."

"Know what?" I almost shouted. Still, she kept silent.

Very softly she whispered but didn't look directly at us, "I found a lump on my breast, and it's not going away."

"Mama!" both Angie and I vehemently responded.

"Why didn't you tell us?"

"When did you find it?"

"Have you seen the doctor?"

"Why don't you want anyone to know?"

Of course this barrage of questions rolled over her, and she began to weep. Watching her cry heaped guilt and fear on me at the same time. Mama has always been very strong—my rock. And she most definitely does not cry, at least not very often.

"Okay, Mama, let's take it a bit more slowly from the beginning," I tenderly said, trying hard be the voice of reason. Silence—long,

long silence—filled the air. We quietly waited for her to respond. Finally, very reluctantly, Mama explained that while showering she felt a lump in one of her breasts.

"It was fairly small, so I let it alone, thinking it was just a cyst and would go away." My sister and I simultaneously gave her an admonishing glance. "Well, it hasn't gone away, in fact it is quite a bit larger," she added.

"When was the first time you felt this lump?" I asked.

Mama looked between Angie and me with a diffident look before finally answering, "June."

"What!" we both shouted.

"Shush, I don't want this to be a big deal. Please girls let's not spoil Christmas," Mom returned.

Gently taking my mother's hand, I firmly stated, "Mama it already is a big deal. You have to see the doctor right away, and you have to tell Daddy."

After some hesitation and with tear filled eyes, Mama promised to call her doctor first thing in the morning. She also promised to tell Daddy everything right after her appointment. We tried in vain to convince her that Daddy should accompany her to the doctor's office, but she dug in her heels, firmly stating that she will wait until after the appointment. "I want to have the facts. I don't want to alarm anyone unnecessarily," she responded.

"All right, Mom, but please, call me as soon as you schedule that appointment," Angie said.

"And by the way, we are going with you to the appointment," I stated. "No ifs, ands, or buts about it."

The guys dutifully shoveled out the cars, and the snow had actually slowed down to a light flurry. No one had any inkling of our private conversation, and so we nonchalantly loaded the cars and began our goodbyes.

"Hey Angie, I'm off tomorrow, how about we grab some lunch, just the two of us?" I inquired, pushing aside my concern.

"Sure, love to," she responded knowing me well enough to suspect my ulterior motive. Leah and Mia caught wind and started pleading to go with us, but we gently explained this is "sister time."

"We're sisters," Leah reasoned, causing some weak laughter from Angie and me.

"Not this time kiddo," I responded as I tickled her ribs.

"Let's meet at that cute little restaurant we went to last summer, the one at the Methuen Mall?" Angie suggested.

"I love that place—quiet, great food, and not expensive," I affirmed. That was settled and no one was the wiser that we actually needed to talk family business.

As we drove home Sal chuckled, saying, "Buddy must be crossing his legs, patiently waiting for us to get home and let him outside."

"Uh-huh."

"Apart from my blunder, I'd say it was a perfect Christmas. And what's more, that dorky hat Angie gave me is beginning to grow on me."

"Mmm hmm," I murmured.

"Out with it," Sal said grabbing my hand from across the car seat. "You're way too quiet for just having left your family. Usually you are talking my ear off with all the gossip and details of the day. Something is wrong, out with it!"

I really didn't need much prompting, since the tears were right there ready to fall, and fall they did. By the time we pulled into our snowy driveway, I had unburdened my load onto my husband's broad shoulders.

"Let's get the car in the garage and Buddy out, then we'll talk, okay?" he said gently.

Agreeing to leave the shoveling until tomorrow morning, we unloaded the car and tended to Buddy. He was one happy dog, romping in the fresh fallen snow, acting more like a puppy than a full grown dog. *Oh, to be so carefree!*

"I'm in the mood for some fireside hot cocoa," Sal said while starting a fire. This man is my rock and knows me so well. Something warm and comforting is just what I needed.

"Sure, I'm just going to get into my comfy robe. I'll make it when I come back downstairs."

As the fire came to a nice roar, I settled down on the sofa next to my husband with Buddy snuggled at our feet. Silently staring into the fire and sipping hot cocoa, I broke the silence, stating, "You were right, it was a perfect Christmas, until Mama dropped that bombshell on us. Sal, I'm worried about her. She found the lump way back in June and never said one word to us."

"Your mother is one of the strongest women I've ever known. She's otherwise healthy, and there isn't a living soul with a more positive attitude."

"I know. You're right, but still … June! That's an awful long time for a lump to go unattended, don't you think?"

"It is, but you have to keep a positive attitude, and I know that's not easy for you … my little worry machine," he said tweaking my nose. "It could be a harmless cyst."

"I pray you're right."

"She's going to be just fine, Trina," he whispered as he embraced me, "just fine!"

While sitting at a window table waiting for my sister, my eyes were drawn to the clumps of snow melting from the trees.

Winter sunshine is the best. I should be enjoying this beautifully crisp winter day. But how? My heart weighs heavy in my chest.

Mindlessly staring out that window yanked me back to the wonderful days of my youth. I blinked, and there was Mama standing over a pot of simmering spaghetti sauce or singing while pounding chicken breasts to be used in her famous chicken parmesan. She was always there, in the kitchen or in the living room, tending to the needs of her cherished family. For Mama, me-time as my nieces would say, was as simple as digging in the warm, rich earth of her glorious garden. Many of our neighbors praised and envied her ever blooming garden, inquiring how she managed to grow such beautiful flowers—an array of dazzling color in spring, summer, and fall. Mama would just shrug off the comment as though cultivating such a lush garden was the easiest thing in the world. Just about every flower she planted thrived with the exception of one, which was of a tropical origin. Daddy's domain was undoubtedly growing the vegetables, but Mama was queen of the flower beds. There were none prettier!

When I closed my eyes, I imagined the feel of Mama's cool hands touching my feverish brow. Somehow that simple gesture comforted me, gave me a sense of security. Even in my so-called rebellious teen years, the two of us could be found sitting at the kitchen counter, she patiently listening while I talked her ears off.

I also vividly recalled the first fifteen years of my marriage. Through all the physical and emotional pain of four miscarriages, Mama was there. She didn't always say a lot, she didn't need to. Her presence was like a magical balm to my wounded spirit. I often wondered if I could ever become as strong and compassionate as this woman I call Mama, my role model.

My thoughts were unceremoniously interrupted, "Hey Sis," Angie blurted out as she peeled off her outer layers while she simultaneously plopped down on the seat across from me. "Beautiful today, huh! The sun feels great," she remarked, "glad you got a window table."

"Did you talk to Ma?" I immediately asked not bothering with our normal greeting.

"Yup, I did. She seemed a bit more settled this morning, and *yes* she did make the call. She's waiting for a call back from the doctor's office. Her composure amazes me; she appears stoic at times. We'll get a better fix on her true emotions once she actually connects with Dr. Lowe. It better not be a long wait for this appointment or they will have me on their door step."

"I hear you! Can you believe she waited six months before spilling the beans?" I replied just as a cute little waitress politely interrupted our conversation by rattling off her name and the luncheon specials.

When she paused to catch her breath, Angie asked, "Don't you go to school with my daughter Mia? Mia Trayer?"

"Sure do, I'm in her English class. Hey, she looks just like you."

"Poor kid," I joked. "Just kidding, we're sisters so I have trashing rights."

Ange rolled her eyes at me and continued, "I'll tell Mia you gave us excellent service ... Cindy is it?"

"Yes, Cindy from English class," she returned with a bright smile while pointing to her name tag.

"And you can also tell Mia that her mom gave you an *excellent* tip for that *excellent* service, right Cindy?" I chuckled. Angie rolled her eyes again and giggled as we got to the business at hand of choosing lunch.

"Okay, Trina, we need a battle plan." she stated. "Just so you know I'm off from school until January 5. But ... whatever the appointment date, I'm going with her even if I have to schedule a personal day," Angie said with an air of finality.

"Well, I'm definitely planning to take a personal day, so we'll both be there. Ange, I've been turning this over in my head, and I think Joey ought to be pulled into the loop if we're looking at anything serious ... I mean anything more critical than a cyst."

"That just might put us on shaky ground with the folks. But we have to be willing to take that chance. We can't, in good conscious, leave him out of the loop. She's his mom too and heaven only knows how he idolizes her. Typical Sicilian son!" Angie joked. "I expect Kevin will drop me on the door step of any old nursing home when the time comes," she laughed.

"Come on, Angie, your kids are terrific. They'll find the nicest one they can afford and still keep their inheritance," I snickered.

"Funny!"

"Anyhow, I agree. But I don't want to make any moves prematurely. Let's just see what happens, then if need be, I'll call him. Hopefully he'll answer my call. He wouldn't even pick up yesterday."

"Same here, my finger went numb from dialing his stupid number."

"I still cannot pry a single word out of either Mama or Daddy why Joey is being so aloof. They seem to be in another zone whenever I press them for answers or even hints. And Joey is no better. He's like a stone wall. I even tried to get together with Ellie. She was friendly enough, but had a million excuses. Obviously she's being loyal to her husband and honoring his wishes to stay out of it. She's a good wife to him. It looks like you and I are the only ones that don't have a clue," I said.

While Cindy silently poured our coffee, my sister and I decided to pool our limited medical knowledge and analyze any potential problems Mama might be facing. After hashing out more medical issues than I ever wanted to consider, we courageously took it to the extreme and broached any worst case scenarios she may be forced to encounter.

Emotionally spent, we joined hands and prayed for Mama. We couldn't possibly know what lay ahead, but what we did know is that our God has always been faithful to care for our family. We prayed with confidence that He would bring good out of this bad situation. Right in that little restaurant, we committed our mama and our family to Him and soon a deep, abiding peace washed over us. We opened our eyes, looked at each other, and smiled.

"So what was up with Daddy yesterday? I felt like I was watching a cloak and dagger movie whenever Donna's name came up. Really, what was the big deal about acknowledging he saw or spoke to her? I don't get it. Was it my imagination or was he being purposely evasive? Do you think I should I press him for an honest answer?" I asked. I suddenly realized I had unloaded too many questions on my sister.

Angie, being Angie, just rolled with it. "It sure was obvious that for whatever reason, Daddy didn't want to talk about it. If we weren't facing Mama's situation, I'd say, we press him. But under the present circumstances, it's probably best to let it alone, for now," she answered.

"You're probably right, why add more stress to their lives. Good advice. I'll back-burner it for now; it's probably nothing anyhow. But for some reason, it still raises my curiosity."

Cindy served our salads and we congratulated each other for exercising enough will power to choose *rabbit food* rather than one of the delectable dishes pictured on the menu. Subconsciously, we must have felt obligated to balance out the calories we had consumed at yesterday's feast. As we moved to lighter conversation while eating, I noticed that Angie hadn't taken her eyes off Cindy; something deeper was on her mind.

"Hey, what's up? Your eyes are glued to our waitress."

"Oh, sorry. It's just that ... well … I feel so badly for that little girl, she comes from a really horrible home life," she confided. "It's probably not very different from some of your more difficult cases. I think I'll ask Mia to reach out to her, try to make a connection. Maybe she can become a friend. You know, sometimes one friend can make all the difference."

"You're a good gal, Ange! I admire your desire to help. Maybe you missed your calling and should have been the social worker. I think Mia is cut from the same cloth as you and would be a good friend to her."

When Angie mentioned Cindy's last name, I nearly choked on my salad. Taking a second glance at Cindy instantly transported me to her bedroom approximately ten years ago. Of course I wouldn't have recognized her after all these years, but now I vividly recalled a six-year-old girl huddled in her bedroom closet, shaking and crying hysterically. She was a beautiful child with curly red hair and sad eyes. The place reeked of alcohol and dirt. I will never forget the filth in that apartment!

Her father, Ted, had a reputation of being a hopeless alcoholic. He wasn't an overly large man, but his grim face held a perpetually menacing expression. On one particular night I remember a major fight erupting in their home. It quickly escalated from yelling and screaming to him trashing the place. One neighbor, never wanting to get involved, finally could take it no longer and called the authorities. Poor little Cindy ran to the safety of her hiding place, scared to death and shaking uncontrollably.

Cindy's mom, Lana, took the full brunt of Ted's anger and was badly beaten that night; hospital medical records later revealed a long history of physical abuse. She was a frail-looking woman who also appeared much older than her actual age and was obviously malnourished. Though Cindy suffered emotional abuse, fortunately she had never been beaten. Children and Youth Services adhered to their policies and procedures and removed Cindy from the home. Eventually, she was placed with her aunt, Lana's sister, where she safely remained for several months.

Once Ted was released, he and his wife agreed to work toward reunification. Lana followed all the rules and worked hard to become a family once again. For a while they appeared to be on track and on their way to that reunification, until without warning, he abandoned his family and disappeared into the night. Lana confessed relief when she was later informed by the authorities that Ted was once again incarcerated for various crimes he'd committed. She could finally breathe!

Another social worker and I were heavily involved in that case; we routinely conducted home visits over a period of eleven months. The source of volatility was no longer present in the home, so Cindy was permanently reunited with her mother. Lana was thrilled to have her little girl back home where she belonged.

Much as I would have liked to, I was not at liberty to share this privileged information, even with my sister. As I studied this now spunky teenager through new eyes, I was actually surprised and delighted that the once traumatized little girl appeared to grow into a normal, stable young woman.

Breaking out of my memories, I wholeheartedly agreed with my sister. "Yes, Ange, I think you're right on target. It's a terrific idea for Mia to befriend Cindy, but I think since you're aware of how turbulent her home life had been, wouldn't it be wise to initially have them meet at your house or maybe even at the mall? Or, you know I love Mia's visits, so my house is always an option."

"Sounds terrific, I'll tell her."

"There's always room for one more around my popcorn bowl?" I smiled.

Chapter 3

"Pinch me! Vincent, I still cannot believe you're actually going to shut down the garage for an entire week. I don't recall us ever taking a family vacation, I mean a real family vacation—one without you running back and forth to repair someone's broken down car?" Mama cajoled as she hugged Daddy's neck.

"Well believe it Maria! I am truly sorry it's so long overdue; you deserve better."

"Oh Vincent, it's fine."

"Times have changed dear. It seems there's an auto repair shop on every corner now, and that means pretty stiff competition for my small garage."

"So are you managing to stay competitive?"

"Well, sure, but in order for my business to survive, I need every job that comes through those doors, no matter how small. Like I always say, every small job could lead to bigger ones, not to mention those satisfied customers are our best advertisement. They bring in new business."

"It says a lot that you have such loyal customers."

"I know and I'm thankful for them. Don't get me wrong, we're doing okay sweetheart. We are keeping our heads above water, and I believe things will get better."

"Thank you Lord."

"But, I've decided this vacation is a priority; there is nothing more important than family time. Before we know it, the kids will be married and gone," Daddy said as he kissed the tip of Mama's nose. "Then, just like the song, 'It's just you and me babe.'"

"Daddy, you mean, 'I got you babe,'" I corrected.

"Whatever! Anyhow the cottage is booked so I guess you can start planning your menu. The time is passing quickly and before you know it, we'll be off. If we cook most of our meals at the cottage and then have some occasional snacks from the boardwalk, we'll be just fine. Besides, your cooking is much better than any restaurant at the beach or anywhere for that matter."

Fifty or more vacation brochures were scattered over the kitchen table. Angie and I could not resist riffling through them trying to guess which one our parents had chosen for our dream vacation.

"Come on Daddy, please tell us which one it is. You promised you would tonight," I nagged. Angie joined forces with me, and I think Daddy knew it was no use prolonging the surprise any longer. We already guessed it was Salisbury Beach, we just didn't know which cottage. To a twelve and fourteen-year-old, this was very important information. Cottages nearest to the boardwalk were the most fun, offering the best of both worlds: the sand and surf and the action of the boardwalk. Daddy consented to allow me to invite my best friend Donna to come along, making our vacation even better.

"Okay, okay, okay, I give up," he joked while pretending to snatch us up like a big angry bear. "Here's the deal, my sweet girls, each of you gets one guess," he said pointing to the brochures. "What's it going to be? Trina? Angie?" My little sister was sure it was the Surf Side because it was pink and pretty. My more mature guess was Boardwalk Lane because of its perfect location. We were both wrong. Wrong. Wrong!

Daddy's green eyes sparkled as he grinned and placed his hands around his mouth and loudly trumpeted, "And the 1968 vacation spot for the Agosti family vacation is ... Polly's Villa!" I couldn't have been happier with their decision. It was not far from the boardwalk where the action was, which meant lots for Donna and me to investigate. At fourteen, I was beginning to enjoy a bit more freedom, so I was sure that heaven was just a few weeks away.

At this point in our raucous celebration, Joey entered the back door wanting to know what all the excitement was about. "We are going to Polly's Villa at Salisbury Beach for a whole week in July," Angie answered excitedly.

Joey's predictable response was, "Cool!" At fifteen, Joey epitomized cool, and I idolized my big brother. Some of his friends were hard to take, conceited show-offs, but I liked to flirt with a few of them. One of those friends, Lenny, was also coming with us to the beach. Mom and Dad knew bringing our best friends would surely make our vacation more fun. Lenny was a quiet, polite, and very cute guy. Yes, this would be a wonderful vacation!

I confess to frequently shadowing my big brother. Wherever he went, I'd be ten steps behind him. I so admired him, and he patiently tolerated me. I don't think he was ever aware when I stayed hidden in the corner of our basement watching him working out; his physique was changing before my very eyes. His muscles were becoming so defined, and I quietly giggled as he flexed in front of the mirror. At only fifteen, he had morphed into the stereotypical Italian male: dark, thick, wavy hair, and oh so handsome. It was easy to see that in another year he'd tower over Daddy. He vehemently denied he was trying to attract any particular girl's attention by working out for hours on end. I teased him unmercifully whenever a girl hung around. His smile was easy and frequent and those teeth, well, they were perfect!

Joey and Daddy always had a unique father-son relationship, especially for the 1960s scarred by teenage rebellion. I sometimes felt twinges of jealousy at the depth of their bond. They loved to fish together whenever Daddy had time, that is. He delighted in teaching Joey about tools and cars. For countless hours I sat in the garage as motionless as a mannequin, watching them hoist or jockey various car parts or fittings. Without fail, they became completely immersed in their interaction, making me invisible to them.

Joey greatly respected and I would guess, even admired, Pops. What's not to admire? He is a special man. Angie, Joey, and I grew up watching our parents joke, tease, and tenderly wrestle with one another. Often this signaled an invitation for us kids to jump into the action, which frequently became an Agosti free-for-all.

Joey, like Daddy, always treated Mama like a queen, as is the old world custom. Sons take care of their mamas. Anything else would bring shame on the entire family. He couldn't do enough for her, yet he managed to spread his wings and fly solo; never by any stretch of the imagination could he be described as a mama's boy. No, never! Being the oldest, he set a standard for Angie and me, and it never crossed our minds to lower that standard by behaving badly. We had normal sibling squabbles, but generally speaking, our home was a place of refuge. We definitely felt nurtured, secure, and loved. My happy childhood prompted dreams that were always the same. I desired nothing more than a husband like my daddy and lots of happy children.

The rest of that evening was spent making plans for our vacation. Mama sat with her notebook and pen, meticulously planning out the entire week's menu for seven. I thanked them a hundred times over for including our friends, which I knew to be a sacrifice; I overheard them discussing our tight budget. I gave her ideas for kid-friendly meals. We begged her not to include any of those lentil or stuffed peppers dishes that she sometimes made. Pizza and burgers for the entire week … yes that would be perfect.

Since even the smallest charter boats were cost prohibitive, Daddy and Joey explored the idea of fishing at Black Rock Creek, a stone's throw away from the Salisbury Beach State Reservation. The state reservation was gigantic to me—over five hundred acres with a beautiful four-mile-long, sandy beach. Lots of our friends camped there if they were not fortunate enough to rent a summer cottage. For many, living so close to the ocean afforded them the luxury of taking day trips simply to picnic or enjoy the beach. New England summers are short, so most beach lovers take full advantage of every sunny day.

"Hey Maria, let's plan a drive over to Plum Island while we're there," Daddy yelled over his shoulder. "It's worth taking the time to show the kids ... It's so beautiful! I have always loved that island. Remember that crazy date we had? We never intended to drive up that way, but it ended up being one of our best times. Remember?"

"Oh Vincent, stop, you're making me blush." We all erupted into laughter at her embarrassment, knowing he surely left so much more unsaid. "But you're right it is a beautiful place, and I would dearly love to see it again. If my memory serves me correctly, I was especially impressed by that charming lighthouse right on the town square. It's such a lovely structure, and I must give credit to the town for having the interest and foresight to preserve it."

"I seem to remember the town's people organizing a fundraiser a few years ago for the purpose of saving their local lighthouse. I guess the town fathers also saw the value in preserving a piece of local history," Daddy said.

"Aren't we fortunate to have all of these beautiful sites and wonderful history in our backyard, so to speak? Oh girls, wait until you see it." Mama said.

The days and weeks taunted us, crawling by ever so slowly, but finally, finally vacation week was on the horizon. For two days prior, we talked about nothing else. One would have thought the entire family was taking a fancy cruise liner to Europe. For us, it was that big!

The Friday night before our trip, we packed up our reliable old 1962 Chevy Bel Air wagon so tightly that Daddy began to complain and yell that we wouldn't have room for our friends. He didn't have to tell us. We were well aware that seven in the wagon was already pushing the jalopy to its max. Needless to say, that comment put enough fear and trepidation into us that we immediately, without a word, began the task of streamlining our load. Nothing was more important than including our friends on this trip. I'm not sure how, but we managed to drastically reduce our baggage, making Mama very happy. She had been insisting we leave enough room for her kitchen items, which we finally managed to accomplish. "I was beginning to think you kids didn't want to eat for the entire week," she joked.

We sniped at each other, arguing over what was more important, Joey's tackle box or my transistor radio, little as it was. Daddy strapped his lawn chair on the car roof, bellowing that he hated lying on a sandy beach blanket. Angie's only request was the instamatic camera she'd received from Aunt Connie; it was the last Christmas gift from her and my sister handled that camera with kid gloves.

When the packing was finally completed, we simultaneously, as if on cue, stood back and studied the bulging station wagon. No one said a word, but I wondered if we all were thinking the same thing: Will it get us to the beach? Being a mechanic, Daddy painstakingly kept our cars in topnotch shape, but I guessed we were expecting a lot from this vehicle regardless of the fact that Salisbury Beach was less than a forty-five minute drive.

Saturday morning even before the birds were singing, I was awakened by voices in the kitchen. Laughter and shushing sounds funneled up the stairway. Jumping out of bed, I half slid down the banister, joining the whirlwind of activity that was already well underway. The sight before me was like watching an ant hill: movement at full throttle, each scurrying rhythmically … coming and going, coming and going. At long last, the perishables were the very last items that were packed into the back end of the car. Angie and I shoveled cereal into our mouths standing up, too excited to sit at the kitchen table.

As the hubbub of activity came to a screeching halt, Daddy loudly yelled, "You have fifteen minutes to get dressed and get in the car. The Agosti train is ready to pull out of the station! And give your friends a quick, and I mean *quick*, call. We'll pick them up shortly, and remind them to bring only one bag. Now let's get this show on the road!" It was still dark, but in exactly sixteen minutes, we did indeed pull out of the driveway, en route to our dream vacation.

None of us kids minded being squeezed like canned anchovies. It was kind of fun because I artfully managed to sit next to Lenny. Our silly and non-stop antics during the drive gave the impression we were much younger than our actual ages of twelve, fourteen, and fifteen. We sang rock and roll songs, challenged one another with riddles, and played silly word games as our trusty station wagon chugged along. I imagined it was chanting, *I think I can, I think I can!*

Although Mama and Daddy joined our chorus whenever they recognized a familiar song, I think they were anxious for our arrival and some much needed peace and quiet.

Donna and I squealed with delight when we caught the smell of the ocean long before we actually saw it. That distinctive salty, fishy scent still rouses within me a feeling of wellbeing. What a wonderful and familiar smell it was. We approached the shoreline and what the locals call the center of the beach—where the food and game kiosks would soon be bustling with activity.

Dawn had given way to what promised to be a beautiful summer day. Our heads were on swivels, attempting to take in every single sight as Daddy slowly followed the narrow road to Polly's Villa. When we pulled into the cottage driveway, people were already milling about, walking on the beach and generally speaking, doing what vacationers do.

Anxious to begin our own vacation, our crew sprang into action and began unloading the station wagon without coercion. Once again that ant hill came alive. With all hands on deck, unloading took less than thirty minutes; we were done and eager to vacation. Mama, as usual, was the only one still working, puttering with the refrigerator and stacking our supplies in makeshift cupboards.

It was a modest cottage with peeling grey paint and a missing shutter, but its ocean front location made it extra special to us and desirable to renters. The brochures boasted of a spectacular view and it surely had that. The hypnotic sound of the roaring ocean surf and the salty smell in the air delighted me right from that very first day. I fell in love with the old fashioned wraparound porch, complete with weather-worn rocking chairs and side tables. Donna and I staked our claim on this quaint and comfortable porch. Most of our early mornings and late nights were spent there, whispering and sharing our most guarded secrets.

We looked at each other and grinned as we grabbed hands and raced to the beach, collapsing into the white sand. We yielded to the sensory overload we were experiencing … No, we completely and totally surrendered to it. Could it get any better than this?

Eventually the center and the boardwalk would come alive, and Donna and I were already scheming how we would savor every bit of it.

Recalling our day trips from years past stimulated my senses. I could almost conjure up the tempting smell of onion rings and fried clams as they sizzled until done to perfection. Tripoli's beach pizza, as we called it, maintained first place at the top of my got-to-have list. Some of the more popular food stands would regularly serve long lines of waiting customers. It was not uncommon to see lines five across and five or six deep. Not many complained or grumbled; how long was "too long" to wait at these iconic food stands? My babysitting money was destined to be quickly spent.

From day one, we broke into our comfortable groups: Mama and Daddy, Joey and Lenny, and of course Angie stayed with Donna and me. Mama insisted we have meals together, but the remainder of time, we were free to explore. True, we had our boundaries but surprisingly, they were looser than in Lawrence. Everyone was either singing or laughing. The relaxed environment spontaneously promoted cheerfulness, as if there was not a care in the world.

We took full advantage of the perfect weather, mostly lying on the beach or taking quick dips in the frigid Atlantic Ocean. *What an awesome sight.* I was spellbound by the repetitious pull of the foamy tide. Sea gulls gracefully glided on the wind currents then frenetically swooped down for their next meal. Even though the water was freezing cold, and I mean freezing cold, Donna and I bravely plunged in, feigning to be unaffected. We giggled and played like young children in the lapping water. When we were no longer able to hide or control the shivering, we'd hastily retreat for the warmth of the sun. There will always be a soft spot in my heart and memory for this special ocean paradise.

Later that day as Angie, Donna, and I walked along the beach good naturedly teasing and jabbing each other, we caught sight of a beach volleyball game. I recognized one girl from Lawrence High School where we attended, but the rest were unfamiliar. The group was so friendly and after we watched for a short while, they invited us to join in the fun. No coaxing was needed. We were in!

We made new friends and later chattered endlessly about our perfect first day in the sand and surf. With promises to meet together again, the group broke up, and we walked back to the cottage, intent on laying claim to a couple of rocking chairs for ourselves.

We found Joey and Lenny hanging out in front of the cottage with *my* radio, listening to "Penny Lane." If Lenny weren't there I would have ripped into my brother for swiping my transistor radio, but I meant to maintain my image. I was guilty of flirting with Lenny for sure, but Donna convinced me he had a crush on me. It would be a very interesting week.

Lenny grabbed my hair and pinched my now sun burned back. "Quit it!" I weakly protested.

"Hey, think you boys are capable of putting the grill together for me?" Daddy yelled from the screen door.

"Sure, where is it? I'm getting hungry for those burgers anyhow," Joey responded.

Daddy was out the door in a flash carrying a huge box. "Go to it guys."

Except for Angie, we all got involved in assembling our new Kmart brand grill, never once reading the instructions. Admittedly, it would have taken half the time had one of us at least glanced at the printed sheet.

"Voila! Truly a work of art," Lenny proudly yelled pointing to the grill and simultaneously whipping around pushing me down in the sand with one smoothly executed move. The chase was on. I was after him quick as a racehorse.

"Ready, Pops. Bring on those burgers," Joey yelled.

"Come on, Donna, let's help my mom with the rest of dinner," I suggested as I walked past Lenny, surprising him with the hardest shove I could muster. He would have been after me in a second if Daddy hadn't appeared with burgers in hand. I turned to him, stuck out my tongue, and waltzed into the kitchen, smugly claiming victory.

Everything tasted better at the ocean. We wolfed down perfectly grilled burgers along with a crisp salad. It was a perfect meal for the first night at the ocean, but we didn't want to linger for even a minute. We were ready to slide away again, this time to roam the boardwalk.

"What, no dessert?" Mama questioned as the screen door slammed behind us. "Stay together! Joey, look after the girls! Be home before dark! Do you have any money?" Mama fired off in rapid succession. We had skillfully convinced my parents to keep Angie at the cottage, since she was only twelve, and we bucked the whole babysitting concept. Angie was not happy!

Wandering through the center was magical. Every booth, seen through our eyes, was more exciting than the last, with vendors hawking their wares or foods to passersby. We did, for the most part, stay together. And Joey did, to a degree, look out for us. But Donna and I were on a mission to experience every sight and sound, not unlike dying men granted a mere twenty-four hours to live.

We made our way straight for the arcade to play skee ball, which was probably the most popular game in the arcade. We reminded each other of those adorable stuffed bunnies we had won last year, even though it had taken the entire summer of day trips to achieve that goal. "Imagine what we could win," Donna blurted, "by pooling our resources until Saturday or even by the end of this summer." But honestly, the real reason the arcade ranked so high on our list was the plain fact that boys loved the machines, hence we loved the arcade.

I quickly zeroed in on Lenny playing a machine at the far end of the building. Not surprisingly, he and Joey had attracted some attention from female admirers. "Let's scoot over to see the boys," I said as my game wound down. I guess I was acting out of jealousy, but hopefully it never showed. The four of us finished with the games and left the arcade laughing and clowning around as we walked together, our heads swiveling trying to capture every sight.

Instinctively, we gravitated toward The Frolics. Ignoring the fact that we were too young to enter the well-known club, our curiosity was peaked; we had resolved to ascertain exactly which famous celebrity was on the marquee. People came from hundreds of miles away attracted by big name performers. Frank Sinatra, Sammy Davis Jr., and Ella Fitzgerald were just a few of the stars who graced this dine and dance supper club. As we slowed our pace in front of the iconic club, The Monkees' "Daydream Believer" blasted from every window and door. We were pumped, but disappointed we had years to wait before stepping over that threshold.

"Let's just sit on the side steps and listen just for a while," Lenny suggested.

"Great idea," I concurred as Joey and Donna followed Lenny and me, already making our way to the steps. Within ten minutes, lots of other kids had the same idea. It quickly became crowded and unruly, and it wasn't long before a humongous bouncer appeared and made quick work of shooing us away. Moans and groans could be heard from the gathered crowd but that giant left us no other choice except to move along.

Dusk was fast upon us, forcing the end of our first sightseeing tour of the center. We promised each other that we would continue tomorrow night, picking up where we left off. We were determined to enjoy every night of this special week.

We arrived back at the cottage but were definitely not ready to end the day. We joined Mama, Daddy, and Angie who were unsuccessfully attempting to start a bonfire on the beach. The older boys sprang into action gathering driftwood, and before long a roaring bonfire enkindled from the previously wimpy fire.

Scanning the shoreline, I realized we weren't the only firebugs. Dozens of bonfires glowed in the dark, sending sparks upward toward the heavens. Angie couldn't get her fill of gooey, drippy toasted marshmallows, but all I wanted was to lie on the sand, spellbound by the stars. Beautiful! Breathtaking!

Quite the opposite of our daily habits at home, there was no need to wake us or coax us out of bed here at the shore. Each of us was up at the crack of dawn, each for our own special reason. Daddy made his way to the corner store for a newspaper and then enjoyed a tranquil walk along the beach. Mama got a jump on her daily meal preparations, freeing her up to enjoy the beach without hurrying home to fix dinner too early. The boys were up because they liked to perch themselves on the front porch to watch the girls parade by the cottage. Angie, Donna, and I habitually gulped our cereal on the front porch and raced to the water. We didn't always immerse ourselves since the surf was rough, often having dangerous undercurrents especially during high tide. My best friend and I made a pact; we would return home with the best tan in town. It was the thing to do back then. Two or three times I coaxed the boys to join us when we went clamming in the wet sand, which took all the sweet talk I could muster. They hated digging the clams but loved any opportunity to meet inquisitive girls.

The morning of our third day, we found another beach volleyball game in full swing. This time there were six or seven from Lawrence High School, and we had more fun than a barrel of monkeys. The laughing never stopped and we were soon functioning as a team, wildly and frequently spiking the ball and diving for it like our very lives were at stake. During one particularly competitive game, I noticed a girl walking past us very slowly and thought she looked familiar, but I brushed it off, getting right back into the game. She was gone by the end of the game, and I didn't give it a second thought.

By the end of the week, our games had become quite competitive, but never mean or nasty. I would like to boast I was always on a winning team, but honestly, I was never on the winning team. It didn't matter in the least. It was great fun just being together with this crowd. We hung out with our new-found friends at the arcade, ate with them at the food stands, and nightly sat with them around bonfires. In fact, a few of these kids became good friends through my remaining high school years. Hanging out with this gang was some of the best times and most special memories of our vacation week.

As Daddy promised, one afternoon we did in fact make the drive to tour Plum Island. Anxious to know if the lighthouse in the center of town was still standing, Mama prodded him to drive in that direction. Spotting it from a distance, she exclaimed, "There, there Vincent. Let's get out and walk around it," which we did. They walked hand in hand with their heads bent together, whispering like a young couple in love.

Daddy treated us to soft ice cream from a local stand. The heat of the day made it close to impossible to stay ahead of the dessert and the sticky mess melting down our arms. Nobody could lick that fast.

We ventured toward the shoreline, but I just had to run ahead for a closer look. Spread before us was a breathtaking display of hundreds, no thousands, of wild beach plums growing in the dunes. Their vibrant rose color was an awesome sight! This alone was worth the hours away from the volleyball game. Angie shot some amazing pictures of them with her little camera. Throughout the week she also captured a couple of stunning sunsets, powerful high tides, and anything else that tickled her fancy. She flaunted her talent for photography, and she was probably right, but we were sick of hearing her endless bragging. Nonetheless, we were glad her camera recorded some of our best memories. Satisfied and happy, we trundled back to the car and home to Polly's Villa.

Our nights were immersed in the boardwalk experience, not the least of which was surrendering to the tempting smells wafting from the kiosks. Our plan was a simple one: pool our money and share the variety of goodies. We also set aside some money for the amusement park. We just couldn't go home without riding the Dodgem bumper cars. Lenny was relentless, chasing me down like a hunted rabbit. Breathlessly, I shrieked with every one of his hits to my car, and no, I didn't mind one bit.

Finally, our adventures wouldn't be complete without taking multiple spins on the Flying Horses carousel, which for some unknown reason New Englanders called dobby horses. I found those beautifully hand carved and hand painted horses to be romantic, even enchanting. Predictably, the boys protested, saying it was a girly ride, but they gave in to us; they patronized us would be more accurate.

On Friday, the last full day at the beach, we decided to have a grand finale game—the championship beach volleyball game! It went on and on. Even though the sun was punishing, we played like professionals, sort of. Intermittently, someone could be seen running into the surf; resuscitated from the brutal heat they would jump right back into the fray.

Later, while sitting in the sand with Joey watching from the sidelines, I caught a glimpse of that girl again. She glanced at Joey and me for only the briefest second as she strolled by the game.

"It will come to me," I muttered to myself.

"What did you say?" Joey asked distractedly.

"Oh rats, you missed her. A couple of times I saw a girl watching us play. She is so familiar, but I just cannot place where I know her from. It will come to me, never mind," I offhandedly replied.

Mama and Daddy gave us permission to build one last bonfire on the shore, reminding us we needed to get a few things packed that night. We all inwardly moaned at the very thought of leaving this place. Our camping skills developed over the week and in no time at all, we had a roaring fire. We quickly threaded marshmallows on sticks, and before long were combatively shoving them above the fire. Lenny repeatedly nudged me with his shoulder as if to push my marshmallow away from his perfectly toasted masterpiece. The marshmallow war quickly escalated; he and I were soon chasing one another in the sand leaving Joey, Donna, and Angie to tend the fire. Suddenly and unexpectedly, Lenny spun me around and planted a sloppy kiss on my unsuspecting lips. We stood there gazing at each other, both of us shocked at what had just occurred. I smiled at him, and I think he blushed but couldn't be certain in the dark. *My first kiss*, I thought to myself as we ran back to the bon fire carefully guarding our little secret. That is, until I could get Donna alone to spill the beans. And spill I did!

As a young teenager I privately dreamed of someday making this place my home. Continually listening to the pounding surf and shrieking seagulls, I believed, would be the perfect lifestyle for me. I will forever be in love with this place and this chunk of my childhood.

Within seconds of my key clicking into the front door, I snickered at the familiar sound of Buddy thundering to greet me. His often repeated ritual never gets old: toenails clicking on the foyer floor and tail wildly wagging as he proceeds to slobber all over me. I should know better, but I swear during these antics he's actually smiling at me.

The phone began jangling off the hook just as I tossed my coat onto the rocking chair. More than once Sal has laughed at me when I attempted, in vain, to explain that there are *good rings* and there are *bad rings*. Something in my gut whispered, *this is a bad ring*.

Without so much as a hello, my mother breathlessly blurted in my ear, "Dr. Lowe wants to see me Tuesday, the thirtieth, at ten o'clock. And before you say a word Trina, I want you to understand that I am perfectly capable of going alone. I've been doing it for years. You do realize that I'm a big girl," she joked, trying to come off as unconcerned.

"Nope, uh uh! You're losing this battle, Mama. Angie and I have already decided that we are going with you … period … end of story," I countered, leaving no room for further discussion. After chatting for a few more minutes about absolutely nothing of any significance, we ended the conversation with my promising to call Angie to coordinate our trip.

Tuesday morning dawned another crisp, yet sunny day. What a gift! After letting Buddy out for his morning constitutional, I quickly showered, dressed, and drove the short distance to pick up my sister. My stomach too unsettled to handle breakfast, I suggested we take Ma to lunch after her appointment. "It will be a perfect opportunity to review whatever was discussed at the appointment and also settle each of us before returning to our respective homes," I said.

"Sounds like a plan," she agreed.

We picked up Mama and although she appeared composed, we knew her well enough to notice the waving red flags. We drove together in silence.

This feels oddly like a blind date. We were all cordial, saying exactly the right things, yet awkward as all get out. Fear loomed heavy over our heads.

My eyes were glued to Mama, watching her every move; her shaking hands were not lost on me. Of course she chose to enter the examining room alone, but following the examination his nurse wordlessly ushered the three of us into Dr. Lowe's office. This particular nurse perfectly fit the well-known caricature of an army nurse—shaped like a bulldog and just about as pleasant. Both our parents have been under this doctor's care for at least twenty years, and it goes without saying that she trusts him explicitly.

Dr. Lowe, probably in his late fifties, has always maintained a professional demeanor, yet fatherly. I was taken aback by his totally white head of hair. *When did that happen?* He also appeared to have gotten a bit chunkier than when last I saw him. *Who hasn't?*

The important thing is that Mama holds him in high esteem.

His office may have been attractive thirty years ago, but now it simply feels like a cave. It's still a dark, depressing, wood-paneled room, and it has reeked of some indefinable stale odor for as long as I can recall. *Would it kill him to add some light fixtures to brighten this place up just a wee bit?* He's probably never given a single thought to redecorating—the, "If it ain't broke, don't fix it," kind of mentality. *I guess it makes a lot more sense to have this trusted, skilled physician rather than an untested doctor in a fancy uptown office. After all, what does décor matter?*

After exchanging the expected pleasantries—So, how are the husbands? How old are the kids now? —We settled into what I could already see written on this doctor's face. Angie saw it also.

Dr. Lowe cleared his throat and began, "I am not going to lie to you girls. Maria, I do not believe this lump is a cyst. It definitely feels like a solid mass." At that, my heart started racing. I reached for Angie's hand and she grabbed Mama's. I had a sudden urge to run, but I forced myself to sit stock-still and listen.

"Okay, so tell us, what is the next step, doctor?" I calmly asked. Mama remained silent, but I watched her reach across the desk for a tissue. We all squeezed hands and waited for his answer.

"First, I am sending you for a diagnostic mammogram. Maria, may I ask why it has been so long since your last one?" he questioned while abruptly riffling through her medical records. He looked at Mama with questioning eyes and sat still waiting for her response.

"I am sorry to say that I cancelled a couple of them, but ... I ... can't remember the reasons. Then, time just passed, and I guess I didn't realize ... I don't know." She sheepishly answered his question.

At this revelation Angie and I wanted to jump out of our skin. *Why didn't we pay more attention? Why didn't I ask her about these appointments?*

Willing myself to calm down, I asked, "Okay doctor and then what?"

"I am also setting up an appointment for an ultrasound study. It can be done at the same women's clinic directly following the mammogram, which will be convenient and save some time. *Time is an important factor here Maria. Let's just take this step-by-step, okay?"*

Time … has time become our enemy?

Just then, his assistant placed a note directly in front of him and without a word, left the office. "Ah, here we go. The appointments are set for Friday, January 2 at ten thirty. Do you know where the women's clinic is?"

"Yes, yes I do, but the appointments are so … well … soon," she softly replied as she fidgeted before his gaze. Dr. Lowe, Angie, and I could not hide our scowls at her response. He then firmly reiterated that she could not afford to waste any more time.

"Maria, I do not believe you are grasping the gravity of your physical condition," the doctor firmly stated. "I will call you just as soon as I receive the test results." Mama silently nodded. Angie and I thanked him as we robotically stood and left the office without making the slightest sound.

For the second time in a week, we sat at a window table in what was fast becoming our favorite restaurant. We were unusually quiet with each other as we individually navigated our own mine fields of mental images. Mama hadn't uttered more than two words since leaving Dr. Lowe's office.

Angie and I were jolted from our thoughts, expressing delight at having Cindy wait on us once again. Her smile is nothing short of contagious as is her charming upbeat mannerism.

"Wow, we meet again," she said with a welcoming smile. "But just so you know, I won't be here if you come again next week. Christmas vacation is ending soon so I'll only be available to work after school."

"That's understandable."

"Guess what? Mia called the other day and invited me to the mall. What a coincidence, huh? Anyhow, we're going Friday night, if I don't have to work. So … what can I get for you today?"

After taking a few minutes to introduce Cindy to Mama, we ordered lunch. Silently, I was thrashing around exactly how we should approach this conversation. Unexpectedly, Mama was the one who broke the ice, taking the lead. Angie and I communicated with knowing glances.

"Girls," which never fails to amuse me, since we are forty-one and forty-three years old, "I have decided to meet this head on and beat it!"

"Good for you!" Angie cheered, embarrassing herself by her sudden emotionally charged outburst and by the attention she received from other diners.

"I have been thinking almost nonstop about this and there is no reason to weep and wail or give up. I know what you are both thinking, and the answer is yes, I will tell your dad today. You are both right, what was I ever thinking? He will most certainly want to be involved in this, and I'm not waiting for the test results."

"Mama, we are so proud of you," I interjected, "and we will be right by your side, whatever direction this goes."

"As so many times in my past, I have placed my hand in the hand of my Lord. He alone holds the power of life and death, and I trust Him with my life," she said with a confident and steady voice.

"Mama," I carefully broached the subject as though stepping into a mine field, "what about Joey?" I asked, noticing the tears that quickly flooded her eyes. "You … we cannot keep anything like this from him. He has a right to know. He needs to be in the loop alongside Angie and me."

"I … I don't know what to say, girls. Let's not talk about that just now," she firmly stated, ending the conversation.

I can't believe it! I just got stonewalled again … yet again! I felt anger rising up from the depths of my belly, yet I understood unloading on my mother would be grossly misplaced. Nonetheless, it took every ounce of self-control for me to keep a lid on that anger, which miraculously I managed. At least for now!

And so, we muddled through New Year's Eve with barely an acknowledgement of the year to come. Sal and I shared a nice dinner with Angie and Jake and the kids. Mama and Daddy spent the evening alone, as is their usual custom, enjoying a special seafood dinner. That was that! Nothing to write home about! It seemed quite evident that we were simply marking time until the next appointment.

Mama kept her word, and we were so proud of her. Daddy did indeed accompany us to the appointment at the women's clinic. It was plain to see he was obviously nervous and probably felt like a fish out of water; normally only women sat in that waiting room. Thankfully, not more than five minutes passed before her name was politely called.

We watched her back as she entered the mammogram area, and I personally wondered what 1998 would hold for the Agosti family and especially for Mama. Not long after she entered the room, I caught a glimpse of her being directed into a different room. I guessed it was the ultrasound room. We waited. Finally and very casually, the technician assistant guided Mom back to us, stating that her doctor would be in touch after their technician studied the mammogram and sent his report. We thanked her and quietly left the clinic.

Not expecting to hear anything for several days or even a week, I naturally resumed my regular case load, returning to work on Monday, January 5, as did Angie. Thoughts of that lump never completely left my mind; it hovered over me like an ominous cloud. At the most unexpected times, fear would drop down on me, not unlike a black veil.

Waiting is hard for me, always has been. Admittedly, my mind often betrays me, serving as my worst enemy, relentlessly assaulting me with sinister or inauspicious situations.

Late Wednesday afternoon as I clumsily entered my front door, the sound of my telephone sliced through my troubled thoughts.

Bad ring, I said to myself.

I reached for the telephone. Angie began speaking rapidly and breathlessly from the other end.

"Whoa, slow down, Ange, what is going on?" I almost yelled.

"Dr. Lowe wants to see Mama first thing in the morning," she rattled off.

"That can't be good, Angie," I quickly stated. "Okay, let me think a second … I'm calling my boss and taking a personal day."

"Same here," she concurred. "But how about we visit them tonight? I'm thinking a little moral support couldn't hurt!"

"Okay, I'll meet you there in a jiffy," I agreed.

Scribbling a quick note for Sal, letting Buddy out, and changing my clothes all happened in a flash. Even though I couldn't find my boots, which slowed me down yet again, I still made it to Lawrence in record time. Thank God it was only flurrying; lately we have been enjoying a milder streak of weather.

Angie and I visited with our parents for a couple of hours, chatting and lending moral support. I believe Daddy was grateful for our visit. It allowed him the freedom to ask some serious questions he'd been somewhat reluctant to verbalize with Mama. We kept the tone positive and never once entertained a negative outcome.

Being together was a good idea, but Mama began to look exceptionally tired. We took the hint and headed home agreeing to meet them at Dr. Lowe's office in the morning.

I'm guessing none of us slept very well that night. Yet, I took comfort through most of the night in Sal's reassuring arms. I have thanked the Lord a hundred times for His gift to me: Sal's compassion and love, supporting me through the best and worst of times.

Walking into that dreary, dark office the next morning sent a ripple of chills down my spine. I doubt the heat had come up yet, but it was more than the physical cold that gripped me, I noticed we simultaneously pulled our coats around us just a little snugger. Dr. Lowe is not known for mincing words, and today was no exception. Almost immediately after greeting Daddy, he shuffled through the reports on his desk and fixed a compassionate gaze on Mama.

Oh God help us, I silently prayed, feeling something like electricity in the air.

"Maria, Vincent, girls, I do not have good news for you." Again, my heart started to race as my sister shifted in her chair. Mama and Daddy didn't move a muscle, seeming to not even breathe. They patiently waited for him to continue.

"Let me explain. The mammogram and ultrasound both confirmed my suspicion that this lump was not a cyst as you had hoped. It is in fact a sizeable, solid mass. Furthermore, the fine needle aspiration that was done for biopsy purposes, confirmed it as a stage three cancer. I'm so sorry to have to tell you this, Maria."

"Wait, wait," I interjected. "When did you have a biopsy, Mama?" I asked, feeling woozy.

Again giving me that sheepish look, she proceeded to say that she hadn't wanted to alarm the family needlessly, so she requested it be done immediately following the ultrasound.

"Mama, you should have told us, all of us!" Angie rebuked.

The four of us sat in shock, holding hands and listening to the purported course of treatment. My head was swimming as I listened: mastectomy, chemotherapy, and possibly radiation. Tears were now freely flowing from my sister and me. My parents were stoically motionless.

Surprisingly, Mama broke the somber mood just as she had in the restaurant and declared, "I am going to beat this thing. I am a fighter! Right, Vincent? Tell Dr. Lowe … I am a fighter."

Nodding to my mama's passionate proclamation, yet unconvinced and afraid, I gathered the informational brochures strewn over the desk. I don't remember what else was said. I drifted into a foggy place in my mind.

Dr. Lowe recommended three oncologists from which to choose, and he stressed that every one of them is highly skilled and of the highest reputation. He strongly suggested we make that decision today before leaving his office; he wanted his nurse to schedule the first appointment.

While Daddy and Mama tended to the remaining details, Angie and I waited in the outer office, clinging to each other in a ferocious embrace, saddened and overwhelmed.

Lord, oh Lord … I cannot begin to know what our future holds. But I do know … I do know … I know You hold Mama and our family in the palm of Your hands. I'm struggling, but … I put my hope and trust in You!

Chapter 6

The year 1998 began and continued with what seemed a never ending parade of appointments. Daddy, Angie, and I coordinated our work schedules so that Mama never underwent any procedure alone, never went unaccompanied to any appointment. She protested, but I suspected she secretly was comforted by our concern and grateful for the companionship.

There was no doubt in my mind that the time had come to bring Joey up to speed, which I did without Mama or Daddy's permission. At this point I didn't give two hoots about stepping on toes or offending anyone. The gravity of this situation, I reasoned, overshadowed all of their petty squabbles.

After leaving several general phone messages, I was finally rewarded by the sound of his mellow voice. "Joey, I am so glad you returned my call. I didn't want to leave any details on the machine … you know … in case the boys overheard. Anyhow, Angie and I feel it's only right that you should know the details of Mama's situation. I don't know what is going on between you and the family, and frankly at this point of the game, I don't care. But you need to be aware … Mama's medical condition is very serious," I began, paused and continued when I realized he wasn't responding. "She

… she has stage three breast cancer, Joe, and she's in for a rough ride. We can't take anything for granted here."

"Oh God, not Mama! She's, she's … she doesn't deserve this," he wept bitterly into the phone. I waited for his weeping to subside. Then after a period of long, awkward silence, "Trina, I'm sorry to put you in the middle of this ugly situation and *no*, I won't talk about the details of this family fracture. Suffice it to say, I only care about what's going on with Ma. Thank you for including me. I really do appreciate it," he said still emotionally raw.

"Of course, how could I not include you? The mastectomy date has already been scheduled. Chemo and possibly radiation will follow."

"Oh my God, and … and how is she taking all of this?"

"Like a rock, but I'm not so sure it's a good thing. Can I please call you and Ellie from time to time, just to fill you in?"

"Yes, of course. If I don't pick up, just leave a message. I promise I'll get back to you as soon as I get your message."

"I love you Joey," I said through tears.

"Me too. Bye."

Mama came through the mastectomy like a champ. We were all truly amazed at her stamina and determination. Sustained by her unwavering faith and family support, her recovery was faster than the doctors had anticipated. After regaining most of her strength, the chemotherapy began. In the beginning, she truly seemed unaffected by the treatments, which delighted us to no end. But then … oh then … it hit her hard … really hard. My heart broke watching her go through these horrible treatments. Just about the time she began to feel human again … *bam*, she was scheduled to receive another sickening treatment.

Through it all, Daddy remained her knight in shining armor. He did over and above whatever needed to be done. Never once did he utter a single complaint while caring for the love of his life, and some days it wasn't pretty.

January through April proved to be the most trying of times. Yet, it was during these dark days that Mama's church friends demonstrated their loving support in a hundred unique and wonderful ways.

Apparently, Mama's illness served as the catalyst that birthed a new outreach from her church: Baskets of Blessings came straight from the heart of their women's ministry team. On conveniently prearranged days, one of the women from her church appeared at the Agosti front door, carrying a lovely basket. Each woman prayerfully and creatively filled a basket with Mama in mind.

The outreach was aptly named; she was indeed blessed by their visits as well as by each overflowing basket. The treasures tucked into those baskets were precious to her, not because of their monetary value, but because they expressed love. She was the grateful recipient of fragrant lotions and creams, devotional books, scented candles, music tapes, picture frames, journals, books, and magazines. Thoughtfully, they included homemade soups and desserts, to which Daddy readily laid claim.

One particular woman, who herself was a cancer survivor, brought a new scarf on each of her visits. She was well aware of the dignity issue related to hair loss and taught Mama a hundred different ways to wear those lovely scarves. Each woman included a passage of scripture into their basket that they hoped would encourage their dear friend, and well they did.

A while after she finished her last treatment, Mama confided in me that she frequently felt undergirded by their prayers, which undoubtedly strengthened her resolve and thus gave her a victorious outlook. I felt tremendous gratitude toward these lovely God-sent women. Each one lovingly showering her with unique and inspiring items and more importantly, with their tender touch. And so, although those were dark months, the light of their expressed love was nothing short of dazzling.

Inspired by the efforts of these kind ladies, Angie and I jumped on board, but in a slightly different manner. We regularly made extra meals, packaging and delivering them straight to their freezer. I'm sure Daddy didn't go hungry during those times when Mama wasn't up to cooking, in fact he may have gained a pound or two because the refrigerator was always full and a selection of snacks were readily available.

Mia and Leah were also faithful to visit their grandmother, delivering their own homemade brownies or cookies. Mama told them that their visits were like medicine to her soul, which delighted the girls to no end. They, like the rest of the family, grabbed hold of every opportunity to spend precious time with Mama.

One lazy afternoon, I caught Mia reading to her grandmother from a teen magazine. I doubt Mama was the least bit interested in teen magazines, still she feigned rapt attention, that is until nodding off in her favorite recliner.

Chapter 7

Since Angie was fortunate to be enjoying Good Friday through the following Monday off from school, she happily offered to host our family's traditional Easter dinner. Without prompting or coercion, she boldly made "the Joey call," graciously extending the invitation to join us, completely ignoring the possibility she'd be rejected. Ellie, affable as ever, promised to pass the information along to her husband, but we weren't surprised when they politely declined the invitation.

Sunday morning service was extraordinarily uplifting and quite moving. Resurrection Sunday, as I like to call it, has never failed to bring me back to center. I stand, awestruck at what Jesus accomplished on the cross for me, for us. Forgiveness so freely extended at an incalculable cost. After a period of introspection, I questioned whether I'm willing to proffer a fraction of the same forgiveness He so freely demonstrated?

Honestly Lord, you know I have been wrestling with my heart attitude toward my brother. Is there a more appropriate day than Easter for me to receive forgiveness … for allowing that root of bitterness like an ugly bramble bush, to take up residence in my soul? Yes Lord, I freely confess my sin and desire to move forward clean and free. Thank you Lord!

Feeling as though the weight of this old world had been lifted from my shoulders, I eagerly faced the day with renewed hope. *Yes, truly it is Resurrection Sunday!*

After church, Sal and I made our usual Sunday morning run to our favorite bakery. We simply cannot sit down to Easter dinner without Tripoli's famous bread, not to mention those scrumptious Italian pastries. The familiar aroma in that bakery is … nothing short of amazing! Like Pavlov's dog, I began to salivate the second I stepped across the threshold of this iconic bakery. Eyeing the glass display case filled with every creamy, sugary dessert imaginable, I smiled sweetly at the clerk and nonchalantly stated, "One of everything, please," to which Sal's head spun around to me like the creepy girl from *The Exorcist.* "Just kidding," I whispered.

Mama was between her scheduled chemotherapy treatments, which almost gave her strength enough for a full day. We joked with her that she was getting a free pass on the cooking and serving this year only. Angie and I happily prepared all of the food with some so-called organizational assistance from the kids. It was actually a fun day and relatively stress free. Completely unflappable, my sister kept the party moving along like the mechanisms of a fine Swiss watch.

The kitchen, always the hub of activity, is where every Agosti wants to hang out, and Easter Sunday was no exception regardless of the confusion and chaos we were certain to create. The cacophony of kitchen activities rattled my teeth. Pots and pans were clanking, and bodies were bumping into one another. Jake was desperately trying to find a bit of counter space for the huge ham that would need to be carved. Sal was smart and removed himself from the madness of the kitchen. He took responsibility for pouring (and spilling) the wine.

Busying myself with various side dishes, I began to identify with the witch of *Hansel and Gretel* lore. At times, I was dreadfully close to being shoved into the oven by my loved ones. However, I was confident someone would rescue me before I became too well done. Angie enlisted help from the kids, assigning the table settings into their capable hands.

Mama sat in the living room with a serene expression on her face, watching the comedy of errors playing out in the kitchen. I could almost read her mind: "I should have done this many years ago."

Daddy, ever the sergeant, ordered everyone around, and I mean everyone, making the confusion much worse than it already was, or needed to be, I might add.

Just as the sounds of clanking pots and pans began to abate, the doorbell rang. Kevin was the first to break free from the task at hand, making a run for the door.

"Are you expecting anyone else?" I asked my sister.

"Are you kidding me, isn't this crazy crew enough?" she laughed as we craned our necks to view the front door. To the person, every jaw dropped, but surprised facial expressions were quickly replaced with broad and welcoming smiles.

Admittedly, I personally was speechless when Ellie, Anthony, and Sammy waltzed in and marched directly to Mama. They embraced in a tearful reunion. Not one wanted to let go of the other; it was a big, beautiful group hug. The boys were so thrilled to see their cousins, they forgot how cool they were and how they were supposed to behave. Punching, jabbing, and performing their ritual head locks were obviously how they expressed their love for one another.

"We can't stay long," she apologized. "We just couldn't stand to let one more day pass without seeing you, Mama, and of course all of you," Ellie said with great sincerity.

"Please, sweetheart, sit for a few minutes," Mama begged.

"Okay, just for a minute. You look good, Mama. How do you feel? Did you get my cards? What about my packages?" Ellie asked.

"Yes dear, I did, and I so appreciate them. Thank you, but your hugs are the best gift of all, I … we have desperately missed you."

I couldn't help but notice that Daddy stayed in the background the entire visit, allowing Mama to enjoy this special time with her other grandsons.

He didn't hear when I whispered in Ellie's ear as we hugged, "Does Joey know you're here?"

"No, he doesn't. I told him I needed to make a quick run for a couple of last minute groceries. We're cooking at home today. I think he might have suspected though, since the boys tagged along, but he didn't question me," she softly responded.

They stayed a little longer than a grocery run would actually take, especially for the scant items they were picking up as part of their cover story. Mama soaked up every word from her grandsons and daughter-in-law like a sponge, rehydrating before our very eyes.

I believe prayers were answered today, at least in part, and we couldn't have hoped for a nicer Easter gift for our dear Mama.

As I watched Ellie and the boys backing out of the driveway, I was lost in thought. *What a beautiful Resurrection Day! Maybe, just maybe, Lord, there is hope for this family to become whole again.*

We all returned to our assigned kitchen posts, resuming the food preparations we'd left undone. The sun streaming in Angie's kitchen window seemed to shine a little bit brighter.

Finally we heard Angie's sweet voice, "Let's eat!" to which we all yelled, "Amen!"

Chapter 8

"Come on in, girls, I'm in the kitchen. I just knew you couldn't resist my offer of homemade pizza," I called out to Mia and Cindy as they made their way to my kitchen counter.

"Hey Buddy, how ya doing, boy?" Mia whispered as she ruffled his long fur. Never did a dog love being petted more than Buddy.

"He'll settle down after a while. You know how he is. He just has to check everyone out, give them the once over, and then welcome them to our humble abode."

"Mia told me on the drive over that you make your own dough. How cool is that? Can't wait to taste it," Cindy said.

"Sure do. It's Mama's recipe handed all the way down from her mama who was born in Sicily. I have never changed it one tiny bit. I don't dare mess with perfection," I laughed. "But today, we are going to make it together. If you like it, I'll share my recipe … Mama's recipe and then you can enjoy it in your own kitchens for many years to come. I thought it would be fun."

"I always love coming here, Mrs. Lamazo. It's so … I don't know … peaceful. I mean it's like an oasis or something."

"You are always welcome here Cindy, and I am delighted that you and Mia have become such good friends. Besides, I'm happy to have your company, especially on nights like these when my husband has business dinner meetings," I responded.

"Oh, we'll be out of your way long before Uncle Sal gets home. Kevin said he'd pick us up before nine o'clock."

"Now look here, little girl, Uncle Sal loves your company too, so don't you scoot off too early. That dough needs another twenty minutes rising time, so let's sit and relax a little until it's ready. Mia, grab some cold soda, would you? I'll get the glasses."

Settling into the living room, Mia and I chatted about family. "How do you think Gram's treatments are going? Mom seems to think she's doing well."

"Honestly, honey, I believe she's a little depressed, but physically, I agree that she's doing pretty well," I responded as I noticed Cindy distractedly pulling threads from her sweater.

"Hey Cindy, are you okay? You don't seem quite like yourself tonight," I tenderly asked.

"No, she is definitely not okay Aunt Trina, not okay at all," Mia loudly interrupted.

Turning my full attention to Cindy, I cautiously pressed her for some kind of response. Very reluctantly, Cindy finally warmed up, slowly at first, and then it was like watching a flood gate burst open.

"I am so ashamed to tell you this Mrs. L., but my dad has been in jail for a long time. He's got a history of assault, robbery and … well he was always drunk," she said in a husky voice, pausing to judge my reaction. I said nothing of my prior knowledge and sat perfectly still, listening. After a period of silence, which I assumed was her defensive way of cautiously discerning any negative response, Cindy then continued. But she was now crying so hard we could barely understand her words. I moved closer to her and placed a reassuring hand on her back.

"Go on, honey," I gently encouraged.

"Well, he just got out and … and he's been harassing my mom something terrible. She's turned into a completely different person.

I hardly know her, she's acting so jittery. I guess it's because he's got her so frightened, and I'm scared to death that he's going to hurt her just like he did years ago."

"Has she notified the authorities?" I asked.

"Yes, she just started the paperwork for a restraining order, but the judge hasn't completed it yet. In the meantime, she's living in fear, constantly looking over her shoulder. Yesterday she opened up and told me that once, a long time ago, he beat her senseless," sobbing again.

Now Mia moved closer, taking her hand.

"We've been doing great, just the two of us all this time. It's been hard for Mom, but she went back to school while working a full time job. Mrs. Lamazo, she's truly a great mom, and … and I'm so scared."

"What can I do to help? You are welcome to stay here with us until this is all resolved," I offered.

"Really? That's so nice of you, but I can't leave my mom alone," she returned through sniffles.

"Well, I know of safe houses through my work. How about I check into that for both of you, even if it would only be temporarily?"

"I don't know how she'd feel about that. Can I ask her and let you know?"

"Sure, sure. Let me do some quick research tomorrow. I'll stop by your house after work and explain it to your mom if that's okay," I quickly reassured her.

"You and Mia are the best thing that has happened to me in a long, long time. Thank you. You're both … special to me," she said smiling at us with those sad eyes.

"Okay, enough tears, let's get that pizza going. Mia, grab the cheeses and pepperoni, if you like it, that is."

"If we like it? Are you kidding me? We love it."

"I'll punch down the dough. Cindy, you oil that pizza pan," I ordered while smiling at these beautiful girls.

In a flash the three of us were up and busy in the kitchen. It was fun to have them here; we worked well as a team and enjoyed each other's company.

"Hey girls, maybe we should open a pizza parlor," I joked.

Turning to look at him, I was acutely aware that my dog was intently staring at the kitchen door, not moving a muscle. "Buddy, what is your problem? What the heck are you growling …?" Suddenly, the kitchen door flew open and crashed into the wall. I immediately recognized the angry man who was yelling obscenities as he staggered through my door. There stood Cindy's dad, drunk and wildly out of control. As if time was standing still, we numbly just stared at him, not knowing exactly what to do next.

Buddy was now beside himself growling, snarling, and baring his teeth. This normally gentle animal was defending his territory against this unwanted intruder. Without any warning whatsoever … *womph!* Buddy took a hard blow to his head. The sound from Ted's heavily booted foot sickened me. My precious dog was knocked to the floor, unconscious or dead.

"What have you done?" I shrieked, as I leaned over my dog. "What do you want?" I screamed again.

"What are you doing here?" Cindy yelled. "Did you follow me? What do you want? Get out, get out now!" she verbally fired at him. "What is the matter with you?"

I turned around, looked up at Cindy and blinked. Instantly I saw a frightened six-year-old, huddled in her bedroom closet. But, now, she was fighting back. I also observed that my niece had protectively pushed Cindy behind herself.

Stroking my still unconscious dog, I looked up with as much composure as I could muster, saying, "Please, calm down. Please. I don't know what you want, but can't we sit down and talk about it?"

That was apparently a big mistake. This enraged man, reeking from alcohol stood before me with an evil expression that I will never, ever forget. He became more and more infuriated as I made every effort to diffuse the situation.

"I'll tell you what I want! I want my daughter back! You took her from me once, and it's not going to happen again … She's *my* daughter," he slurred as he lumbered toward me. As I attempted to stand, I could feel and smell his spittle all over my face. It instantly soured my stomach.

Suddenly and without warning, that same heavy boot hit the side of my jaw with such force that I crumpled into a heap next to my dog. Everything went totally black for a few seconds. It was as though the world was moving around me in slow motion—very slow motion. I heard the girls screaming at what seemed like the top of their lungs. Before I could focus or protect myself, he was on me, punching, slapping and kicking me. I remembered whimpering and curling into the fetal position.

I desperately tried to maintain consciousness, but knew I was slipping away. Oddly, I was cognizant of some of the sounds swirling around me, yet they were fuzzy and unclear. I'm not certain exactly how much time passed, but I became aware of Kevin and his friend running through the door and tackling this brute. Slipping into a dark pit, I vaguely recalled Kevin frantically screaming, "Get off! Get off! Get off of her! You animal! I'll kill you!" They, no doubt, pummeled him into submission and had him restrained long before the police arrived.

I was in and out of consciousness but managed to discern the sound of crying and the wail of an ambulance. Confusion clouded my thinking, yet I remember worrying if Buddy was dead or alive. Then blackness came over me like a rug. I fought for every breath.

As the medics lifted me onto a litter, I regained enough focus to hear Mia crying into the phone with Sal then with Daddy. I tried to say, "No, don't worry them," but I was unable to utter a word. For a short time my senses seemed heightened: The taste of blood was nauseating, the ambulance lights assaulted my eyes, and then I slipped away once again.

When next I opened my eyes, I was in the hospital. Sal was holding my hand and weakly smiling at me. Mama stood at the foot of my bed clinging to Daddy with one hand and holding my foot with the other hand. They were watching me, staring at me as though I were a ghost.

Do I look that bad?

I desperately wanted to ease their concern but felt restrained and was unable to communicate with them.

Sal whispered to me that Angie and the rest of her family were in the waiting room.

"Hospitals have their rules. Only three visitors at a time," Daddy said.

When I tried to speak for the second time, but couldn't, panic gripped me, and I began thrashing around the bed. Sal's soothing voice and gentle touch eventually calmed me down.

"Honey, your jaw is wired. Don't try to speak. You took a nasty beating, but the doctor said you are going to be fine," he whispered in my ear and kissed me at the same time.

I knew the girls were okay; I had a vague recollection of them hugging each other after the beating. But I needed to communicate with Sal. I needed to know … Just then he leaned in and smiled, saying, "Everyone is okay, and Buddy is going to be just fine."

I gave him a knowing look and drifted into a deep sleep.

I thought I was dreaming when I awoke to my brother Joey's beautiful face looking down at me with such concern. Again, I tried to speak, but could not. He was alone.

Where was the rest of the family?

As if anticipating my question, "I know it's late, but I had to come and see you and I … I didn't want to run into the whole family," he said with what seemed like shame. "Angie called to tell me what happened. I'm glad she did. I just want you to know that I love you and will be back to see you soon." With that, he squeezed my hand and turned to leave. I felt tears stream down my face even before he closed the door.

I was rudely awakened the next morning by my doctor as he unceremoniously examined my injuries. I struggled to unglue my sticky eyes while he jabbered away, quite unaware of my sleepy state. He explained to me that my jaw would probably remain wired for approximately four weeks. Further explaining, we don't actually treat cracked ribs, except to keep them immobilized. "They would heal on their own," he assured me. "The abrasions and contusions will heal fairly quickly," he said smiling.

Nevertheless, I groaned. *On the upside, a liquid diet meant shed pounds.*

When he finally asked how I was feeling, I smiled slightly, which I could hardly muster. *Like I was hit by a New England Patriots linebacker, repeatedly.*

"I'll check in on you tomorrow, Trina. For now, no dancing," he joked as he patted my knee and left the room. *Funny man!*

I was grateful to have the use of my right arm. *Thank you Lord.*

The hospital chaplain was obviously quite experienced with cases like mine. He brought me a small chalkboard, which allowed me limited communication with my world. It was surprisingly awkward at first: holding the board away from my painful ribs, keeping it steady, and positioning myself in just the right way. After fumbling several times I began to get the hang of this primitive yet effective method of communication.

I looked up in time to watch the door slowly open and Kevin peeking around the corner whispering, "Aunt Trina? Are you up for a visit?" I wanted to jump out of bed and give him (and his friend) a big bear hug, but for now he'd have to settle for a weak smile.

He was the first to have the privilege of deciphering my chalk-board chicken scratching. I couldn't stop the tears from flowing as I attempted to express how thankful I was—how proud of this brave young man.

"It's okay, Aunt Trina, I know, I know," he said while attempting to blot my tears. "By the way, he's back in jail, for now. You are planning to press charges, right?" he asked, revealing such deep concern. "Hopefully this time they'll throw away the key."

Wanting to arrest his concern, I nodded my affirmation to his question and began clicking away with my chalk: *How R girls? How is Gram? How is Buddy?*

"All are doing okay. The girls are coming to see you later this afternoon. We're coordinating our visits so we don't wear you out. I think Gram plans to visit after breakfast, but honestly she looks pretty tired. I doubt she'll stay too long."

I nodded my acknowledgement, hopefully conveying that I understood. *Kevin, what made U come back 2 my house early? Mia said U picking them up around 9,* I intently clicked on my board, trying to think of creative ways to abbreviate my words.

With that boyish grin, he simply said, "We were broke and hungry. Mia told me you guys were making pizza."

I couldn't help but smile (although it hurt) as I went to work on my board again writing, *I'm so gr8ful 4 ur appetite! I owe U a pizza.*

We both smiled as he bent to kiss me good bye and gently squeezed my hand. "I love you, Aunt Trina. See you soon."

Right on schedule, Mom and Dad appeared in the doorway. I couldn't help but giggle as I watched the two of them clumsily pushing through the doorway, each wanting to be the first to get to me. She was laden down with balloons and a small Tupperware bowl of something sloshy. Daddy was carrying a beautiful flowering gardenia plant. The fragrance was irresistible.

Could anyone have better parents?

I watched as they fussed with my blankets before they made themselves comfortable.

Mama spoke first, "Sweetheart, I realize you are on a liquid diet, so I brought Italian Wedding Soup … broth only. I'm well aware that you love the tiny meatballs and ancini di pepe pasta, but for now you'll have to settle for broth only. When you're ready, I'll make you the real stuff," she said patting my knee.

Tapping on my trusty chalkboard I responded, *Thank U both. Too much for U, Mama?*

"No, no, I'm feeling stronger every day. I'm doing good, huh Vincent?"

"You can't keep a good woman down," he said with those beautiful green eyes twinkling at me. Yet, there was no way to deny it, Mama looked worn out, and I felt badly that I added to her burdens.

Daddy thought my chalkboard was quite ingenious. "Can't keep my little girl quiet," he teased.

I interacted with my folks via my chalkboard as best I could. They made every effort not to cause me pain by inducing laughter. However, Daddy told several stories of how our friends and family were extolling Kevin's bravery. Daddy couldn't control his laughter as he explained how his friends had dubbed him King of the Agosti Family.

I tapped out, *Will I have 2 bow B4 him? Kiss his ring?*

"No, no, I don't think so. But seriously, princess, we're all very thankful he and his friend were strong and brave enough to overpower that savage," Daddy said with glistening eyes. "I shudder when I think what might have happened to you if they didn't get there in time."

I knew they didn't want to tire me out and would soon be leaving.

Now's my chance; I have nothing to lose. They wouldn't harm their poor defenseless daughter.

I took a step off the proverbial cliff and tapped out, *Joey here late last night, only few minutes, kissed me, told me loved me, left.* There was that deafening silence once again, hanging heavy in the room. They looked at me then each other, and Mama squeezed my hand, not uttering a word.

Clearing his throat, Daddy said, "Maria, I'm going to find the men's room. I'll be right back." With that he left, and I gave my mother a mournful glance.

She chose not to respond to my message, but not long after Daddy walked away, she leaned in close to my ear and whispered, "He's been visiting me all through my treatments, when your Dad is not home." We both smiled and with that revelation, I rested. I was so very thankful that Mama entrusted me with that nugget of hope.

As I watched them walk out of my door, I purposed in my heart that when I was strong again I would get to the bottom of this horrendous rift that is threatening to destroy our family. I would attack it like a pit bull, not letting go until I knew the truth of it, no matter how ugly. Not just know the truth, but hopefully see it through to a resolution and to healing.

When Sal pulled the car into our driveway, I released a long, satisfied sigh. "Good to be home, huh?" he said with that beautiful smile. I could only muster a nod, moved by a feeling of contentment. Had I been away from my cozy little home for only a few of days? It felt more like weeks. *Ahh … there is truly no place like home!*

The first order of business was for Sal to restrain Buddy for a short while before he helped me into the house and got me settled; his excitement was unbridled. I half expected this bundle of love to jump into my lap. Needless to say, I wept at the sight of my best four-legged pal. I couldn't endure losing my furry friend at this point in my life, but here he was, perky as ever.

We recuperated together, Buddy and I, although he appeared to be almost back to his normal playful self. He only left my side when absolutely necessary. He lay by me when I was on the sofa, by my fireside chair, by my bedside, and he even attempted to follow me into the bathroom. I still couldn't talk to him, but I nearly rubbed his lush fur off with my continual petting.

I wasn't the least bit surprised when Donna appeared at my door. She carried an armful of casseroles, soups, and desserts. I pictured her chained to her kitchen, cooking up a storm the whole time I was hospitalized. Ever so gently my dearest friend embraced me, "I'm so glad you're home and healing," she sniveled. "I don't know what I would have done if anything happened to you, I mean worse than happened … I mean, I'm so glad you're okay. I love you." After composing herself she declared with a broad grin, "You look good, and for once, I get to do all the talking."

She always makes me happy. *Don't make me laugh, hurts,* I wrote, still depending on my chalkboard.

"How about a cup of tea?" she asked Sal and me, already making her way toward the tea kettle.

"I know you can't eat those casseroles yet, but Sal can pop them in the oven and you can be a lady of leisure. The broth and soft stuff is for you. Yummy, huh!"

I wrote out, *U R the best! Sorry, I fell asleep your hospital visit.*

"That's okay. But I've got to tell you, you looked so exhausted that you actually kind of scared me. Also, your family was there so often, I didn't want to overstay. Better that you got your rest. That's was hospitals are for, right?"

"Donna, can you hang out for a bit, I need to pick up Trina's prescriptions," Sal called from the foyer.

"Sure can, take your time, I have nowhere to go," she replied while fixing our tea. He thanked her and was quickly out the door.

She set our tea on the coffee table to steep a bit and then asked, "One- or two-word answers Trina. How are the girls doing? How are Kevin and his buddy?" Buddy raised his head and wagged his tail at the mention of his name. We smiled and settled him back down.

Chalk dust flew with my answers, *Girls and boys doing great!*

"I don't get it. Why did that evil guy come after you? You have nothing to do with Cindy, other than being Mia's aunt."

Trying hard to simplify this story into a few characters for the blackboard, I simply wrote, *I was SW their case long ago. All I can say now.*

Donna smiled and accepted that answer with her usual grace. "Okay, but you are all safe now ... right?" she asked with those deeply concerned eyes.

Hope so. In jail 4 long time.

We sipped tea and she babbled nonstop until Sal returned with my medications. Noticing my drooping eyes, she cleaned up the kitchen, kissed me on the cheek, and headed for the door. "I'll be back in a couple of days. I love you, kid, and no jitterbugging while I'm gone."

Donna, always so easy to be with ... my truly faithful friend.

"Honey, I picked up deadbolts for all the exterior doors. I'm aware that Cindy's dad is behind bars, but that whole incident got me thinking, it's a simple and smart thing to do. I should have done it years ago; it was careless of me to ignore something so basic to your safety. I'll get them installed before I go back to work, okay?" he explained in a rather downcast manner.

I held his gaze for a moment, and then realized he was blaming himself for the attack. I hastily tapped out, *NOT your fault!!!*

My prince charming smiled back at me with glistening eyes, "You would say that," he softly responded while tenderly kissing my forehead.

I nodded, immensely grateful for this man who is always concerned for my safety and wellbeing. Feeling relaxed for the first time in days, I began to drift off in my comfy recliner when Mia and Cindy strolled through the door carrying get well balloons, big smiles radiating from their beautiful faces. I was delighted they were so upbeat and chipper. I don't recall Cindy coming to the hospital. If she had, I likely slept through her visit. So today, being the first time seeing her since the incident, I desperately wanted to be sure she wasn't carrying any misplaced guilt. She needed to understand that she bore no responsibility for her father's behavior. These precious girls smothered me with warm hugs and kisses, and I loved it. Even with the twinges of pain, it felt good.

We visited for a while, but Sal had quietly clued Mia in that I was still very tired, because they repeated several times they wouldn't be staying very long.

It came toward the end of their brief visit, the question I had anticipated. "Mrs. L., I've been thinking about something … and if it's okay with you, I have a question. It's probably nothing, but I can't get it out of my mind. Just before my dad attacked you he screamed something at you, but I just don't understand what he meant," Cindy solemnly ventured.

What's that? I scribbled.

Hesitantly she proceeded, "Well ... he said, 'you took her away from me once and it's not going to happen again,' or something close to that. Do you have any idea what he meant by that?"

Did U ask your mom? I wrote.

"No, I was so upset when I got home, and when she heard what happened she sure wasn't up to any questions either. Besides, I have my doubts that she would have known."

When I get voice back more details, but I was social worker. I jotted away.

But before I finished my sentence, her gaze penetrated me, as though she was seeing me for the first time.

"Wait ... I think I remember! You were there! You ... I think you carried me out of my closet! You saved my mom!"

Mia was confused, totally in the dark as she listened to her friend unfold some long ago scenario. Not to mention her aunt's confirmation of that scenario as it continued to be brought into the light.

"Now I understand, now I get it! He's held on to resentment, maybe even hatred for you all these years. He blames you, instead of admitting he was a drunk. He should have just looked in the mirror, but instead ... he shifted the blame to you. My dad refuses to admit he's the one ... the only one responsible for destroying our family."

I simply nodded, searching her troubled face.

"I'm really sorry he did this to you; you didn't deserve this." She sat still looking pensive then said, "Thank you so much for ... saving my mom and ... me."

She hugged me until it hurt, literally hurt.

I simply wrote, *I will heal. U and your Mom will heal 2,* taking her hand as she surprised me by kissing my cheek.

And heal, we did!

By the end of June, I was almost as good as new—almost. Sal's teasing was relentless, but probably true. I readily pleaded guilty to talking nonstop for several weeks, indeed appearing to make up for lost time. And of course it was so satisfying to once again put solid food in my mouth. I pledged to never again eat gelatin or plain broth. My first solid food request was pasta. No surprise there. Not just any ordinary pasta but Mama's raviolis. By now she was feeling well enough to make a small batch for Sal and me. I savored every last scrumptious morsel. Those tantalizing sauce-covered pillows were a bit of heaven on a plate. If I live to be a hundred, I doubt I could ever duplicate her cooking skills.

While recovering, Angie kept me well informed of Mama's chemotherapy sessions. She's an amazing woman. She never whined or complained throughout the entire course of treatment. Never a whimper! In all honesty, I cannot make the same claim.

Knowing how Mama relishes time in her garden, I was delighted that she finished her treatments early enough to get back to digging in the earth. She could make anything grow, and grow lively and lush. During this time, Daddy's creative juices began to flow. He built two beautiful garden benches enabling family and friends to sit and visit with her in this special place she called her Garden of Hope.

I was scheduled to return to work August 3, which was fast approaching. But for now, I planned to enjoy every precious minute with my family. Priorities get quickly set in order when confronted with real life obstacles—life and death obstacles. I've come to better understand the old adage, life is too short! *Life is indeed, too short!* It would be a travesty to fritter away one single moment of this beautiful life.

It was a sunny July afternoon, not a cloud in the sky. I picked up some Italian ice (and yes, I did have lots of it while wired shut) and drove to my parents' for an afternoon visit. I was not at all surprised to find my mom scrunched down next to her beloved roses. Watching her serene face, one would never guess she had just come through a serious round of chemotherapy.

"Hi. I brought refreshments," I sang as I approached the garden. "Let's sit and enjoy your beautiful garden."

"Wonderful! Good timing! I need to rest. Ah, Italian ice, just what I have been craving, but you must be tired of it?"

"Actually, it is the only thing from my wired-up days that I'm not sick of."

"Well, I could never get sick of it either. Thanks, honey!" she said grinning at me.

"Where's Daddy?"

"Just ran to the garden shop for me. I need a few supplies."

"Mama, how did you ever get this garden looking so good? We were sure you would have been forced to let it go, at least for this year. Your energy levels can't be normal yet?"

"It would have greatly saddened me to look out here to see weeds and neglect. I just did a little every day. Your dad pitched right in; he managed to do the heavy work. Besides, it's therapy for me, you know."

"Yes, I do know that. Tell me what you were doing with those roses when I got here. It looked like you were cutting into the stem. And what is that jar of honey for?"

"Well, I'm a little bit like a mad scientist," she said with a snicker. "I have been experimenting with this for a couple of years now. I'm grafting roses. It's quite simple and very exciting when it works. I'm loving it!"

"What do you mean?"

"Well, if you really want to know, here is my Garden of Hope lesson of the day," Mama continued, encouraged by my inquisitiveness. "Trina, I'm delighted that you are interested in this process. Okay, here's how it works. I want that beautiful red rose, which has a tendency to be rather sickly and weak, to be grafted or joined with this lovely pink rose, which is hardier and more vigorous."

"Okay, I'm with you so far."

"I begin the process by cutting a single stem from that weak rose and dipping the cut end into my container of honey."

"Why honey?"

"The honey adds moisture, nutrients, and encourages growth. Now watch while I make a V-shaped cut into the more vigorous rose. I carefully scrape away only the outside layer from the stem. Next, I carefully insert the honey dipped end into the cut. Finally, I use this gardeners' tape to secure the stem."

"Wow, I never realized you possessed this level of expertise! But Mama, what results are you trying to achieve?"

"Sweetheart, any rose bush, however strong and healthy it appears, has the potential to become one of even greater beauty and strength. You see, every plant, roses in this case, have their own unique qualities and the blending of two plants can potentially create a more vibrant, healthier, and sometimes magnificent rose. That blending is accomplished through the process of grafting."

"I'm impressed."

Turning her full attention on me and with as much sobriety as ever I've witnessed she said, "Trina, please hear me. My sincere prayer is that each of my children will come to understand the lesson I have learned from this beautiful process. Once you have learned this lesson, I am confident you will reap its many joys and benefits."

"Mama, I don't understand what exactly you're trying to say …" I started to respond as Daddy bounded into the garden, carrying what appeared to be heavy bags of topsoil.

"Let me help you, Daddy," I said starting toward him.

"Not on your life. You are not yet ready for heavy lifting. You two beautiful ladies just sit there and enjoy the flowers," he chuckled, somewhat out of breath.

"Let's go inside. You look tired, Mama," I suggested.

"I think an afternoon nap may be in order. Never in all of my life have I taken naps; they always seemed like such a waste of precious time. Now at age sixty-seven, I seem to need them. I even look forward to a little afternoon shut eye."

"You have been through so much. There is no shame in taking an afternoon nap. It's good for you, right Pop?"

"Sure, sure … I encourage her to rest," he agreed.

I desperately wanted to talk about Joey's visits with Mama, but the timing was never quite right. Now, with Daddy hanging around, is definitely not the right time either.

"Well, I'm off to the library and then home. I've been enjoying lots of leisurely reading and being released to drive again was such a treat. Funny how we take simple things for granted."

"When do you return to work, sweetheart?"

"I'm starting back August 3. I sure wouldn't want to go through that attack again, but I really enjoyed being home, if only for a short time."

"I thank God every day for your full recovery."

"Mama, before I go, I'm curious about something. What, if anything, prompted the name, Garden of Hope?"

"As a matter of fact there is a very good reason I chose that name. Grab my Bible for me, would you?"

"Here you go," I said as she immediately began thumbing through the pages.

"Ah ... I'm very fond of this scripture that says it perfectly: 1 Corinthians 13:7 says 'love bears all things, believes all things, hopes all things, endures all things.'"

Honestly, sweetheart," she whispered, while glancing around, I assumed for my father's whereabouts, "I asked God to help me love like the Apostle Paul talked about in Corinthians. I have experienced a number of ... shall I say ... hard things in my lifetime. They could have robbed me of my faith and my ability to love, but in my garden I am reminded of His perfect love, and that includes the gift of forgiveness."

"Mama, thanks for sharing that. You are an amazing woman!" I whispered. "Now, I think you need to take that much deserved nap. But I'm delighted you are enjoying your garden once again. Have I ever told you how proud of you I am?"

"Oh Trina, I'm just an ordinary wife, mother, and grandmother. Nothing special."

"Wrong, Mama, wrong. You are so very special!" I smiled and kissed her, wanting to stay longer to soak in her warmth but knowing she needed to rest.

Chapter 10

When all else fails, sneak attack! I've had just about enough of this family division. It's a beautiful autumn day, perfect for a family get-together. *I am a woman on a mission.*

Sal was in Boston for the entire day, leaving me without any obligations on this lovely Saturday. I convinced myself I would have a good chance of finding my brother at home. Without any hesitation or worse yet, analyzing it to death, I made an executive decision, making a beeline for the telephone.

"Hi, Ellie, it's Trina," I nonchalantly announced and was met by uncomfortable silence. "Look, Ellie, I would really love to see all of you. How about it? Dinner is on me. I'll bring pizza from Napoli's. Are your boys home?"

Ellie responded, almost in a whispered tone, "I would love that, Trina. I've missed you and the family more than you know. Everyone should be home around five o'clock. Ah … can this be our little secret?"

"Sure can. I don't care how we have to do it, let's just do it and get this family healed. See ya around five," I cheerfully responded to my dear sister-in-law. "Yes, let's do this!" I shouted to no one but Buddy, who raised his head, wagged his tail, and went right back to sleep.

I can only imagine how difficult this separation has been for Ellie and the boys. They have been just as tight with my parents over the years as the rest of us. I'm hoping and praying this visit initiates a crack in the wall. *Lord, widen that crack and break down the wall.*

For no obvious or apparent reason, my mind yanked me back to our childhood. Joey was the most compassionate and forgiving, yes, forgiving kid on the block. It simply was not in his makeup to idly stand by or watch bullies jeer or beat up on smaller, weaker kids. He never appeared to worry about his own safety. Jumping right into the fray, he wouldn't stop until he'd rescued the downtrodden. I am unable to understand what has happened to that compassion, that forgiveness. It appears to be in short supply when he's dealing with his own flesh and blood.

Lord, how can this be?

The hands on the hall clock seem to mock me, ticking by at a snail's pace. I tried to pass the time by tackling my ever-growing pile of laundry. That didn't work.

Still antsy, I began puttering in the kitchen. That didn't work either.

Feeling like a stick of dynamite about to explode, I decided to call Angie and share my plan.

"Hey, Jake, how goes it? Is Ange around?" I casually asked.

"Sorry Trina. She's out with a high school friend. You're stuck with me. Can I help?"

"No, it's okay—just sister chat. I'll call her after church tomorrow." With that I hung up and soon realized I'm on my own here.

The hours continued to move like molasses in February to quote my dear mama. It was torture. Finally, I settled onto the sofa with my Bible in hand. I began to read, praying for peace and guidance.

I felt compelled to read a portion of scripture from the Old Testament. I quickly turned to "Isaiah 26:3 You keep him in perfect peace whose mind is stayed on you, because he trusts in you."

It wasn't long before a soul-quieting peace gently bathed me. *Lord I do trust in you. Thank you God!*

After calling Napoli's Pizza to place my order, I changed into clean jeans and a nice jersey. The air was crisp now but undoubtedly would turn quite chilly before my drive back home. So I grabbed a jacket and whistled for Buddy. "Come on, Bud. Let's go for a quick walk around the block." As always he took me for a walk with his powerful pull and puppy-like energy.

I steeled myself for just the briefest second before ringing the doorbell, then took courage that this visit could very well be the first step toward the restoration of our family. *Wholeness!*

I heard Ellie yell, "Joey, I'm busy here. Can you grab the door?"

Hmm, smart cookie that Ellie, manipulating my brother into answering the door.

Slowly the door opened, and he blinked as though not sure what or who he was seeing. He didn't say a word, causing me to almost lose my determination—almost.

"Hi," holding up the pizza boxes like a peace offering. "I brought dinner. Can I come in or do I have to eat these all by myself?" I tensed as I caught the hesitation in my brother. I felt a jab of pain.

"Sure, Sis, come on in," he finally … finally said.

"Well, look who's here," Ellie said feigning surprise as she rushed forward giving me that familiar, warm embrace. I melted into her, but it was my brother's hug I desired. We stood there awkwardly when after what seemed like an eternity, Joey stepped forward, giving me that familiar bear hug I had been craving.

Anthony and Sammy, like Frick and Frack, lumbered into the foyer, grinning from ear to ear. "Hey, Aunt Trina! Good to see you!" Anthony said as he gave me a sideways hug. "You brought pizza?"

"They're pizza boxes aren't they?" Sammy said mocking his older brother. "He's always hungry, Aunt Trina. But it's definitely good to see you, even without the pizza."

"Well thank you for that, Sammy."

"I'll set the table; we don't want that divine-smelling pizza to get cold. Please, come on in, Trina. Be comfortable," Ellie said nonchalantly as she retreated to the kitchen. The boys also disappeared, as though prearranged, leaving Joey and me alone.

Joey led me to the living room, still not talking. The air was definitely charged.

"Hey you guys painted the walls," I said as I dropped my jacket on the sofa while looking around. "I love the color. It's soft, warm, and inviting. I think it's similar to Mama and Daddy's living room," I said, thinking it was a good segue to the subject we both knew was on my agenda.

"Joey, I first want to say … thank you for your hospital visit. It meant the world to me to look up and see your face," I started.

Squirming, he said, "You're my sister, I was worried about you. I'm glad they put that joker away, hopefully for a long time."

"Mama confided in me that you also visited with her throughout all of those nasty chemo treatments, and for that I am really thankful. Those visits were more precious to her than you will ever know."

"Trina, I'm not a monster. She's my mother, after all."

"Don't go there, Joey. No one thinks of you with anything but love … and longing," I quickly added. "We just don't understand what happened between you and Daddy and …"

"Trina, before you go any further I just want to say that I appreciate you coming today and trying to fix this. But, I refuse to talk about … it. I can't. Not yet."

"Can't you talk to Dad about it?"

"Nothing to talk about! Nothing!" he firmly retorted with glistening eyes and a set jaw.

Maybe I should have pressed, but suddenly it seemed wise to back off. This was at least a start. Weak as it was, it was a start.

"Please convey my love to the family. I don't know what else to say."

"Joey, I'll … we'll always love you! Let's have some pizza," and with that I backed off.

I cried all the way home and headed right for the sofa, trying to pray away the heaviness that shrouded me. Good old Buddy was quick to nuzzle me, never leaving my side. He probably sensed my raw emotions.

Later that night when Sal finally waltzed in the door, he impatiently questioned what had happened, fearing the worst. "Your eyes are all bloodshot … Why have you been crying?" he inquired. Once again, I completely dissolved into a puddle of tears as I unloaded the whole conversation that had transpired between me and my big brother.

I felt so completely defeated. But Sal, my eternal optimist, didn't see it that way. "Trina, you have a lot of love in that little body of yours, and I love that about you. I think it was a terrific gesture to head over there, pizza in hand. Really, I do."

I smiled at him and wrapped my arms tightly around his waist."

"I have no doubt in my mind that your brother was greatly impacted by that love today, whether or not he'd admit to it. He just isn't emotionally ready yet to come to grips with whatever has wounded him so deeply. He will, he will."

"I'm really hoping you're right Sal, but honestly, I'm not so sure."

Chapter 11

Jarred by that annoying ring, Daddy wiped his greasy hands and scrambled to grab the phone. "Agosti's Garage," he gruffly stated.

"Vincent," came Mama's familiar voice, "Joey and his family are here—waiting; dinner is drying out. I thought you'd be home by now. Why are you still working?"

"I know, I know. This repair was more than I bargained for, but I'm almost finished. Give me another fifteen minutes to wrap things up. I should be home in twenty or thirty minutes ... promise."

"Alright, I'll make bruschetta to stave off their hunger. You know these teenage boys, always famished!"

"Okay, okay. See you," he impatiently replied.

Now feeling additional pressure to complete this job, Daddy quickly rolled back under the car. His skilled hands wasted no time in methodically working on this repair toward its completion. "There we go," he said, as if fitting another puzzle piece into place, "ten minutes and I'm done here."

While quietly working, he thought there was an unfamiliar sound in front, possibly near the reception desk. Not moving a muscle, he silently listened but heard nothing. "My imagination. I'm tired... and hungry." Minutes passed, then came a distinct clanking noise.

"Who's there? I'll be right with you, just give me a second," he nervously yelled in the general direction of the front door. No response came back, not a word, not another sound.

Feeling sweat break out, he rolled out from under the car and stiffly stood, feeling every bit his sixty-five years. Wiping the grease from his hands, he gingerly walked toward the reception area, but didn't see a soul at the counter. "Just my imagination," he muttered.

But just on the outside chance that a customer had taken a seat in the waiting area, he started into his normal spiel as he approached the threshold to the reception area. "Sorry to make you wait, but ..." *Thunk*! Daddy took a punishing blow to the back of his head. Blackness blanketed him instantaneously as he fell onto the concrete floor—hard.

"This is not like your dad; it's way after seven o'clock," Mama said as she fixed her gaze on the kitchen clock.

"I'll scoot over and see what's keeping him. Maybe someone stopped by needing an emergency repair. You know how that goes. We'll be back shortly. Save us some bruschetta, boys, Grandpa will be famished when he gets home," Joey said over his shoulder as he promptly left the house.

Pulling into the parking lot, Joey spied Dad's car in its regular spot, but there were no others. "Ma is going to kill him if he got caught up in another job."

Entering the front door, Joey yelled, "Hey Pop, you know you're in hot water; we're all starving, especially my boys!" There wasn't a sound in the shop. "Pop, you here?" he called out again, making his way toward the reception area.

Joey stopped dead in his tracks. The room began spinning as his brain desperately tried to make sense of what lay fifteen feet before him. "Pop!" he screamed, frantically running toward Daddy's motionless body. "Oh God ... Pop," he screamed again, now seeing the pool of blood around his head.

He quickly grabbed the phone and although his hands were shaking uncontrollably, he somehow managed to dial for help. Everything blurred and spun around him and yet it was crystal clear that Daddy was lying in his arms, unconscious and bleeding. "Pop," he whispered, "please don't die! Don't you dare die! Pop, I love you! We all need you!"

It seemed like an eternity had passed but in reality it was only a few minutes before hearing the wail of an ambulance then silence as the paramedics pulled up to the overhead door. They flew in through the office area and without hesitation suggested Joey lift the overhead door. He was reluctant to release Daddy, but he immediately complied knowing it would be much easier for the medics to carry him out on the stretcher.

Joey frenetically bombarded the attendants with questions. "Is he okay? Is he going to make it? Oh God, I should have come by sooner," he chastened himself.

"Listen, sir, we are going to take real good care of your dad, but we must get him to the hospital, now. You can ride along with us or meet us there," the attendant explained, already moving Daddy toward the ambulance.

"I'll … I'll meet you there. Lawrence General, right?"

"That's right. Are you going to be okay?" the older medic asked.

Nodding but feeling more alone than he had ever felt in his life, he stood in the parking lot, sobbing as he watched the ambulance disappear around the next corner. "Mama," he shouted aloud as if being jolted awake from a nightmare. "I've got to get back to the house."

Only after locking up the side door and walking toward the front door did he notice the cash register was slightly open. "Robbery!" But that would have to wait until after he brought Mama to the hospital.

Speeding away from the parking lot, Joey willed himself into some semblance of composure before attempting to spring this on his mother and the rest of the family.

Hesitantly walking into the kitchen, he heard Mama and Ellie conversing in their affectionate and easy manner. Anthony and Sammy were shoveling bruschetta into their mouths like normal eighteen- and sixteen-year-old boys, not even looking up as he came through the door.

"Well it's about time," Mama said as she half turned to see Joey standing alone in the doorway. "Where's your father?" Time seemed to stand still as she and Ellie studied his face.

"What's wrong?" Ellie was the first to ask, noticing blood on her husband's clothes.

"Joey," Mama was next, "tell me what has happened?" she managed with a trembling voice.

"Mama, Ellie, we have to get to the hospital. There was a robbery at the shop. Dad's unconscious, bleeding from his head," Joey stated as calmly as possible. His hands were still shaking and as she moved toward him to pull him into a comforting embrace, Ellie could see her husband had been crying.

"Oh dear God!" Mama cried out, running to snatch up her purse. "Let's go, I must be with Vincent!"

"Boys, you stay here. Call Aunt Trina and Aunt Angie," Joey ordered.

"Not on your life," Anthony protested. "We're going with you."

"Okay, okay. Then please call them from here quickly," Ellie responded. "Tell them to meet us ... where Joey?"

"They took him to Lawrence General."

"I'll call the police later to report the robbery after we see how Pop is doing."

Stunned and frightened, Angie, Sal, and I arrived at the hospital and gathered in the designated waiting area, which was cramped and sterile, not to mention its pukey-green walls. Never losing her sense of humor, Angie whispered to me, "Someone failed Hospital Interior Decorating 101, big time!" as she looked around the room.

One by one, the rest of our family members trickled in until the room was jam-packed. Joey immediately stepped up to the plate, assuming the responsibility of regularly interacting with the emergency room doctors.

The hours passed in painfully slow motion and forthcoming information was minimal. Normally talkative and gregarious, this family was now eerily quiet as we shuffled around that waiting area, thumbed through tattered old magazines, and generally speaking, sat like automatons … waiting. Angie initiated the first of many prayers as we huddled together, pleading for Daddy's full recovery.

Hospital policy dictated that only the closest of kin should be allowed into the trauma unit. Unquestionably, we agreed that Mama should be with Daddy for now. Sammy and Anthony thoughtfully made coffee runs for us as we ticked off the minutes, then hours. No one dared speak of the …what ifs. Some unwritten rule prompted each of us to verbalize only positive, hopeful statements.

I was filled with compassion as I witnessed a young woman crying hysterically; a fatherly doctor whispered what we could only assume was extremely bad news. I sat mesmerized, watching as she pulled her small child to her bosom, rocking the little girl more for herself than for the child. The doctor accompanied by a very young nurse led this fragile woman to a small office just off the waiting area. My heart broke for this woman; I could only guess what she might be facing. I desperately wanted to go to her aid, but knew my place was here with my family.

So much hurt in this world. So much hurt!

Finally, after what seemed like time and eternity had lapsed, we received news that he was conscious and appeared to be lucid. We breathed a collective sigh of relief that prompted another volley of hugs. Good news for sure, but still we waited. Whether from the gallons of coffee or the stress of this situation, my hands trembled uncontrollably. Sal reached out, taking one of my hands and Mia grasped the other, until they finally steadied; I imagined our family linked together, standing firm against the horrors of this world.

More than an hour passed when at long last the attending physician was kind enough to join us in the waiting area, gather Daddy's children, and provide us with the most recent information. His bedside manner, whether practiced or natural, quickly calmed our ragged emotions; he expressed concern for each of us and of course for his patient. Eventually, when I guessed he was confident none of us would freak out, he explained that Daddy received a severe blow to his head causing a concussion. His vision was impaired, but would hopefully clear with the passing of time.

"We expect him to make a full recovery, but it's imperative that he rest until totally healed," the doctor declared with a slight smile. Words like joy, exuberance, or thankfulness fail to remotely describe how I actually felt at that exact moment.

The doctor gave approval for Joey, Angie, and me to join Mama. Everyone else would have to wait until he was moved to a regular room. Thanking the doctor, we quickly made our way to the trauma unit, nearly stampeding the poor guy in the process.

Mama sat as close to his bed as humanly possible, refusing to loosen the tight grip she had on his hand. Fear was still written all over her face.

"Hey, Mama, did the doctor talk to you yet?" I tried to reassure her with a steady voice. "You know he's going to be all right."

"Yes, yes, the doctor just left. But I … I was so frightened. I thought we'd lost him."

"I can hear you, *mio amore*. You know I'm right here," Daddy whispered, keeping his eyes closed. "You can't get rid of me that easily," he huskily joked.

"Pops, you gave us quite a scare," Joey broke in. "Did you see him … the guy that clobbered you?"

"I saw nothing," he said trying to focus on my brother. "I only heard movement in the office, came out, *wham!*"

"Thank God, you're a tough old bird," I joked.

"Can't whack an Agosti that easily," Angie added in her usual light hearted manner. "Don't do this to us ever again, Pops."

"I'll try to accommodate," he said, his eyes half-lidded.

"It was a robbery or attempted robbery, Pops," my brother said. "I'll know better tomorrow after I check it out, then I'll head over to the police station and make a formal report. The police will want to know how much was stolen ... Any idea?"

"I had just made a bank deposit so there wasn't much in the cash register, maybe seventy-five dollars," he said, desperately fighting sleep.

We stayed together until he was settled in his own room and then allowed the kids a very brief visit with their grandpa. This man detested hospitals, and I knew he was going to be a terrible patient; these poor nurses were in for the ride of their lives.

We had already been advised he needed to be checked out, but still Mama was reluctant to leave him there alone. Joey was successful in convincing her that his body had been traumatized, and it was wise that he stay for additional observation and some much needed rest.

"We'll be back tomorrow, Vincent. You behave yourself, and stay out of trouble," she teased. "Do whatever the doctors and nurses tell you."

"Good luck with that," Angie laughed.

A local police officer met with Joe the very next day. He scanned the garage and robotically completed the robbery report, but it appeared to be nothing more than a formality. He clearly conveyed the message to my brother that there were no solid leads or clues. The cash register was cleaned out, but receipts reflected a mere sixty-eight dollars had been stolen.

From time to time Joey made phone calls to follow up with the reporting officer, but we were not deluded enough to believe the thief would ever be caught, and admittedly, the officer never gave us any false hope.

The days following the robbery were difficult for Joey. He was wracked with guilt, blaming himself for somehow not being there for Daddy. None of us expected that of him, nor did we in any way hold him culpable for the intrusion. The blame rested squarely on the shoulders of that vile robber. My brother alone put that unrealistic expectation on himself despite our attempts to mitigate his guilt. Ellie confided in me that Joey was haunted; he could not erase the memory of Pops lying in a pool of his own blood with him only minutes away.

Joey also made his living as a mechanic, but with a well-known, reputable chain of large garages. He was fortunate enough to have been recruited and hired right out of trade school, the same year he and Ellie married. He had no complaints about the company; they treated him exceptionally well. There was no denying that this man still loved auto repair as much as that first day Daddy placed a wrench in his little hand. My father was proud of Joey for striking out on his own, and God knows he was being well compensated—much more so than Agosti Garage could possibly offer. Yet, now Joey wondered. Pop was sixty-five, and the signs of his slowing down were more than apparent.

For days he struggled, wrestling hard with this dilemma, when unexpectedly one day he had a vision—a seedling poking up through fertile soil, a promise of new life, new growth. He knew what it meant and was anxious to talk it over with Ellie, but in his heart, my brother had already made the decision to join Daddy in the shop. He vowed to himself that Pops would never suffer this kind of brutality again—ever!

Daddy, being the rugged individual he was, made a speedy recovery. He astonished everyone by meticulously following doctor's orders, and Mama waited on him hand and foot (nothing new there). We took advantage of every opportunity to dote on him and probably were guilty of spoiling him back to health.

During Daddy's recovery time, I began to worry about my brother. It was evident that he was burning the candle at both ends. He worked his normal hours at his own job, but also worked well into the night hours taking care of Agosti Garage's regular customers. He was concerned that losing customers would put financial pressure on our parents.

At long last, Joey called a family meeting, which isn't a common occurrence. When it does happen, however, we each make every effort to attend. My sister and I anticipated what was on his heart and exactly what he would lay out for family discussion. Call us psychic, or maybe we just know our brother so well; we saw the handwriting on the proverbial wall.

No family gathering ever happens without food and this get-together was no exception. After Mama fed us her delicious lasagna, salad, and hot Italian bread, we settled into the living room for our family meeting, which included every one of the kids.

Attempting to bring this chatty crew to order, my brother started, "You're probably all wondering why I called a family meeting," clearing his throat as he began. Now directing serious attention to Daddy he continued, "Pop, I normally would have come to you first with this, but Ellie and I both strongly felt that the whole family should be involved in this decision." With that, Daddy smiled as he nodded to his son.

"It's not that I consider you old, but you *are* sixty-five," prompting our laughter. "No … seriously, you should be taking life a bit slower, taking vacations, but instead you're working your butt off," causing a second round of laughter. Joey seemed to abruptly change his demeanor. We all took the unspoken cue and quieted ourselves for what we knew he felt compelled to share.

"The truth of the matter is … I cannot handle Pop being alone in that garage any longer. He could have been killed," he said with a quivering voice, which started the waterworks trickling down Angie's and then my cheeks. "No one can dispute that the old neighborhood is getting rougher every day. Ellie and I are well aware that it's not feasible to move the garage out of that location; it's too cost prohibitive," to which Sal and Jake nodded in agreement. "But …" he continued cautiously, "but, here's the deal …I strongly believe that I should leave my job and work with you, Pop," now directing full attention to Daddy. Of course, all of our heads immediately swiveled toward the family patriarch, waiting for some kind of response.

It was quiet except for the sound of squirming kids and shuffling feet. Then Daddy smiled, looked at Mama, and said, "Son, I am well aware of my age, but thanks for the reminder," which was again met with laughter. "Your mother and I have discussed this at length since the incident at the garage. We have come to a wonderful conclusion ourselves." With an impish grin, he said "I want to ask you to become the '& Son' part of 'Agosti & Son Garage,' but with the understanding that it will belong to you, free and clear, when I do decide to retire," which was met with nodding heads and applause.

"So son, I guess we were on the same track. Actually, I have wanted this for many years but always felt it would have been a financial strain on your growing family. My concern has always been that I could never pay you what the big boys were able to pay … not to mention, what you are worth. Mama and I were also concerned about my ability to provide adequate health insurance; our plan is not very good. You must have good health insurance for your family."

"Actually, Dad," Ellie interjected, "my company's health benefits are outstanding, and I will simply add Joey and the boys. I can make that adjustment whenever you are ready."

"So it's settled then, Pop?"

"I would say you have taken a great weight off my shoulders. Yes, son … it is settled," he said with a warm smile.

Joey jumped up, draped his arm over Dad's shoulder, and loudly proclaimed, "Agosti family, I hereby present to you the Agosti & Son Garage!" We raucously cheered in complete agreement, which delighted my brother. Sensing the timing of this announcement to be perfect, it was confirmed, and not one person disagreed with this business decision. Daddy was nearing retirement and Joey, at forty-one, was brawny and energetic. He also possessed extraordinary business acumen; he would succeed in this new business venture, even excel.

Needless to say, we celebrated with, what else … more food.

"I'll put on a pot of coffee," Angie yelled.

"Music to my ears," I agreed as I headed back to the dining room to slice up the Italian rum cakes I had brought along.

I could already hear excitement bubbling over, primarily from Anthony and Sammy. They were eager to spend time helping their dad and grandfather at the garage, especially Anthony with his shared love of cars. He jumped into this venture with both feet, offering to repaint the tired old sign out front and clean up the dingy entrance.

Sammy on the other hand, had his eyes fixed on modernizing the waiting area. He caused ripples of chuckling when he asked if we really needed five-year-old ladies' magazines in the front room. "I'm taking charge of getting some new 'guy magazines' for the waiting customers," he firmly stated.

"What kind of guy magazines are you talking about?" Ellie asked with raised eyebrows.

"Mom, you know, hunting, fishing, cars … guy stuff," he retorted.

"You do realize that women actually drive cars these days," Angie joked. "And they too occasionally need repairs on those cars. So include a few 'gal magazines,' if you don't mind."

"All right, all right, one or two maybe."

Even Kevin was getting drawn into the charged atmosphere. He idolized his older cousins and hoped this venture would provide the perfect environment to spend lots and lots of meaningful time together.

Leah and Mia, now eight and thirteen, were rather indifferent to the entire endeavor. But for the sake of Uncle Joey and Grandpa, they whooped it up with the rest of us.

Sal, being a numbers guy, offered to make available whatever expertise may be needed in the future. Jake simply said, "Whatever you need, whenever you need me, just give a yell … happy to lend a hand."

And so it was! One month later, on December 15, 1994, Agosti & Son Garage was birthed, and we couldn't have been more proud.

Chapter 12

Despite Ellie's insistence that Anthony apply to a four-year college, he would not be deterred. His decision to follow in his dad's large footsteps appeared to be set in stone. "If it's good enough for Dad and Grandpa, it is definitely good enough for me. Besides, I'm not the student that Sammy is; it's not my bag. I love working on cars—period! That's that, Mom. It's already settled. I'm finishing my studies at community college and then trade school. There are several good ones locally to choose from," he firmly stated.

Ellie wasn't happy about it; she was often frustrated by the number of hours and how hard Pop and Joey worked every day. She didn't want that for either of her boys. On the other hand, she acknowledged that the business was indeed prospering, and it was honest, respectable work. Ellie wrestled with Anthony's decision for a long time until she came to the place of being brutally honest with herself. Only then did she bow to her son's wishes.

"If the truth be known, it was very likely the garage would soon need another set of hands. Why not Anthony's hands? 'Agosti & Sons Garage' may not be too far in the distant future," Ellie finally surrendered, "Can't fight city hall or the Agosti men! Guess I have no choice but to hop on board this fast moving train," she relented.

Not long after their grand reopening, new customers began to come out of the woodwork. Joey was concerned they would not be able to meet the growing demand. However, father and son carefully set their work schedule and accomplished much more than either of them ever thought possible. Pop was thrilled to have his boy (of forty-one) working with him, not to mention the resulting spread of the Agosti name in the community.

Ellie and Mama often brought meals to the garage, affording the men more time to complete their scheduled repairs. The shop soon became a hangout for Kevin, his cousin Sammy, and their friends. They were visibly proud of the family business, notwithstanding its greasy environment.

The prospering garage became the subject of many conversations during family gatherings. Every single family member was thrilled with their success, and we praised them unabashedly. Joey felt free to exercise his creative side; however, he had so many ideas that Daddy sometimes grew weary of listening to the tedious details. Still, he encouraged his son, and the entire family encouraged them both.

Snow fell continuously that winter, causing even the most stalwart New Englander to grumble. But from Agosti & Son's perspective, it was obviously heaven sent. Joey purchased a sturdy plow for his truck, adding plowing to the garage's services. Anthony, Sammy, and occasionally Kevin were enlisted into the plowing service. Of course, the women became anxious if the roads turned treacherous suggesting … no, insisting the boys be kept off the roads during those times. Nonetheless, Joey's creative thinking added dollars to the business' bottom line. The plowing business became very lucrative.

It wasn't long before he added car inspections to their growing list of services much to Daddy's chagrin. For years he had wrongly assumed lots of rigmarole would accompany adding inspection services, so he avoided offering it, like the plague. Loving a challenge, Joey researched the entire process and learned those fears were completely unfounded. The so-called mountain of additional paperwork, he determined, was inconsequential when compared to the resulting steady stream of new customers. Joey possessed the power of persuasion and knew how to make a strong case with Pops, who eventually bowed to his wishes. The business began to take on an entirely different image, and its standing in the community grew to be more and more respected.

Just when we assumed winter was about to make its final exit, one of those freak snow storms blew through, blanketing the region yet again. In New England, you just never know! Joey recruited the boys to help with plowing since he and Daddy were up to their elbows in automotive repairs. The boys were familiar with pretty much every road in the immediate area but loved the challenge of zeroing in on some new location.

The standing protocol was for them to always ride in pairs and always get clear directions before starting out on each call. Sammy was exhausted; he'd worked some long hours and had enough for the day, so Kevin was elected to ride shotgun with Anthony on this last scheduled call. Kevin loved these calls if only to be with his cousins.

This call was over by Marston Street near the hospital, so at least they wouldn't be gone long. Or so they thought!

Several hours had ticked by when finally Joey verbalized that he was beginning to worry about the boys. "They should have been back by now, Pops," he said. "Don't you think?"

"My thoughts exactly," Daddy agreed. "I was going to mention that half an hour ago, but didn't want to worry you."

"I can finish this clutch tomorrow. I'm going to check with the caller."

When Joe returned to the bay, he nervously said, "Pops, our truck never got there, so the customer called another garage," now clearly with concern in his voice. "I'm driving over there to check it out, Pops."

"Wait, wait, I'm coming with you."

"Okay, let's lock it up and get going. It's freezing out there. No telling what happened to the boys."

The swirling snow made for poor visibility. They drove slowly, scouring both sides of the road but saw nothing. "This is way past the call site. Do you think they headed back to the garage and we missed them?" Pop said.

"I don't know what to think, but it's definitely getting worse by the minute. I'm turning around to double check," Joey responded. "If we don't see them, I'm calling the cops. They'll freeze to death out here tonight."

"Shh, shh, don't say that," Pop said with a shaky voice. "You're scaring me. God will watch over those boys. You'll see."

"I'm really struggling, Pops. It's getting so slippery I can hardly stay on the road. Wait … what are those lights? Off to the right, do you see them, Pop?"

"Yes, yes, I see."

"I'm pulling off the road. We'll have to climb down that hill to get closer. Hold on a second … I think … It's them! It's them! They went off the road. It looks like they lost control and slid down this embankment."

"Oh, I should have grabbed the good flashlight. This thing stinks."

"You wait in the car, Pops. It's a pretty steep embankment."

"No, no way. I'm coming, you might need help. I'll be fine."

"Anthony, Kevin," Joey yelled at the top of his lungs into the blowing snow. "Hold on boys, we're almost there. Anthony, Kevin … are you okay?" frantically yelling once again when no answer came back. Finally, they heard Anthony's familiar voice through the whirling snow.

"Dad, oh Dad, thank God! We're freezing. I can hardly feel my toes. I'm so sorry … the truck … the plow …"

"I don't care about that. Are you guys okay?"

"Yeah, think so. Don't think anything is broken, probably just bruised. I'm embarrassed and so sorry; I lost control of the truck. It was so stinking slippery," Anthony cried.

"I know, son, I had trouble too. I never should have sent you out in these conditions. It was just plain stupid. Can you both walk?"

"Yeah, I think we're fine," Kevin responded.

Pulling both boys into a fierce hug, Joey said, "Let's just leave the truck for now. I'll tow it out tomorrow and check the damage then. Let's get you guys home and warmed up."

Climbing back up that embankment was no easy feat for any of them, but Kevin noticed Grandpa was really lagging behind, almost losing his footing.

"You okay, Gramps?" he asked trying to support him as they trudged up the embankment.

"Sure, I'm not as young as I used to be you know," he struggled to say with winded breaths.

He was out of breath most of the ride back to the garage, but refused to admit it. Those strapping young men, however, were just fine. A few bruises, but otherwise none the worse for wear and tear on their sturdy bodies.

"The women are going to wring my neck for allowing you out in this storm," Joey lamented, "and I honestly wouldn't blame them. I could kick myself for that poor decision; you guys could have been seriously hurt."

"What storm? Was there a storm?" Anthony grinned. "Dad, there is no sense in worrying them. Look at us; we are both fine. Why not let this be our little secret, right Gramps."

Joey wrestled with that type of rationale, but finally decided it was a valuable learning experience and upsetting the girls was not necessary. All the same, he wondered if it would come back to bite him. He was certain the "mother hens" of the family would not agree with his decision. But in the end, the men unanimously decided to keep their little secret!

The witch hazel bush near the garage door burst open in glorious full array, declaring that spring has finally broken free from winter's icy grip. Those beautiful sunshine yellow blossoms were certainly a welcome, if not a dazzling sight. Spring had not abandoned them, and at long last it was on the horizon.

With the arrival of nice weather, Joey began pressing Daddy into offering roadside assistance. Try as he might, Pops unsuccessfully attempted to ignore this most recent suggestion. Tow trucks were expensive, and he disliked the idea of leaving the shop in order to rescue disabled travelers. Once again, Joey argued that competition dictated they had no choice but to include towing. The days of a successful small community garage were numbered; vying with the big boys was the key to prospering, if not just staying afloat.

Occasionally I'd find myself with a block of free time between home visitations, and I took full advantage of those little serendipities. I loved to drop in the garage, unannounced, with coffee, soda, and sometimes sandwiches from Jim's Submarines, our favorite shop.

On one particular day, Joey repaid me with a kiss on my nose when he spied the familiar lunch bag I was toting. "Oh man, are you trying to butter me up for something? I love these hoagies. Thanks, Sis," he snickered. "Come on, Pop, take a break. Let's eat."

"Hi ya, Princess," Daddy yelled from the washroom. "I'm coming. This is so nice of you!"

"You really have this place in shipshape condition, Joe. How do you manage to convince a stubborn sixty-six-year-old Sicilian to see it your way? I salute you dear brother."

"Trina, in his gut he knows it's either run with the pack or get eaten by them. He's been great to work with, even with my barrage of suggestions for new growth. Between you and me, I wouldn't be surprised if he begins to introduce the R-word into his vocabulary."

"You mean retirement? Are you kidding? He will never retire. He'll hang around here until he is physically unable to roll under a car," I giggled, unwrapping my hoagie.

"Hey, what are you two gabbing about? Glad to see you, honey."

"I was just telling Joey, and now I'll tell you, what you've both done here is really quite impressive. Amazing!"

Daddy shrugged his shoulders and smiled, "Progress, right?"

"Guys, I'm actually here on a mission on behalf of *the family*," I started.

"Wow, sounds like a mob related mission," Daddy said while snickering.

"Very funny, *Don Agosti*," I cajoled in kind.

"The plain fact is that we never had a family get-together to … you know … officially acknowledge the birth of the acclaimed Agosti & Son Garage. Ellie, Mama, and I were kicking around the idea of having a family outing at Canobie Lake Amusement Park for just that purpose."

"Hmm, really?"

"Why at Canobie Lake?" Joey asked.

"Well, we ladies have an ulterior motive. No one would have to cook, not that we don't love to cook for you wonderful guys. But it would be an opportunity for all of us to just kick back and enjoy the day and each other."

"Okay, keep talking, sweetheart."

"They have every imaginable kind of food stand, and the lake is so pretty. We know that the kids would love it; they would probably spend most of their time on the rides. Then, if it's okay with you, we can regroup and head back to my house for dessert and coffee."

"Sounds like you've thought this out pretty well."

"Yup, but first, we need to get a date from you guys since I hear your repair schedule is so full. After all, a celebration picnic must include the two very special guests of honor. So … what do you guys think?"

"What do I think? I love it!" Daddy shouted. "Joey, please grab the appointment book. Why don't you go ahead and pick a date for the lovely lady? You are right, honey, we would love a day off, and nothing is better than being with the entire family. Let's do it!"

"All right! Let's do it!" I shouted back in agreement as Joey and I high-fived each other.

Chapter 13

It has literally been years since I have gone to this park, even though Salem, New Hampshire is so to speak, in our back yard. I must confess that I have never outgrown the magical sway it holds over me. I felt like a teenager again as I showered and dressed, full of anticipation and excitement. Sal and I enjoyed many dates at Canobie Lake screaming on the rides, devouring the fantastic foods, and reveling in endless paddle boat trips on its picturesque lake. Even now, romantic memories stirred within me!

The lake itself is not very large—a mile by a mile and a half—but only a handful of area lakes can match its beauty. The amusement park has been operating uninterrupted since 1902, which speaks for itself. They continually and systematically add new rides and concession stands. Their advertising slogan says it best: "Just for Fun!"

The plan, although my family is not known for adhering to plans, was to meet at one o'clock at the main gate. I fervently try to always be punctual, *try* being the operative word. But in reality more often than not, I'm guilty of running late. Angie, on the other hand, is up with the roosters and by all outward appearances, she never tires of crowing. Staying together will be a monumental task. The teenagers, ranging from thirteen to eighteen, should be fine unless they connect with school friends, in which case we'll probably have to send out the Royal Canadian Police to rein them back into the fold. Leah, at eight, is livelier than an entire litter of puppies and just as cute. She, no doubt, will require every adult pair of eyes to be firmly fixed on her tiny body. Even then, this precocious child may get it in her head to hike in the woods … alone. One never does know with that kid, adorable as she may be.

The local weatherman promised a beautiful, sunny day, and I'm holding him to that promise. I'm also acknowledging it as an answer to my prayers.

My giddiness was not lost on my husband. He too recollects our many dates and stolen kisses at this wonderful park. We were newly in love in those days, exhibiting a gushy kind of love. Now, still deeply enamored, we've settled into a more mature, less gushy way of expressing our love. It's stronger, deeper, and it's nothing short of wonderful.

As we drove into the parking lot, I wasn't the least bit surprised to spot Angie and her family congregating by the main gate. Yup, very predictable!

Leah bolted, running toward us even before our car came to a full and complete stop. I hadn't opened my door yet, and I could hear Ange warning her daughter to be careful.

"Honestly, that girl will give me a heart attack one day," Angie cried.

"Leah, Leah, you have to be careful. This is a parking lot with moving cars. Please, honey, stay with your folks today. This is a big park with some dangerous areas," I half whispered to her as we made our way to my sister's waiting family.

We only had to wait a few minutes before spotting Joey, his entire family walking zigzag toward us in some silly animated dance, laughing and grinning as they approached. The boys eventually broke into a run, attempting to draw their cousins into their crazy horseplay. In my brother's typical style, he quickly set about teasing and harassing the kids by jumping in the middle of the fray. The boys acted annoyed, but when Joey stopped, they would inevitably egg him on, and it started all over again.

"I'm starving," Kevin moaned. "Where are Grandpa and Grandma? I'm craving fried pizza dough. It's the best here."

Seconds later, Mama and Daddy pulled in the parking lot and began making their way toward the rest of the family.

"Hail, hail, the gang's all here," Jake sang out as he spotted them. "So what's the plan for today? Every man for himself or do we attempt to keep thirteen people together?" he inquired.

"I suggest we give everyone two hours to run amok, go on some rides, whatever, then meet at the lake by the rock wall and wander back together toward the parking lot. That way, we'll pass most of the food stands before reaching our cars."

"With their appetites, just that procession alone could take a couple of hours," Joey said elbowing his two sons. We couldn't help but chuckle, knowing the truth of their voracious appetites.

"Remember, I have desserts back at the house, so don't eat yourselves into oblivion," I reminded them. "Plus we do want some time to actually be together in order to really celebrate."

"Sounds like a good plan," Sal added, "you both up for the walk?" looking at Mama and Daddy.

"Sure, sure," said Daddy, "you just lead the way, and we'll follow like a good mama and papa," he said with those green eyes twinkling in the sun. "But children wait, wait … here, here, I bought some tickets for any rides you want," handing tickets to the adults to dole out.

"Thanks, Grandpa," Mia was the first to blurt out.

"You're the best, Grandpa!" Anthony shouted, followed by cheering from the rest of the grandchildren. Leah was jumping up and down as though springs were attached to her sneakers.

They will be too sick to eat anything.

Everyone synchronized their watches as though they were about to initiate a James Bond-style mission. It didn't take much to make these kids happy, and happy they were.

Sal and I stayed with my parents, maintaining a much slower pace. They were happy just to be with their children and grandchildren and wanted nothing more from the day. Arm in arm, Mama and I strolled while perusing the jewelry and souvenir kiosks.

My dear husband desperately tried to win a cuddly soft panda bear for me without much success. For his efforts, I rewarded him with a big kiss. We laughed, remembering his many failures eighteen years ago at the same kiosk. "I'm convinced those stuffed animals are glued to the platform," he joked.

"Sure, sure," said Daddy, consoling him with a pat on the back.

"Vincent," a voice shouted from some distance away. "Vincent, how are you?" came the question as we all turned to see our family lawyer taking long strides toward our group.

"I'm well, Reggie, how are you?" my dad responded.

"I see you're enjoying a family day as am I," he said lifting his chin toward his grandson who was throwing darts at balloons also hoping to win a prize.

"We are celebrating Joey and Daddy teaming up at the garage," I jumped in.

"Wonderful, that's just wonderful! I'm happy for your success, Vincent. I sincerely wish you the best, both of you."

"Thank you," my dad humbly replied.

"Well, I should go, but please remember to come and see me," he said to my father over his shoulder as he returned to his grandson.

"He's such a nice man," Mama said.

"Yes, yes, let's walk okay," Daddy responded.

"Dad, why do you have to see him? Does he have anything else to do for the business?" I asked.

"No, no … we just … I stop to see him periodically. That's all. Let's walk," he said again, more brusquely this time.

"Whatever!" I mumbled. *Much as I love this guy, it truly annoys me when he is obviously blowing me off.*

After purchasing a few little trinkets and enjoying a refreshing snow cone, Mama was happy to simply sit by the lake and appreciate the wonderful view while waiting for the rest of the clan to regroup. I found myself mesmerized as I wordlessly gazed across the lake. What a sight! Watching the swans gracefully float across the lake was nothing short of heart stopping. Surprisingly, they appeared to be totally unfazed by passing paddle boats. Children were firmly instructed not to harass the swans; signs were posted everywhere in the park. Although lovely, the males could be quite aggressive if threatened.

We sat quietly, taking in the sights and were fascinated by what appeared to be diamonds reflecting off the lake. I couldn't guess how many days of my youth were spent right here in this very same spot.

Angie and family were the first, as usual, to reach our park bench. They too were carrying little bags filled with their treasures. Mia immediately shoved her ringed finger at my face, excitedly explaining it was her birthstone. Kevin didn't buy a single thing; at fifteen years old nothing was cool enough to entice those dollars out of his wallet.

I glanced around curious to see what Leah had to brag about. Not seeing her I asked, "Where's Leah?"

Angie's face went white. "What? She was right here a second ago. Jake, did you see her?" she said with a shaky voice. Everyone panicked as together we scanned the area. It was Mama who shouted, "There, there, she's leaning over the rock wall, toward the lake."

"Oh my God, she's losing her balance," Jake yelled, running toward her.

Instantly, we were all leaning over the rock wall. Jake stretched out his hand in a frantic attempt to reach her, she went under, and we all gasped.

I sensed more than saw a blur fly by me, and within seconds, already pulling off his shoes, Joey dove into the lake. By now all of us were gripped with fear, holding our breath … waiting. Tears were streaming down Angie's face; I wrapped my arms around her. Time stood still. We couldn't see anything as we collectively peered into the lake. We were silent, not uttering a single word and just waited.

Much like a rocket had jettisoned up from the bottom of the lake, Joey and Leah were propelled to the lake's surface. Leah's eyes were closed as Joey laid her on the grass, but she immediately began sputtering and coughing.

Onlookers began gathering around us in a free-form circle. Just as she opened her eyes, the park attendants arrived on the scene ready to begin CPR if necessary. But, thank God, this little girl was only wet and frightened.

Crying uncontrollably, she snuggled into Angie's embrace, "I was only trying to feed the ducks," Leah explained through tears.

Filled with thankfulness, we spontaneously descended on Joey smothering him with hugs, kisses, and atta boys until he finally broke free shouting, "Okay, okay!" not liking the accolades at all. "She's going to be just fine. Just a little dip in the lake, right, Leah?" he winked at his niece. "Who's ready to go home?"

"Wait!" Kevin said "I didn't get my fried pizza dough." With that we laughed while wordlessly exhaling, deeply relieved.

"Okay, okay, I won't renege on my promise," I quickly reminded the rest of the crew. "Meet you all back at our house for dessert. Whoever gets there first … you know where the key is … and put on the coffee."

"All right! I knew you wouldn't let me down, Aunt Trina," Kevin smiled broadly as he attempted to wrestle with me.

My sister and brother both made quick stops at their homes for dry clothes, but it wasn't long before the entire entourage arrived. Leah appeared to be none the worse for her little water escapade, and she was certainly not shy about diving into the waiting cannolis.

"Those ducks were so cute weren't they, Mommy?" she innocently exclaimed as she pushed the remaining cannoli into her mouth with the tip of her finger.

"Absolutely adorable!" Angie grimaced as she rolled her eyes. "But don't, I repeat, don't ever attempt to feed them again! Got it?" she sternly admonished. "Your swimming skills are no match for a deep lake, at least not yet."

"I won't. That water was so cold," Leah sighed.

"Tell me about it," Joey chimed in. "And I don't want to ever swim with the fishes again," he said while tweaking her nose.

"Well, it certainly was an eventful day," Mama said "but probably not exactly how we planned to celebrate, huh Vincent?"

"You got that right, sweetheart," Daddy responded.

Again we settled into our normal style of banter, enjoying our desserts, coffee, and each other's company, when I heard the phone ring.

"Got it!" yelled Sal from the other room.

"Kevin, how can you possibly put another thing in your mouth, aren't you …" joking as I looked up to see Sal entering the room, his face white as chalk. "What is it? Who was that? Sal, tell me what's wrong?" I pressed.

"Trina, that was Donna's neighbor, Jeannie."

"Really, she's never called me before, what's up?"

"Sweetheart, Donna and Peter's house is … it's … on fire."

"Oh good Lord, Sal! Are they out? We have to go there," I yelled as my hands began to tremble.

"Okay, okay, I knew you'd want to go," he said while wrapping his arms around me in an effort to calm my emotions and my imagination, which was running amok.

"We're going, don't worry, we're going," he calmly said.

Angie yelled after us as Sal and I wasted no time getting into the car, "Let us know what's happening … We'll be praying."

They didn't live very far, but it felt like an eternity before we arrived. Sal grabbed my hand at the first sight of smoke spiraling into the sky, yet we were still more than a block away from their home. Crying and praying, I desperately fought to suppress every evil thought my imagination conjured up.

The fire police stopped us from parking anywhere near the house, which was still actively burning. It was like looking into the fires of hell ... frightening. The instant Sal stopped the car I took off like an Olympic runner, desperate to reach Donna's house, yet scared to death of what might await me.

"Trina, slow down!" Sal hollered. "We need to find someone we can talk to, someone who can give us some accurate information. Come on now, calm down, and stay with me."

"You're right, you're right," I conceded, patting his arm.

The smoke was billowing out of every upstairs window and flames ... the flames were ... horrifying. Several fire departments were called out and on location, valiantly battling the flames. We scanned the entire area, not seeing Donna or any of her family. I was overwrought.

"Hey, hey," I heard Sal yell to a passing fire policeman, "Did the family make it out? Please, we're close friends. Did anyone make it out?" he repeated to the stone-faced man.

With tears streaming down my face and my eyes fixed on this man, I heard myself pleading with him, "Please, please, we have to know. She's like a sister to me."

"Ma'am," he softly replied as he soberly looked into my eyes, "you should check with the rescue truck ... over there," he half-smiled while pointing to the red truck several houses away.

"Thank you so much," Sal said as he abruptly dragged me by the hand like a rag doll toward the truck.

Cautiously, we approached the back of the truck, frantically searching for an attendant. I'm sure it was against all acceptable protocol, but I yanked the back door open hoping against hope to get some information. Instantaneously our eyes met and Donna was on her feet, flying at me at her full speed.

"Oh thank God, Donna, you're okay," I said as I pulled her into a fierce hug. At that moment, nothing on this earth could have pulled me away from my dear friend. Nothing. I looked down at her bandaged hands but didn't say a word. She was alive!

After a few extremely emotional moments, I finally asked, "Pete and the kids ... where are they? Are they okay?"

"The EMT already checked them over. They're next door at Jeannie's house. They are fine, just dealing with some coughing and stinging eyes. I was the last one out; I tried to find Rascal. I scoured the first floor, but I couldn't find him. The kids are going to be devastated; they love that dog."

"Donna, you should have gotten out with them. You could have been trapped," again pulling her to me.

"I know, I know. It was foolish of me. Trina, it was unbelievable how quickly the fire spread. It was raging in what seemed to be only minutes. I've never been so scared in my entire life."

"I can imagine. Well, as soon as you're up to walking, you're all coming to our house. We have plenty of room."

"Are you serious? You do remember we have two hyperactive kids?"

"You and Pete need a place to get your thoughts together. Our house is the second best thing to being in your own home. Besides, you are family!"

"We won't take no for an answer," Sal interrupted, wholeheartedly agreeing with my invitation. "Stay as long as it takes for you guys get back on your feet. And Donna, this may take a while from the looks of your house."

After the medic cleared Donna, we walked arm in arm to Jeannie's house. There sat her dazed family at the kitchen table with sandwiches and drinks in front of them ... safe. Except for an occasional sniffle and a sporadic cough, they were eerily silent.

The second we walked through the door, Suzanne jumped to her feet. "Mom, where's Rascal? I called and called, but he didn't come."

Donna, Sal, and I exchanged glances. "The smoke and fire probably got him so scared that he ran off," Sal interjected. "I'm sure he'll calm down and come home soon. You just wait and see."

"Jeannie, may I use your phone? I need to let my family know these precious friends are okay."

"Help yourself."

"Hey guys, we're going to the Lamazos' tonight," Donna desperately tried to direct the conversation away from Rascal's disappearance. "Pete is that okay with you?" she asked as an afterthought.

"More than okay. Thanks guys," Peter smiled. "Why don't all of you go on ahead? I always leave a spare set of keys in the garage. I'll grab them and drive over shortly. I don't really want to engage those news reporters that are gathering, but I do want to talk to the fire chief. Donna there is no need for you guys to stay here. You know we'll have to come back tomorrow anyhow and search through the rubble."

"I hate the thought of it. Please honey, don't be too long. You look exhausted," Donna said as she awkwardly hugged her husband, trying to avoid bumping her bandaged hands.

Angie and her family busied themselves at my house while they waited, making up the spare beds and freshening the guest bathroom. When we returned home, she immediately grabbed Donna, laying lots and lots of wet sloppy kisses on her cheek.

"All right, all right, girl! I'm going to need a towel if you don't stop," she laughed at my sister's demonstrative antics.

"I'm sorry. Did I hurt you … oh your hands," Angie almost wept looking at the big bulky bandages.

"No, Angie, you didn't hurt me. The medic said they are not too bad. I should be fine in a couple of weeks."

"Well, make yourself at home … I mean … sure it's Trina's home and all, but still … make yourself at home!" We all chuckled at my sister's abundance of nervous energy.

"You're too much, Angie," I laughed. "Seriously, you guys are free to take a shower, eat, whatever," I said directing my attention to her family.

"I'm going to work on getting some fresh, clean clothes for your family," Angie said as she ushered her own crew out the door. "You need to rest, and we need to go."

"Trina, could you help me with … maybe some plastic bags over the bandages? I really would love a shower."

"Sure thing! As a matter of fact, I have plenty of robes and spare clothing you can slip into. If you'll give me all of your smoky stuff, I can run a load of laundry. You will all sleep better if you don't smell like a bonfire."

While fitting two empty bread bags over my friend's bandaged hands, I offhandedly asked, "Any idea how the fire started? Sal and I guessed it may have been something electrical."

"No clue. I'm sure the fire marshal will be there soon to make that determination. At least that's what one of the fire police told Pete."

Everyone managed to enjoy a nice refreshing shower before settling down for a few minutes prior to heading off to bed; exhaustion doesn't begin to describe their condition at the end of a very long day.

"Thank you for the use of your home, your shower, and your bread bags," Donna laughed as she clumsily sipped a glass of iced tea in the kitchen.

Simultaneously, we looked up to find Suzanne standing in the doorway, staring at us. She wore a facial expression that I couldn't quite define. It wasn't fear; neither was it anger. It was … shame. I immediately knew!

"Mommy? I'm sorry! I'm such a bad person!"

"What? What are you saying, honey?" Donna turned to give full attention to her daughter.

Roughly tugging and twisting on the belt of her bathrobe, she said, "I did it … the fire. I started it, but I didn't mean to. It was an accident."

"Oh Suzanne! Come here and tell me what happened?"

"I wanted to see how those birthday candles work. You know the kind Grandma always puts on our birthday cakes for fun?"

"You mean the trick candles that start up again after you blow them out?"

"Yeah, that kind. So I hid in my closet with a few candles and some matches. I never thought about anything catching fire."

"Go on," Donna gently prodded as she stroked her daughter's damp hair.

"Well, I lit two of them then I blew them out. They started on fire again just like they do on the cakes. But I wasn't ready, and I got so scared when my Easter dress caught on fire that I ran out of the closet and down stairs. I thought it would just burn out again; I didn't think it would burn down our house," she wept inconsolably into her mother's neck.

"Why didn't you yell for me or Daddy?"

"I was too afraid. I thought you'd be mad at me. And now Rascal is afraid and ran away."

"Okay, honey, it's going to be okay. We're all alive and no one was badly injured. That's what is important. But Suzanne, listen to me, that was a very foolish and dangerous thing to do. You could have been killed."

"I know, Mommy. I'm so sorry. Do you ... will you forgive me?"

"Sweetheart, of course I forgive you ... and I love you. They held each other for a long time, Donna rocking her daughter on her lap, so thankful that they were all alive and unhurt.

"Now I understand why the Canadians banned the sale of those candles back in the seventies," I commented. "In light of this incident, I can understand their wisdom. It makes perfect sense to me."

Later in the day Donna unfolded the whole scenario to her husband, and he responded to Suzanne in much the same manner, expressing love and affirmation. I was so pleased that no heavy guilt trips were laid on the poor kid. That would be so much more than any youngster her age ought to carry.

The next night, the fire marshal stopped by our home and confirmed what we already knew; the fire had indeed started in

Suzanne's bedroom closet and was fueled by the abundance of flammable materials, quickly spreading to the rest of the house.

Our primary concern was now for Suzanne; she had turned rather sullen in the days following the fire. She had little appetite and other than playing with Buddy, just sulked around the house all day.

A few days later, big brother Joey banged on the kitchen door, "Hey guys, I come bearing gifts," he joked.

"What have you got there?" Donna asked while helping him to unload his packages.

"Well, kid, I've got homemade pasta puttanesca, compliments of my lovely wife."

"Oh my goodness, that is my all-time favorite."

"I knew that ... well, actually Ellie knew that. And for dessert ... Boston cream pie."

"Oh, Joey, this is so nice of you both."

"I figured if you're forced to live with my sister, at least you should eat well."

"Thanks a lot," I said while playfully jabbing his arm.

"Joe, you haven't called me *kid* ... well, since we were kids," Donna reminisced.

"Yeah, well here's the thing ... you'll always be a kid to me. So, how are you all doing?"

"We're all fine except for Suzanne. She misses Rascal. But really, I think she's feeling badly about the fire."

"Where is that little rug rat?" Joey joked.

Donna yelled up the stairs, "Hey, Suzanne, Joey is here and he wants to give you one of his special hugs."

In what seemed like warp speed, Suzanne bounded into the kitchen and softly muttered, "Hi Joey."

"Come here, little lady, and give me a big bear hug. No, bigger ... No, bigger ... No, much bigger." My brother kept up until Suzanne was giggling and jumping all over him. "See, little one, that's how much your Mommy and your Daddy love you ... more that the biggest, tightest bear hug. They will always love you and always forgive you—for anything."

"Even burning down our house?"

"Yes, you little twerp, even burning down your house. Suzanne, you do understand, that was an accident, don't you?

"I guess I do."

"Good, now get over there and give your mama bear the tightest hug you can possibly give her."

Something finally broke in Suzanne as she jumped into her mother's arms, snuggling and simultaneously bear-hugging.

A week and a half after the fire Pete walked through our kitchen door with Rascal on his heels. It was nothing short of the miracle we had all been praying for. Thank you Lord!

Apparently, he had miraculously escaped the burning house, high tailing it across town where he wandered in search of his family. A kindhearted man found and temporarily sheltered the dog while waiting for the SPCA to locate his owner. Fortunately, many years ago Pete had the veterinarian tattoo Rascal's identity inside his left ear, never expecting it would someday reunite their family. It was a joyful reunion, and I must say that Rascal and Buddy became the best of buds during their stay.

Donna and Pete chose to rebuild their home right on the same site. After endless meetings with architects and contractors, they were confident they had made the right decision and were anxious for the insurance to settle so they could begin their new adventure.

It was undoubtedly a long road back, but eventually the construction moved along at a good pace, and they were in their new home enjoying some semblance of normalcy. As were Sal, Buddy, and I!

Chapter 14

The year passed in normal Agosti mode with one notable exception: The Agosti & Son Garage was rapidly growing and prospering as well as making its mark on our community. The city newspaper even ran a special story in the business section: "Local father and son take garage business to new levels!" Needless to say, we were very proud of them; their hard work brought huge rewards. Daddy, however, was growing noticeably weary, showing his age with each passing month. He simply lacked the stamina needed to keep the pace that was second nature to my brother. Joey was acutely aware of it, frequently encouraging Pops to work a shorter week. Our stubborn father would not hear of it. In fact, I'm convinced he stretched himself, working harder and longer in order to pull his own weight.

As Mama was clearing the dinner table, she offhandedly suggested, "Vincent, let's take a ride along the coastline one day this week. We didn't go to the beach once this summer, not once. September is right around the corner, and you know I don't like going when it's cold."

"I don't know Maria. I just hate to leave Joey alone in the shop."

"But he had that fancy new security system installed."

"No, no I don't mean that, I know it's safer now. It's not a one man operation anymore, and sometimes it gets unbelievably busy. Some days the counter takes too much attention away from our repair time. The free advertising was wonderful but honestly, we'll be ready to bring on Anthony as soon as he completes his courses."

"Okay, okay, I'll take a rain check, but just this once. You're not forty years old anymore and you cannot keep pace with your son."

"I can still catch you pretty lady," he joked, pulling her into a bear hug.

"Oh Vincent, you're too much. But, if it's okay with you, I'm going to organize a girl's day outing! I know Ellie is feeling like a widow these days and would probably welcome some fun time with the rest of us."

"Sure, sure, you go and have fun. Do whatever it is you gals do when you're not in our kitchens, but remember to come home in time for my dinner."

"Honestly, Vincent is that all you men think about?" she said with a playful giggle.

I nearly knocked my father down coming in as he was going out the kitchen door.

"Hey, what's the rush little girl?" he said.

"Hi, Daddy! No rush, just thought I'd drop by to say hello, so … hello!"

"And hello and good bye to you," he joked back. "I'm running back to the garage to grab some paperwork," he said and kissed the tip of my nose.

"Don't you guys ever rest anymore?"

"You are sounding a lot like your mother and just as pretty!"

"Don't you try buttering me up! Daddy, really you should slow down a bit. You know you're not a kid anymore."

"Now you really do sound like your mother. Got to run!" And he was quickly out the door.

Turning to face my mother, I said, "He's like the Energizer Bunny, he just keeps going and going."

"You are right, he surely does. But I think he looks tired lately, and he does not like to be reminded of the reality of his advancing years."

"Oops! That's exactly what I just did."

"Sit, sit, I'll make some tea. I'm glad you stopped by; I was going to call you tonight."

"Oh, what's up?"

"Well, I can't get your father to take a day off, and I know Ellie is bored to death with Joey working so many hours. So I thought a girl's day outing is just what the doctor ordered. What do you think?"

"I think you're a very smart lady, and I wholeheartedly agree. Where do you want to go? Do you have a date in mind?"

"I don't know, maybe the Boston farm market? What about Gloucester or Newburyport? You three girls decide. Being together is the important part."

"Leave it to me, Mama; I'll call Ellie and Angie right away. This will be our first annual girl's day outing. You're a genius."

"Yes, I believe I am," she said smiling. She opened a well-worn cookie tin, saying, "Here … I made biscotti."

The very next Saturday we rose early, met for breakfast at a local diner, and we were then quickly on our way. Not wanting to waste one precious minute of this rare getaway, we planned to soak up every bit of this fun day.

Together, we drove to Newburyport, a lovely historic seaport town. This beautiful town is especially popular over the holidays, adorned with dazzling lights and old fashioned Christmas displays. Tourists also flood this town all summer, making it one of the more popular spots in our area. We were in total agreement that this was the ideal place for our first annual girl's day outing. The distance and location were perfect for us, not far from Plum Island or Salisbury Beach, so we were on familiar turf. The picturesque setting is home to more quaint little shops than we could possibly cover in one day, but we made a valiant effort.

At my suggestion, Mama agreed that she was more than ready to stop for lunch. We found a charming seafood restaurant that overlooked the mouth of the Merrimac River and the harbor.

"What a view!" Angie commented, shielding her eyes with both hands to get a good look at the sparkling water. The harbor was buzzing with activity; boats of various sizes were moving in and out of the harbor. I personally could have basked in this setting for the entire day.

There was no shortage of conversation at our table or laughter for that matter. Angie performed her usual straws-up-the-nostrils routine, embarrassing us to tears. That's my sister: always joking and ever the life of the party.

"This was a wonderful idea!" Ellie said toasting Mama with her raised water glass.

"We needed a spark in our daily routine, especially you, honey," Mama said to Ellie as she gently took her hand.

"Those men of ours don't seem to keep count of the enormous number of hours spent at that garage, although I do believe it will eventually level off. Anthony is anxious to enter the family business, which will lighten the overall work load," Ellie responded. "Even so, I am so proud of them."

"We all are, but for now, let us eat drink and be merry," Angie sang as the waitress served our lobster rolls. "Oh these look heavenly. I haven't had one since we were at Martha's Vineyard, and that was two years ago."

"You know, I was thinking …" I started.

"Oh no, we are in deep trouble now," Angie joked.

"Wouldn't it take some of the strain off the guys if someone else watched the register, answered the phones, that sort of thing?" I asked.

"Your father actually was saying the same thing the other day; the demands of the counter pull them away from actual time spent on car repairs."

Everyone was nodding in agreement while devouring their lobster rolls.

"Hey, what about Mia?" Angie inquired. "She's almost fifteen and would love the extra money. Of course, it would only be a couple of hours a day after school, but something is better than nothing."

"Great idea! I'll mention it to your dad. Who could turn down such a pretty young lady? Do you think she would really want to work in that greasy environment?" Mama asked.

"Pizza grease, car grease, what's the difference? It's money!" Angie laughed.

"I'll talk it up with Joey as well. They may soon have to change their name to the Agosti Empire!" Ellie snickered.

We finished ordering dessert when Ellie said with an impish grin, "Guys, I just love being in this family! You love food, and you love each other. That's a recipe for a perfect life."

We laughed uproariously and then Angie said, "We can't believe Joey managed to snag such a prize. You fit right into this whacky family, and we love you for putting up with us."

"Are ya kidding? I'm the blessed one, you guys are the best," she continued. We finished our desserts and lingered over coffee for a short time.

"Who is ready to shop for a couple more hours? Mama, are you up for it?" I said.

"Sure, I can keep up with you young chicks any day."

With our wallets empty from shopping and our tummies pleasantly full, we walked to the car with memories of a wonderful day together. We were in total agreement that we needed to make the time for more days like this one. Angie picked up on that and excitedly suggested our families go to the upcoming church feast together.

Throughout childhood, our parents faithfully took us to the Feast of the Three Saints, which was associated with Holy Rosary Church. We didn't attend that church, but every Labor Day weekend the Feast became a gathering place for friends and families; many were of Sicilian descent so the dishes were familiar, if not family favorites.

There was bandstand entertainment, food, food, and did I mention, more food. As teenagers, it was the best of the best places to meet friends, stroll through the designated areas, and of course gorge ourselves with Italian delicacies.

Pizza, sausage with pepper sandwiches, calzone, and these delightful little items called crispellis, were just a few of the delicious items that could be found at the Feast. The crowds were unreal, cheerfully waiting in long lines at the Italian Kitchen for these fried balls of dough that were stuffed with either ricotta cheese or anchovies. If you happened to be a purest, you'd order them plain. I will never forget the aroma or taste of those piping hot crispellis.

We agreed to forge ahead with our plans for another family outing. Next time, however, the entire Agosti family would be crashing the Feast.

Driving home from Newburyport was bittersweet. We were tired enough, but didn't want this wonderful day to end. We talked of doing this again next year. After all, isn't that what annual means?

Labor Day was upon us in the blink of an eye and that meant back to school, cooler weather and … the Feast. Everyone was in total agreement that our family should grace the Feast with our collective presence. I personally fasted the entire day, hoping to make belly room for an assortment of scrumptious treats. Sal laughed at me, but I noticed he hadn't eaten since breakfast, and that was very little.

As usual, Lawrence officials blocked off several streets for a couple of days, allowing for safe foot traffic, especially where children were concerned. Angie and Jake were, without a doubt, grateful for this as we recounted the water incident at Canobie Lake. They could relax a bit without threatening to harness their daughter.

We started out together but were soon separated by the enormous crowd. Thankfully, the area wasn't so large that we'd be forever lost from each other. As we meandered down the streets of Lawrence, we met many old friends, which was half the reason for coming. I told myself that these catch-up conversations were not unlike reading their Christmas letters. That is, hearing the abbreviated Readers' Digest version of their lives since last we met. All conversations ended the same, with the mutual promise to get together … real soon. Well, some promises fall by the wayside no matter how noble our intentions.

Sal and I laughed every time we passed an Agosti chewing away on something or another but never failing to sloppily grin while giving us the thumbs up. *My family … so precious!*

I felt a tap on one shoulder and then a kiss was planted on the opposite cheek: sneak attack from behind. Could only be one person. "Daddy, Mama are you having fun?" I asked as I spun around to face them.

"Yes, yes, we are. But, oh Trina, so sad to hear of so many old friends taken ill or passed away this year," Mama said.

"Have to expect that at our age, Maria," Daddy said.

"I know, but still sad. Very sad."

"Mama, let's go over to the bandstand. They are getting ready to play," I cheerfully interjected.

As we made our way toward the music, I heard that way too familiar cry. I quickly spotted Leah on the ground, wailing and holding her bleeding knee.

"Leah," I yelled, "are you okay?" I knelt to check her out.

"I was racing my friend and I fell," she said through deep sobs.

Just then Angie and Jake broke through the crowd. "Leah, did you fall again? Come on, let's get you washed up, but it doesn't look bad."

"Look on the bright side, honey," Jake chimed in, "at least there are no lakes for miles around," which earned him a shove from both Angie and me.

After the band concert, we walked past the iconic Tripoli's Bakery, Pappy's Bakery and the Italian Kitchen. My day was complete and my belly full. *If I was a kitty and you listened closely, you'd hear me purring!*

Chapter 15

Autumn was spectacular in New England. The trees seemed ablaze with deep, rich color. I took advantage of every available Saturday, summer through fall, to wander around our local farmer's market. Bringing Ellie and Mama along with me when they were free was an added bonus. They understood the demands of the garage, but occasionally grumbled when it overflowed to a Saturday, so I reaped the benefit of their company. We sometimes made a day of it: poking, sniffing, and squeezing our way through the kiosks overflowing with their abundant harvests of fruits and vegetables. The market would soon close, surrendering to the frigid temperatures that were right around the corner. But for now, we kept busy while the men were hard at work.

My brother's grey matter never slipped into neutral. His newest brainstorm was to expand the business, and to add two additional bays and hire another set of hands. He was anticipating those hands would belong to his own son once he completed his course of study, that is.

The second half of 1995 was passing like a whirlwind. Things at the garage got done in record time and done well. Word of their success continued to spread in the greater Lawrence area. Needless to say, expansion seemed inevitable.

"Pops, have you given any more thought to the expansion we talked about?" Joey asked while finishing up on a new exhaust system.

"Sure, sure, but I'm afraid I still have cold feet. It's a big step that could make us or break us," Daddy responded.

"I really believe we can do this. Our credit is excellent, so I know a loan would be a piece of cake …"

"Let's toss it around a while longer before making a final decision, okay?" Daddy said cutting him off.

"Yeah okay, we'll revisit it right after the holidays," Joey conceded. "Mia is working out really well, don't ya think? She's quite businesslike for a kid, which honestly surprised me. I'm looking forward to bringing on Anthony. It will soon be the Agosti Dynasty," he joked.

"I don't know about any dynasty, but I'm sure enjoying having my family around; I never envisioned this happening," Daddy responded with a wide grin.

"I'm going to make coffee. Either of you up for a coffee break?" Mia yelled from the counter.

"Sounds perfecto!" Daddy yelled back to her.

"I'll second that. Give me another ten minutes, and I'll be there."

Grandpa dropped heavily into in his favorite chair, sipping his hot coffee and enjoying the rich, robust flavor.

"Mia honey, you make a darned good cup of joe! Who taught you?" Grandpa asked.

"A cup of what …?"

"It's slang for a cup of coffee; never heard that one?" Grandpa asked.

"It sure wasn't my sister! Her coffee tastes like dishwater compared to yours," Joey said, tickling her while snorting. "And don't you dare tell her I said that. I'll deny it."

"Hey, you're getting grease on my sweater. And for your information, it was my dad who showed me how to make a good 'cup of joe,'" she laughed back.

"We think you're doing a bang up job here, Mia," Grandpa smiled.

"Thanks, but you do know I heard you two in there," she smiled. "I like it! I can do homework when it's slow. When it's busy ... I like it better. Thanks for giving me the job."

"Eh, keep it in the family, I always say," chortled Joey.

The banter between Joey and the kids was always fun to witness; he was their idol, no two ways about it. Mia intermittently worked on her homework as the afternoon passed by. The level of shop activity was fairly normal.

"Joey, I'm ready to call it a day," Dad called out. "Can you handle it from here?"

"Sure, go on home. You look beat," Joey answered. "I won't be here much longer either."

Watching Grandpa's car pull out of the parking lot, Mia turned to her uncle, "I think Grandpa is working too hard. He looked awfully tired today," she said wistfully with concerned eyes.

"I agree, but he's one tough old bird and doesn't listen to my suggestion to cut back."

"Yeah, I noticed," she said as she picked up the next phone call. "Hi Daddy! Sure, I'll ask."

"Daddy wants to know if you can drive me home. His meeting is running late."

"Sure, kid, no problem."

"Thanks for the ride, Uncle Joey ... Can I ask you something?" Mia questioned on their drive home.

Joey, being the ever faithful big brother type, mentally geared up for what he sensed was an important question, at least in Mia's mind.

"Shoot!"

"Umm, I have this friend; he's a guy," she sheepishly began.

"Oh boy, I am not liking how this is starting."

"Just hear me out. Please, Uncle Joey."

"Okay, okay, continue."

"He's sixteen, and I'm almost fifteen. He's really nice. Mom and Dad won't let me date until I'm sixteen, but the real problem is they don't like Ricky."

"What don't they like about him, exactly?"

"He's sort of, I don't know … lost? I mean, his dad abandoned them when he was only five."

"Yeah, so …"

"I guess the real reason is because he got kicked out of school, twice, for mouthing off and fighting. But that was over a year ago, and since then he's been trying really hard; he wants to be a better person. He loves cars, just like you do."

"So, what are you asking me, honey?"

"Can you talk to my mom? Maybe she'll let me see him in a group setting or at the house?"

"I don't know, kid. This could get messy."

"Please, Uncle Joey, could you just try?"

"Tell you what, I'll talk to your mom and suggest that Ricky comes by the garage so I can check him out. But I want you to promise me something: no sneaking around or doing anything behind our backs. Deal?"

"Deal!" she responded with a giant hug, as she quickly gathered her things and ran from the car to her home.

"How do I get myself into these things?" Joey grumbled as he drove away.

"Good morning, Pop. Crisp out there today, huh?" Joey said as he strolled into the garage.

"Hey there, son," Daddy said, barely looking up to greet him.

"Sheesh, Pops! What time did you come in today? I thought I was up before the birds, but you beat me again."

"I just wanted to finish up some paperwork before I get myself greasy."

"I'm going to ask you, yet again, if you would please allow me to take some of that paper work off your hands. I can at least make deposits, balance the checkbook, something," Joey pleaded. "And why do you insist on keeping that post office box? We get everything delivered here at the shop. It's a waste of time and money running over there."

"No, no, I like to make an occasional drive to the post office. Some of my older customers still use that post office box number. It's okay. We'll keep it," he insisted.

"Pop, it's easy to update them. I can do that for you."

"I said no! I want to keep the post office box. End of discussion!" Daddy briskly retorted.

"Okay, okay, what's the big deal?" Joey reluctantly conceded. "Sheesh! Someone got up on the wrong side of the bed," he muttered under his breath. "I'm going to start on the Ford now."

Daddy just nodded as he watched his son roll under the old sedan. He felt pangs of guilt at his impatient outburst. In an effort to smooth things over, Daddy later gave in and contritely said, "Okay son, you can help with the deposits and balancing the checkbook."

"Terrific, we're making progress here." Joey smiled as he gave his father the thumbs up.

Angie and Jake relented to Joey's suggestion, but only after a long, laborious conversation. They were in agreement that Ricky could visit the shop and be "checked out" by big brother. Angie was confident that not one single shenanigan would get past her brother; the garage seemed a neutral and safe setting for their initial meeting.

The very next afternoon while Mia was busily answering the phones, Ricky sauntered in the front door like he owned the place. Joey's radar started to ping, and he was immediately wary of this guy. He discreetly watched the two of them, trying to get a feel for their already existing relationship.

"Uncle Joey, come out front when you get a minute. I want you to meet my friend. Where'd Grandpa go?" she yelled.

Joey steeled himself for this meeting, expecting the worst but hoping for the best.

"Hey, I'm Joe Agosti, Mia's uncle," reaching to give a *very* firm handshake.

"Pleased to meet you, Mr. Agosti. My name is Ricky. Mia told me nothin' but good stuff about you," he politely responded while extending his own hand.

"Grandpa went on a post office run. He'll be back shortly," Joey added.

He was pleasantly surprised by the kid's demeanor during their fairly lengthy chat that was mostly focused on cars.

"Well it was nice to meet you, but I need to get back to work," Joe said.

"I'd be happy to help you, Mr. A. Just say the word," Ricky eagerly replied.

"Hmm, the kid seems nice and respectful enough, and knows quite a lot about cars. Maybe Angie and Jake jumped to a wrong conclusion about him," Joey mumbled while rolling back under a car.

Later in the day after Ricky was long gone, Joey said, "Okay Mia, here's the deal. He seems likable enough, so he can visit with you here at the shop twice a week after school. But he can't interfere with your work, and maybe he'll learn something watching me. Okay?"

"Thank you, Uncle Joey. Thank you. You'll see, he's a terrific guy, really he is."

Over the next couple of months, Joey grew to genuinely like Ricky. They developed a good relationship. He sensed that Ricky looked up to him, maybe even as a role model. Unfortunately, he felt like his head was perpetually on a swivel keeping an eye on Pop all day and Mia with Ricky on their designated afternoons.

Angie and Jake were satisfied that Mia was abiding by the rules. Big brother was a good influence they had concluded.

It was almost closing time. Joey was underneath a car but he was also watching his niece interacting with Ricky at the counter. He smiled to himself thinking, they actually made a cute couple, that is, once she turns sixteen.

As Mia turned away from Ricky and walked toward the rest-room, Joey caught a flash of something shiny, something metallic. Ricky was tucking something inside his jacket. Oh no, was he stealing something? Don't jump to any conclusions, he admonished himself but hastily rolled out from under the car. Before his niece returned from the restroom, he quickly approached Ricky wanting to be sure, "Hey bud, how's it going?" Joey offhandedly asked, yet focusing on Ricky's jacket zipper.

"Uhm … good! Uhm … no … I'm not good! Oh my God, what was I thinking?" he said suddenly beginning to tremble.

"Excuse me?"

Ricky slowly unzipped his jacket and shakily placed a ratchet wrench in Joey's hand, never making eye contact. "I don't know what got into me. I'm so stupid! I'm thinking you have every tool imaginable and I … I'm sorry. You've been nothing but good to me. I don't know what came over me? Go ahead, call the cops. I deserve it," he said, preparing himself to accept the worst.

"Ricky, let's go for a walk," Joey calmly said.

Once outside in the parking lot he said, "I'm not going to lie to you, kid. What you did back there, well … it's a disappointment. But I'm not calling the cops."

Ricky's head shot up, "You're not?"

"No, I'm not. But here's the deal, Rick … you have to promise me that you'll never, and I mean *never,* steal anything again. You have a bright future ahead of you, and I'm not willing to mess that up because you made one lousy mistake. I trusted you to be with my niece, which is a heck of a lot more precious than a wrench. I'm not going to say anything about this. But … listen to me and listen good …"

"I'm listening."

"I expect two things from you. Number one: finish school. I'm not telling you what to study, but you need to either get a college degree or some type of trade school certification. Number two: make yourself and me proud of you. Got it?"

"Got it, Mr. A. I promise you. No wonder Mia loves you. Thanks, and I mean thanks."

"Hey you guys, aren't you cold out there without your jackets?" Mia yelled as they walked back into the garage. "What are you two up to anyhow?" she asked.

"No, we weren't cold. Your uncle was just explaining some possibilities for my future," Ricky said smiling at Joey. "Thanks again, Mr. A., for taking the time to care about me. It means a lot."

Joey grabbed Ricky in a headlock and ruffled his hair, saying, "Sure, kid, sure. We all need direction and help along the way. You're going to be just fine."

Chapter 16

Sammy and Kevin both suited up for the big game. Neither of the boys possesses the athletic prowess needed to earn them football scholarships nor have they ever deluded themselves by thinking otherwise. But for now, during their high school years, they are content with loving the game and playing hard. Undeniably, it's their recipe for success on the field, as well as making their coach a very happy camper.

For as long as I can remember, Lawrence High School played their rival team Lowell High School every Thanksgiving morning. Of course our whole family has squatters' rights in the blue and white section, frenetically cheering on our home team. Jake and Angie, however, have gone off the deep end more than once when reacting to bad calls. Being typical sports parents; they wildly lead the cheers for their son as well as their nephew. Surprisingly, Joey and Ellie are more reserved in their style of gridiron encouragement. Either way, those boys are keenly aware of our support and our presence in the bleachers. These games against our longtime foe historically take it up a few notches, and adrenaline is free flowing. We've been accused of over reacting to every play, every call, which eventually stokes the Agosti clan into frenetic, animated behavior.

To our credit though, not one of us has ever been thrown out of the stadium … yet.

Mama and Daddy opted to stay home, tending to Thanksgiving dinner. In their ultimate wisdom, they knew we would be ravenous the very second we hit their door. Angie, Ellie, and I dropped off our contributions to the meal earlier that morning. We safely delivered pumpkin and apple pies, squash casserole, and the old faithful green bean casserole, while Mama handled the rest.

Daddy really can be quite helpful in the kitchen when he wants to be. Besides, it gives him the opportunity to get first dibs on everything, insisting he's responsible for quality control. His self-proclaimed job description was simply to taste, ensuring nothing but culinary excellence was fit for his family. We humor him! Admittedly, they are both old pros at getting a big meal on the table with years of experience. Later in the day while enjoying our turkey dinner, we heard hilarious stories of Daddy waltzing around the kitchen while tuned into the game on the radio and tending to every tiny little menu detail.

"Right there in the kitchen," Mama teased, "he would frequently break into loud, robust cheering whenever the announcer mentioned either Sammy or Kevin's name." Covering her mouth in such an innocent, girlish manner, she said, "And your old Papa here once or twice got so carried away that he spun me around, 'tripping the light fantastic!'" she giggled. "His antics are more entertaining than the Macy's Thanksgiving Day parade," she said.

This Lawrence vs. Lowell game was played at the Lawrence Stadium, and it was freezing cold. I have learned the hard way to dress appropriately, even if the frigid temperatures unexpectedly make their unwelcome appearance as early as November. Layering clothing was undoubtedly the only way to survive such an exceptionally cold morning, especially sitting way up in the top row of the stadium. The wind was relentless as it whipped across the open field. But we knew how to mitigate the discomfort: blankets, thermoses of hot cocoa, and twelve pairs of wool socks per person (slight exaggeration). Let the game begin!

The game started with high energy and high hopes, but by the second quarter both teams appeared to be sliding into an abyss. Nevertheless, we dutifully cheered them on, ignoring what we were seeing, hoping for the best. Regardless of all my carefully planned layering, by half time I felt like a block of ice, nuzzling into Sal's chest. Joey pressed from the other side, trying to warm me. As a matter of fact, we all snuggled into each other, wrapping ourselves in blankets. Ah ... shared body warmth.

During the halftime band exhibitions, we all scooted to the much needed restrooms and to refill our hot drinks. As Joey and I were starting to climb back up the bleacher stairs, I saw that gal. I can't explain why, but I definitely remembered her from Salisbury Beach. I was only fifteen and am now forty-two, but that face and her demeanor were unforgettable.

"Joey, Joey, quick look over near the chain link fence. Do you see the woman wearing the red hat and mittens? I would guess she's pretty close to our age? Don't be so darned conspicuous!" I admonished him with a playful jab.

"Yup, I see her. Why?"

"Does she look familiar to you? Try to get a good look at her."

"Yeah I guess. It's kind of hard to tell from here, but there is something familiar about her. Why don't you just go on over there," he suggested, "and say, 'Haven't we met before?'"

"You're right. Maybe I will," I replied, turning just in time to see her disappear into the sea of people. "Oh shoot, she's gone. Can you believe I remember her from that long ago?"

"What, what do you mean *that* long ago?"

"Salisbury Beach ... volleyball ... family vacation. Don't you remember?"

"Man you must be part elephant. What a memory."

He just shrugged it off, but I searched the crowd for the rest of the pitiful game, looking for her … I say pitiful because we lost 24 to 7.

Oh, the boys are going to be so bummed out, but on the bright side, a feast awaits, I thought to my frozen self.

Charging in the door, we pushed and shoved each other, each attempting to plant our backsides as close to the roaring fireplace as possible. Our collective icy bodies must have lowered the internal house temperature by five degrees. The smells wafting through the air were tantalizing, but body warmth was our priority, at least for the moment.

To my surprise, the loss did not dampen the boys' spirits in the least. As a matter of fact, by the time they were showered and dressed, both were laughing and roughhousing, as per usual. *Those kids have their heads on straight.*

Besides, how could any of us dare to be bummed out today? After all, it was Thanksgiving Day. We were toasty warm, abundantly fed, healthy and happy, and oh so thankful!

"Not you too! The Agostis are dropping like flies! Just stay in bed and get plenty of rest; I'm sure Mama will take good care of you," Joey talked into the phone as he ran his hands through his thick, black mane.

"Don't tell me your dad's got the flu too," Ellie muttered as her husband hung up the phone.

"We obviously shared more than dinner and gifts this Christmas," Joey said. "Pops, Mia, and you are presently down for the count. It's looking like more of us have succumbed to this nasty flu than not."

"This too shall pass," Ellie weakly smiled as she padded off to her warm bed. "I'm not going to kiss you goodbye. You're one of the few who've escaped its clutches. I love you and don't work too hard," she called back over her shoulder all the while sniffling into her tissue.

Smiling he said, "Love you too. Call me if you need anything, see you tonight."

"Man, Pops never gets sick," Joey mumbled while unlocking the office door. "Must be one potent flu bug!" Joey flipped through the appointment book and was actually glad for the bit of reprieve he was seeing. "Only one appointment. Maybe all of Lawrence has the flu too, and they're all under their cozy quilts," he said to the empty office. "This just might prove to be an opportune time for catching up. Can't hurt to enjoy a breather every so often."

Being alone in the garage may also provide exactly the right opportunity he'd been patiently waiting for. Still trying to convince Pops of their need for expansion, he decided to use his father's sick time to surreptitiously gather information, which he was confident would make his case.

Dad was a black and white kind of guy; he had to see it to believe it. Determined to prove their financial ability to enlarge, he planned to present Pops with a viable plan, and he was convinced a budget proposal based on hard facts would do the trick. To accomplish this, he needed numbers, cold, irrefutable numbers. His plan was to dig out these numbers today, and tomorrow if necessary.

Single mindedly, he set his sights on accomplishing that goal. Very few outside interruptions sidetracked him from that goal, and that was an extra bonus. Within a couple of hours, every piece of paper he could lay hold to was spread haphazardly across the top of Pop's beat up old desk. "Hmm, this just might take a bit longer than I expected," he murmured. Working until bleary eyed, he desperately tried to make sense of the numbers that lay before him, yet satisfied with his findings to this point. However, as he began to scrutinize income and expenses, he realized pieces of information were missing. Actually, large chunks were missing. Knowing how attentive to detail his father is, Joey was certain this information was simply misplaced or misfiled, but try as he might, the missing information remained elusive.

After scratching his head and pondering his problem, Joey decided the only logical way to proceed was to thumb through every item in the file cabinet. This was turning into a monumental project, much larger than he'd originally anticipated. But his pit bull determination would not allow him to quit. Joey assured himself that the needed answers were hidden somewhere in these files, wherever that may be.

While eating lunch alone, he couldn't take his eyes from the small closet in the corner of the office. Like a thunder bolt, it suddenly occurred to him that he'd never seen the inside of that closet. He now thought it extremely ... odd ... that in all the years he'd hung around this garage, he'd never even seen it opened. Could the missing information have been inadvertently stored in that closet? Once, only once, he observed Pops sliding the storage closet key from his jacket into a tiny box that, at that time, was kept in his desk. He thought to himself, "I wonder if that key is still there?"

A wave of guilt washed over him as he slowly pulled open the drawer in search of that old box. After riffling through the drawer for a short time, he did indeed find the box. Another tidal wave of guilt hit him as he opened it up. There was the key he hoped would answer his questions.

"Oh man! Where do I begin?" he mumbled to himself as he gazed at the methodically stacked boxes—lots of boxes. "Well, I guess I just pick one and give it a go," he blurted out loud. He hit the jackpot on the second box. All his missing information somehow found its way into this closet. As he pulled out the elusive paperwork, he caught sight of a checkbook. Again, he wondered if Dad misplaced it, or maybe it was inadvertently misfiled.

Thinking back to Dad's attack, Joey wondered if he could possibly be foggy from the head trauma and no one noticed. After all, he did suffer a pretty bad concussion.

He opened the checkbook and was surprised ... no, shocked to see that it was a personal checking account, and Mama's name was not on it. And what was it doing in his office closet? "This is really odd, totally against Dad's principles." Reflecting back over the years, he'd adamantly taught his children that once married, you are *one* in everything. He did not condone husbands and wives maintaining separate finances, so what could possibly justify his keeping a personal checking account? Even though niggled by guilt, curiosity spurred him on to further investigate.

His quest to find spreadsheet numbers was quickly pushed aside; his quest to solve this perplexing puzzle became a top priority. Analyzing the entries in the checkbook register revealed the account had been opened in May, 1955. He plopped down at his desk and scanned every single entry, both deposits and written checks. Not able to take his eyes off his father's handwriting, a pattern seemed to emerge.

He noted consistent monthly deposits of sizeable amounts, and he noted they were entered on approximately the same date each month. He was even more befuddled by the checks that were written. Carefully studying each entry, he was certain, yes, positive, it was Dad's handwriting. Those monthly checks were written, not to a name but to a set of initials ... BI. "Who the heck is or was BI?" he questioned himself. "BI, BI," he repeated over and over.

He further noted that those monthly checks to BI continued to be written (no exceptions) from May, 1955 through May, 1973. "Hmm, eighteen years," he played over in his head. "And who on God's green earth could he possibly have owed a personal debt to for eighteen years?" Again he searched his memory and wracked his brain for anyone in the family, friends, or business acquaintances with the initials ... BI. Nothing!

Returning to the checkbook register he then discovered that the checks became sporadic after 1973. No ... wait ... not sporadic, they were still consistent, but now only written in the months of May and December. The entries now changed from BI to LI. He also found two entries with "gr" written in parenthesis: one for June, 1973 and one for May, 1977.

"This seems ... looks like ... this couldn't possibly mean ...!" Joey shouted in exasperation.

Hoping against hope to find a logical answer to his questions, he decided to take a look at Dad's address book. The address book was original to this business, so of course there would be hundreds of entries, many were crossed out but many more were still active. He methodically scanned every single active entry but found nothing or no one with those initials.

Frustrated, he slumped into his chair not knowing which direction to turn. Staring into the closet, by happenstance his eyes fell onto his father's ancient Rolodex card holder. "It's worth a shot," he said, already making his way toward the closet. Carefully carrying the old relic to the desk afraid the old yellowed cards would crumble right in his hands, he very cautiously began to spin it around.

After scanning a few of the dusty old cards, he concluded that this file system had been used for the oldest of the garage vendors, and it was not likely he'd find anything here. But, he dusted it off and painstakingly proceeded to search through each card. It was then that a folded piece of paper taped to the very last index card grabbed his full attention. "Humph, that's odd," he said. "Well, I've come this far, might as well finish the job," and with that he carefully pulled off the tape and unfolded the scrap of paper. There it was … LI. along with two telephone numbers. A line was drawn through one, maybe it was an older number, but both were obviously Lowell exchanges.

Sitting in silence, paper in hand, he decided to call the number. Nervously, he dialed and waited. If it was a vendor, he reasoned, someone would answer stating the company name. It rang, but no one answered. He hurriedly copied the number, stuffed it in his pocket and returned everything just as he'd found it, minus the pile of dust. He decided he would try dialing again from home after business hours. At least, that was his plan.

What, if anything, should he do with the information he had uncovered? He certainly couldn't ask Mama about it since his father obviously had gone to great length to hide this checking account from her. He definitely could not ask Pops about it, since that would surely reveal he'd been snooping into his private affairs.

After grappling with this predicament for a very long time, he decided to just sit on it for a while, at least until Dad was feeling better. And that is exactly what Joey did. But it never left his mind and honestly, somewhere deep inside his being, he was fully cognizant of exactly what it all meant.

Daddy slowly but steadily rebounded from his encounter with that virulent strain of flu, but he was still weak as a kitten when he returned to work the next week. Joey had put everything back exactly where he found it and acted as though nothing had transpired while working alone. Mia also returned to work but was much spunkier than Grandpa. Although business continued to be slow for two more weeks, gradually the work load picked back up, resuming its normal, harried pace.

Joey vacillated between excitement of the proposed budget he'd drafted and being halfhearted and apathetic about their future. He was confused and double minded, unsure at this point in time whether he should even bother presenting it to his father. Completion of his final draft was finally shoved to a back burner, and he repeatedly procrastinated giving it any attention whatsoever.

Ellie frequently questioned why his motivation petered out with regard to future expansion. Something was eating at him but the more she inquired of him, the more he clammed up. It wasn't like Joey to shut her out, so she knew he was deeply troubled and needed space. All she could do was pray for him and give him all her support.

Daddy noticed a change with Joey as well. He was quieter and much less communicative, which was definitely not his personality. And yet, while at work he frequently asked questions that Daddy considered unrelated to their conversation. Some questions hinted at something else, something greater. Even though they had always enjoyed a special father-son bond, he could not quite put his finger on what was troubling his son.

As the chill of winter passed, the chill in the garage grew colder. Conversations had deteriorated significantly between the two men. Joey became sullen and morose both at work and at home, which was fueled in part by *the* phone call.

After procrastinating for as long as possible, his curiosity eventually won out, compelling him to redial the telephone number he'd discovered in Pop's Rolodex. He dialed the number at various times of night from the privacy of his home, never getting a response. By this time he had almost convinced himself that the phone number held no special meaning or significance, but he decided to try one more time.

Dialing but expecting no answer, he was caught off guard when after the fourth ring he heard "Hello" on the other end of the line. It was a female voice, a young-sounding female voice. Standing there mute, he heard "Hello" for the second time, but he was so rattled and off balance, he simply hung up the phone.

He never dialed that number again. That final attempt left him without words and slowly sinking into emotional quick sand. That one phone call disturbed him to the depth of his being, and the memory of that voice cast a shadow over his daily life. Still, he was unable to muster up the courage to flat out ask about the discovery he'd made in January. And so, his imagination was given free reign, his anger grew, and his trust in the one man he'd always deemed trustworthy withered.

The onset of spring proved to be no better, bringing no warmth while the two men continued to work side by side. One day in May after Pops returned from the post office, Joey asked why he insisted on making these trips; he reasoned that they were a waste of their valuable time. Daddy shot back that he just enjoyed getting out once in a while, visit with the old postmaster, that sort of thing. Joey's countenance grew dark, remembering all those checks that were routinely sent in the month of May to LI like clockwork as a matter of fact. Still, he didn't verbally press, but anger swelled in his heart.

Mia took a summer job at the mall that offered more hours, taking with her that buffer she unknowingly provided between the two men. The dozens of menial tasks she had routinely performed now fell back into their laps, and neither handled the added stress appropriately.

Joey was seething in silence. He didn't want to acknowledge it, but he was smart enough to know he was suppressing rage each time he allowed his mind to wander to what he knew to be the reality of his findings.

Everyone in the family noticed the change in his personality. They pressed and prodded him and were genuinely concerned for his wellbeing. He shrugged them off and kept his mouth shut. After all, he knew nothing with any certainty.

Daddy, on the other hand managed to maintain his normal demeanor with everyone else, at least outwardly. He was completely in the dark regarding the heavy weight his son was carrying. Whenever the subject of Joey's behavior came up, he practiced diplomacy and made light of the obvious personality change they had all witnessed. He agreed something was very wrong, but he hated conjecture so he often retreated from family conversations, making himself scarce. But privately, he began to wonder …

One muggy and brutally hot summer afternoon Joey decided he needed to clear the air. This tension and suspicion was eating at his gut; it was impossible to continue on like this much longer, locked in an emotional prison. Daddy was putting some tools back into the tool chest when Joey nervously approached him.

"Pops, I need to talk to you," he blurted out.

"Finally! Thank God!" Daddy said, "I've been wondering how much longer you'd take to get whatever it is off your chest."

Joey half smiled, but was ramrod stiff. "I have a confession to make," he cautiously proceeded.

Daddy nodded and waited.

"I wanted to make you proud of me ..."

"I am proud," Daddy interrupted.

"Let me finish. I wanted to make you proud, so I decided to put together a spread sheet and a very detailed proposed budget ..."

"Let me see it," Daddy interrupted yet again.

"Pops, will you stop interrupting me and let me get this out?"

Daddy quietly nodded.

"I wanted to prove to you that we could well afford to add two more bays. I felt that we needed to expand or be eaten up by our competition," he continued.

Joey was getting very uncomfortable at this point, stammering and grasping for precisely the right words.

"While you were out sick in January, I began digging through the files for the numbers I needed in order to prepare these documents. I had high hopes that once I finalized the spreadsheet, you'd be convinced; you'd see it my way."

"And ..." Daddy nervous and oddly anxious said.

"And ... and chunks of financial information were missing. So I kept looking, going through every single file and still couldn't locate what I needed. My last resort was to unlock the storage closet hoping to find the missing paperwork. I thought maybe the information had inadvertently been misfiled in one of those old boxes."

Daddy's face went ashen. He was instantly cognizant of the burden his only son had been carrying these past months but said nothing.

"Pops," he said almost inaudibly, "tell me, who are BI and LI?"

Daddy seemed to cave into himself for a brief moment before silently commanding himself back to composure. He then revealed an emotional side of himself that Joey had never, ever seen. On some unexplainable level he displayed a mixture of rage and shame.

For a brief time Joey was certain that he would clam up and say nothing more, but abruptly his demeanor softened. Daddy slowly stood up, walked to the door and put the closed sign on the hook. It was obvious he didn't want to be interrupted by anyone.

"Son, let's sit. This isn't going to be easy."

Chapter 18

Daddy pulled two sodas from the machine and handed one to Joey. He plopped heavily in his desk chair and took a long swig of his drink. It was evident that he was none too anxious to tell this story.

"Son, this is going to be very painful for me to tell but probably more painful for you to hear. There is not one soul in this world who knows about this, and I hope we can keep this between us," he started more as a question than a statement.

Joey was not about to agree to anything. He didn't move a muscle and he didn't utter a word. He knew what was coming and was already feeling a choking rage in his throat toward this man whom he'd admired all of his life.

"I'm going to preface this by saying I love your mother more than life itself. I would never intentionally do anything to hurt her. I love my children and my grandchildren more than you'll ever know."

Here it comes, he angrily thought to himself even as his father began to pour out what he already judged to be empty words.

"In March of 1954 we had a freak snowstorm. It was a humdinger! People were off the road everywhere. Unfortunately, I still had to drive to our Lowell supplier for auto parts, which as you know wasn't all that unusual. As I slowly drove back to the shop, the roads were becoming more and more treacherous with every passing minute. I came upon a young woman who had spun out, gone off the road, and was stuck in the snow—I mean, really stuck." At this point Daddy looked into Joey's eyes but was met with an icy stare. "The temperature was dropping like a rock, and she was scared to death she'd be stranded, alone on this desolate stretch of road. Of course I stopped to help her; anyone would have. She was just about buried in a drift. It was unbelievable. Eventually, after a lot of digging, we were able to free her car. I pushed her back onto the road and followed her most of the way to her apartment in Lowell, just to be sure she was okay. It seemed like the right thing to do. I even told your Mama about it. I thought that was the end of it."

"But it wasn't the end of it, was it?" Joey sarcastically shot back as he remembered the Lowell telephone number he'd found.

"I'm sorry to say, it was not. She was familiar with my garage and came by a couple of weeks later with a thank you pie she had baked for me. I graciously accepted it, and we shared a piece together in the office. She left and that was that, I thought.

"She started dropping by every couple of weeks: automotive work on her car, another home baked pie, etc. It was all very innocent, at least for me. Then, she called me one night in August. Her car was broken down, and she needed help. Against my better judgment, I went to her assistance. Mama offered to ride with me, but you were already in bed and Trina was just a newborn; I didn't want to drag you kids out into the night. I expected to be right home anyway, but …"

Joey hatefully glared at his father, thinking of the years of warnings and admonishments he'd passed on to his kids about avoiding this type of potentially dangerous situation.

"Well, her car was indeed broken down," he went on explaining the problem in mechanical terms.

Joey couldn't care less what the mechanical failure was. He felt his heart pounding out of his chest in anticipation of the moral failure that was about to be confessed.

"I tried but was unable to fix it there on the road; it needed to be towed into the garage where I could tear it apart. She agreed and asked me to drive her home, which of course I would have. I'd never leave a lady stranded."

Joey was boiling, but by some miracle he mustered up every ounce of emotional restraint he possessed.

"Son, I want you to know that I did not go into her apartment with any selfish or dishonorable intentions. She offered me iced tea and she ... her name was Brenda ... she began sobbing uncontrollably. She had a terrible home life as a child: no family to speak of at that time to support her financially or otherwise. She was alone and felt like her life was falling apart. I began to comfort her and ... and ... one thing led to another."

The words were hardly out of his mouth when Joey exploded out of his chair into Daddy. He head butted his father, violently grabbed his throat and began wildly choking him. Daddy was like a rag doll in his hands, not even attempting to defend himself.

"How could you do this to your wife ... to Mama ... to us? I hate you for this." He screamed at the top of his lungs as he abruptly released him, suddenly aware of his fierce grip.

Grabbing and rubbing his throat, Daddy sheepishly responded, "I deserved that, I know. But please, son, do not hurt your mother. It was a long time ago and ..."

"Don't you call me son—ever again!" Joey retorted as they retreated to opposite corners of the office.

Joey, calmer now, spat out, "Finish ... finish ... I need to know what happened next. Did you ... did you keep her? You must have kept seeing her ... I saw checks to BI."

"No, no! It only happened once, just that one time, but ... but ... she conceived a child ... my child," he said, weeping uncontrollably into his hands. Hardly able to catch his breath, he looked up, searching Joey's face for some kind of reaction to his awful confession. Joey glared at him with deep contempt, but no words came.

"I felt obligated to care for that child; it was the only morally right thing to do. So ... I sent monthly checks to Brenda after Lily was born in May of the next year. I continued doing that until she was around eighteen years old. After that I just sent birthday cards and Christmas gifts.

"Brenda Iveson never married and sadly she died when Lily was twenty years old. But, son ... I mean ... Joey, I have made a point to be in Lily's life in whatever way I could without hurting my own family."

Joey was slumped forward clutching his head, crying, and trying to make sense of what he'd just heard from this man ... this man he would have walked on burning coals for ... given his own life for.

"I kept the post office box so that Lily could send me letters, cards, etc. She's a sweet young woman. Brenda didn't poison her to hate me or our family; she raised her to be a kind, loving young woman. In fact, Lily has made every effort to keep this painful secret from hurting Mama and the rest of our family. I beg you; don't devastate your Mama by telling her this story. Joey, I know too well that I have sinned. I have asked God to forgive me. Will you forgive me?" Daddy pleaded with genuine sorrow.

"Forgive you? Forgive you! I'm having a hard time even looking at you right now. You were my hero, my role model. I feel like my heart has been ripped out of my chest, and you want me to forgive you?"

Both wept without restraint, and then Daddy tried to comfort his son with an embrace.

"Don't touch me ... I can't bear to be in the same room with you! I need to get out of here," and with those hateful words he gathered his things and walked out the door.

That was the last interaction between father and son, and for a couple of weeks Joey stayed far away from the entire family. Finally late one night, he along with his family entered the shop, packed up, and removed all of his own tools and personal items like thieves in the night. I don't know if Ellie and the boys knew any specific details, but they certainly were aware that something bad, really bad, fractured their once happy family.

Daddy had no choice. He was compelled to tell Mama he and Joey had fought but never revealed the vile root of it. God and only God could possibly know the sorrowful and crushing weight endured by our dear Mama throughout the following years. Separation from her beloved son was at times almost more than she could emotionally bear. Did she press or coerce Daddy for details of their argument? Did she attempt to mediate between the two stubborn men? How was my father able to keep this despicable secret from her, the love of his life?

Joey found employment almost immediately, so they never suffered any real financial loss. However, the emotional loss to him was enormous, not to mention the devastation heaped on the family business, as well as to every single member of our family.

The reality of Daddy's confession left an incredibly deep fissure in the Agosti family; God only knows if it could ever be healed.

Chapter 19

"You girls did not have to drive over here on this snowy day," Mama admonished Angie and me. "As you can see, your dad is perfectly capable of whipping up a nice Sunday dinner. Besides, I honestly don't have much of an appetite these days."

"Mama, there is nothing better than enjoying a nice Sunday dinner with you and Daddy. Besides, it *is* Valentine's Day. I'll grant you that it is horrible out there, but we're all snug and warm with our sweethearts and you guys," Angie said lightheartedly as she munched on a piece of anise celery.

"Yeah, what could be better than sharing our resources to create a scrumptious meal; cooking is more fun when everyone chips in and does part of the meal." I added as the doorbell rang. "Are you expecting anyone else, Mama?"

"Are you kidding, on a day like today?"

"It's not fit for man or beast out there," Daddy chimed in as he hot-footed it to the front door.

"What … for the lady of the house you say," he loudly proclaimed after thanking the flower delivery boy.

Turning around and with great flourish, he presented Mama with a huge bouquet of roses saying, "For my Valentine," as he tenderly kissed her on the forehead.

"Oh Vincent, you shouldn't have, but they *are* beautiful. And you know how I love yellow roses," she said weakly.

"And why shouldn't I, my dear? Since you are the most beautiful of all flowers," he said.

"Oh Mama, they are gorgeous and what a treat, especially in the dead of winter," I commented. I must say, we were impressed and touched by his tender display of affection toward his wife of so many wonderful years. Who knew Daddy could be so poetic? Her love of roses could not be denied; it was in her DNA. She reveled in those countless hours spent in her garden. Pruning, feeding, as well as her experimental grafting, was no chore to this lady.

"Let me put them in water for you."

At the sound of the doorbell my mother said, "My word, now who in the world could that be?"

"I don't know, but I'll get it again," he said gingerly heading for the door again wearing a silly grin.

There before us, yet again, stood that same half-frozen delivery boy. He handed Daddy another bouquet, wasting no time in heading for the warmth of his truck. This bouquet was a stunning mix of daisies, freesia, mums, and tulips, which he promptly placed in Ma's arms. The colors were vibrant. They dispelled the cold and seemed to make the entire living room come alive.

"And these are for my best friend and lover," he quietly whispered, this time planting a noisy kiss on her nose.

"Oh Vincent, what are you doing? You are embarrassing me," she coyly smiled with a blush.

Our mouths dropped open in shock at the scene playing out before us. He was desperately attempting to clearly communicate one simple truth to the love of his life: she is cherished. I was fighting hard to keep the tears at bay and knew too well that if I opened my mouth, I'd lose it.

"Sweetheart, would you mind reaching into the credenza for my favorite glass vase?" she asked Angie. "These are going to need water as well."

"Sure thing. It's the least I can do in light of all this free entertainment we are enjoying," she giggled.

Not five minutes passed and, "Oh my, not the door again," Mama exclaimed covering her face with her hands.

"Hey Pops, you'd better give that kid a big … really big tip," Sal exclaimed, laughing almost hysterically.

Daddy again answered the door, this time yanking the young man fully into the foyer. "Wait here," he said. He proudly returned from the front door for the third time. This time, however, with an absolutely gorgeous gardenia plant. He placed the gardenia plant in her waiting arms and said, "And this is for the faithful wife of my youth."

We gasped and then did cry, full well knowing that Mama chose gardenias for her wedding bouquet on that very special day, and he remembered. She loved them so, and tried repeatedly, without success, to grow them in her garden. This plant was deliciously fragrant and fully in bloom.

Daddy winked at the delivery boy, who by now was dripping all over the foyer carpet. He profusely thanked him for the critical role he'd played in this great charade. And yes, he did tuck a rather generous tip into the young man's pocket while roughly thumping the poor kid on his back. Closing the door, he turned to face his audience with a dopey grin pasted on his face. He was proud of himself; he had pulled it off as planned.

"Happy Valentine's Day, Maria! You are my sweetheart, my lover, my best friend, and my faithful wife. I love you dearly," he whispered as he kissed her tenderly, this time on the lips.

We loudly applauded as we attempted to assimilate the touching scene that had just unfolded before us. These two people were still deeply in love, yet were being cruelly torn apart by the dreadful disease called cancer. But for today, there would be no talk of that ghastly disease. Today, this one special day, was set apart to express love for our sweethearts, and to make precious memories, memories to which we'd cling when the days darkened.

"Hey, Pop," Jake loudly warned, "You're making us guys look bad, really bad. Stupid me. All I got for Angie was a card. What about you, Sal? Did you get Trina three bouquets of flowers?"

"Nope, no I did not. I would have, but the local florist told me they were all sold out. It seems some old guy came by the other day and bought everything off their shelves."

We laughed and hugged each other. I for one, will never, ever forget that wonderfully magical Valentine's Day.

"Well, since no one is standing on the front step, can we eat now?" Angie joked with happy tears streaming down her face.

Chapter 20

While bundled up in my winter attire, I stood at my front door waiting for Donna as I searched the ground, hoping to find the tiniest signs of spring. Nothing yet! Oh, wait! I willed myself to discover a crocus poking up through the packed soil.

Is that a hyacinth? Whatever that teeny green nub is, I'll take it as a sign that spring is right around the corner. I cannot remember any other year where I so badly needed something to brighten my day. Flowers always do the trick.

Donna must have sensed my somber mood, even over the phone. Suggesting we have breakfast together before hitting the soup kitchen said it all. I couldn't fool her, nor do I ever try. Being friends since grade school, we have grown to become inseparable sisters. We know each other inside out, and I love that about our relationship. In light of Mama's declining condition, it probably doesn't take an astrophysicist to figure it out but just the same, I'm thankful for my friend's sensitivity.

Pulling my parka tighter around me against the stiff wind, I turned to see Donna's approaching car. "Jump in," she said wearing that wonderful smile as she pushed the door open. "Don't let the cold in. Man, is winter ever going to end?"

"Tell me about it. I'm ready to burn this stinking parka. I'm more than anxious to drag out my spring clothes."

"So, this is my treat! Where do you want to go for breakfast?" she cheerily asked.

"Let's go to Denny's since it's on the way to the soup kitchen."

"You got it!"

Surprisingly, the restaurant was not very busy, and we were quickly seated.

"I guess the normal breakfast crowd doesn't wander in quite this early, huh?" I remarked while scanning the large room.

"You got that right. Most of them are still home under their ever so cozy quilts."

We both ordered French toast, and enough hot, strong coffee to drown ourselves, which was served almost immediately.

"Hey, Trina," she said grabbing my hand, "how are you doing? I know you're spending every spare minute with your folks. Are you taking care of yourself?" she asked.

"Oh Donna, you read me like a well-worn book. I'm hanging in there, but it's so difficult to watch this happening. My mom has lost so much weight—too much."

"What does the oncologist say?"

"There is nothing he can say. She refused to undergo any further treatment once she discovered more lumps. The breast cancer has since metastasized to her lungs, which is why she is dealing with shortness of breath," I explained as I grabbed a tissue.

"Oh sweetie, I don't know what to say."

"There are no words. Now he suspects liver involvement. She is looking yellowish, but she's refusing any more tests to confirm that. Oh Donna, I'm losing her!"

"I'm so sorry Trina. She is a very special lady. I've always admired her and your entire family for that matter."

"Really? Have you forgotten about our notoriously dysfunctional brother-father relationship?" I scoffed sarcastically.

"Oh come on, Trina. You know he'll come around. Didn't you tell me that he's been faithfully visiting your mom?"

"Yeah, but he and Daddy are still … still … mortal enemies! They haven't spoken for about three years. Three years Donna! Can you even begin to understand how that has affected our once almost perfect family?" I almost shouted as I broke down into great sobs.

"Here's a news flash kiddo, there are no perfect or even almost perfect families," she said with a quirky smile. "Let me just tweak your memory with three words: my Aunt Delores. Need I say more?"

I burst into laughter at the memory of the two of us walking into Donna's house to find Aunt Delores dancing all alone, floating around the kitchen, cackling. She was wearing a hideous velvet gown, adorned with a cheap jeweled crown, and she was wielding a huge knife. We stood still, scared to death, wondering what she'd do next. She simply looked up and asked if we'd like a salami sandwich? She moved out of their home not long after that incident. (She actually moved into another *special* home.)

"You always make me laugh," I said, remembering how, sadly, we mocked and ridiculed her Aunt Delores.

We silently sat there for a while longer while I made a vain attempt to pull myself together. Donna tried, also in vain, to think of comforting words for her dearest friend while maintaining a death grip on my hand. The poor waitress didn't know what to do with herself. Finally, she stealthily placed our bill on the table and retreated to the cash register without a word.

"If you're finished, we might as well head over to the church," I suggested.

"Are you sure you're up for this today? We can volunteer another time."

"No, it will do me good. It reminds me to be thankful for what I do have. I count my blessings as I serve those poor souls. I just feel badly that my nieces and nephew have quit coming with us."

"Like I always say, there are times and seasons. It's just not their season to volunteer. Maybe next time," she added with her typical optimism as we started toward her car.

"Man, I'm still freezing," I commented as we pulled into the church parking lot. "I'm guessing it will be busy today with these temperatures," I commented. "Hi Pastor, I didn't think you'd be here today. Isn't Saturday a busy day for you, what with sermon prep and all?"

"Never too busy to help out," he returned. "Besides, I'm only here through the lunch meal. I'm officiating at a wedding later today."

"Oh that's nice, but it surely is a cold day for a wedding."

"Their love will keep them warm," he said with a twinkle in his eyes. "So Trina, what do you say we get going on that homemade soup of yours?"

"Okay, okay, what a hard taskmaster you are, Pastor," Donna said with a snicker.

We worked on the soup preparation for a couple of hours then began the process of setting up to serve Mama's Italian Wedding Soup. Everything was out and ready for our clientele.

Grinning from ear to ear, Donna nudged me and lifted her chin toward the main door. In bounded Angie with my nieces and nephew. Of course Anthony and Sammy would not be joining us.

"Hey, let's get this show on the road," yelled Kevin. "I don't have all day. I have places to go, people to see," he laughed.

"I'm so proud of you all for coming," I said.

"What, did you think we weren't going to show?" Kevin jested.

"Oh ye of little faith!" Mia self-righteously exclaimed.

"Can I do the drinks?" Leah asked her mother.

"Sure you can," Angie responded.

"But remember to stay on the opposite side of this table. You're only thirteen, and I don't want any aggressive guy messing with my cute little sister," Kevin protectively ordered.

The six of us worked almost nonstop all morning; I had predicted correctly that it would be extremely busy. Every time the door opened bringing in another group, a burst of what felt like arctic air also blew into the dining area. It was almost impossible to keep the place warm.

We had served a record number of men, women, and children, leaving the kettles almost bone dry. With their bellies now full, the once hungry crowd had significantly dwindled down. But as I approached one of the last men to be served, he lifted his bowl to me as though toasting. Our eyes locked. I immediately turned icy cold right down to my core, and my hands began to tremble uncontrollably. I was looking into the eyes of the one man I had hoped never to see again—Cindy's dad.

My eyes darted back and forth, searching for assistance should this encounter turn violent. Panic started to rise within me, not unlike a thermometer just plunged into boiling water. But something gave me pause. Something in his demeanor was ... different.

"Mr. Walker?" I questioned, yet knew.

"Yes," he said as he bowed his head then blurted, "I ... I'm so very sorry for what I did to you. What I did was ... cowardly. I've played it over and over in my head ... like a nightmare. That day ... that scene continues to haunt me. I cannot shake the awful shame that overtakes me."

I fixed my gaze on him, attempting to assimilate what he was saying to me.

"I have been ... out ... for a while, but I haven't made contact with anyone. I'm sober now, and I want to stay that way. I knew you volunteered here; I saw you twice before, but you didn't see me. I thought this would be a safe place to ... to apologize," he meekly said with what seemed to be genuine sorrow and regret.

I was stunned; so taken aback that I lacked adequate words. Finally, I managed to break the silence hanging between us.

"Mr. Walker, I am truly happy for you. What you are attempting to accomplish is admirable. It will not be an easy road back, but I believe you can do it."

His gaze on me was steady and piercing, but it was slowly softened by a warm smile.

"I … I do forgive you," those words surprised even me, "and I will be praying for every good thing to come your way."

"I assume you two know each other," the pastor interrupted as he smiled at Ted, affectionately clutching his shoulder. "This man has come a long way, Trina, he's one of the success stories I was boasting to you about last week. Right, Ted?"

"Wow, I'm beyond thrill'd to hear that, Pastor," I added, smiling at Ted's now relaxed face.

We spoke for a few more moments before I excused myself to finish up my duties. Anxious to explain this surprising turn of events to my family, I wandered over toward their group. Apparently they hadn't noticed or recognized Cindy's dad, and they were shocked beyond belief as I quickly retold what had just transpired.

Kevin listened respectfully; to say he was guarded would be a huge understatement. "Aunt Trina, I can't forgive that man. Have you forgotten what he did?"

"No, I certainly have not forgotten, but I think he's made an honest turn around."

"Humph, we'll see," he said casting a glance toward Ted.

"I understand, Kevin. I'm not asking you to forgive him this very second. Just be open to it."

"Well guys, ya just never know what's going to happen here at the soup kitchen, do you, Sis?" Angie commented while drying pans.

"You got that right," Donna agreed. "Isn't life an adventure? Aren't you guys glad you came along?" She playfully nudged Mia and Leah.

"Yeah, it's pretty cool here. I wonder if Cindy is ready for a dad in her life," Mia remarked. Only time would prove whether or not Ted Walker had actually turned his life around, but I for one honestly hoped and prayed that he had. I'm sure the desire of Cindy's heart, if she were to verbalize it, was to have a sober, loving dad back in her life.

Our gang watched as Ted pulled up his coat collar, yanked down his cap, and sent us a salute as he braved the cold, but he somehow now radiated a certain glow.

It was still freezing cold outside, but with all that had occurred, I now had a feeling of warmth deep down to my bones.

Chapter 21

"This was so much fun," Leah cheerfully exclaimed as the train chugged along. "Why don't we shop in Boston more often?"

"I don't know? Could it be that you tend to spend all my money?" Angie ribbed her daughter.

"Come on, Mom, admit it, you love riding the train into the city. And the shopping was even better with Cindy along," Mia added.

"Just kidding, girls, I do indeed love the sights and sounds of Boston, and the shopping ranks high on my list," Angie admitted.

"By the way, thanks for paying for my ticket Mrs. T. You guys are so good to me," Cindy said.

"You are entirely welcome, honey. After all, you've become part of the family, right, Trina?" Angie replied.

"You sure have. It wouldn't have been any fun without you."

Fixing her eyes on the passing suburban sights, Mia appeared to be lost in another world as the train chugged toward home. "I really missed having Grandma along with us. I know she's not up to it, but she was always so much fun on these excursions."

Mama had taken a radical turn for the worse. Her weight loss was frightening and she had clearly grown weary of the fight. We continually attempt to coax her into eating something, even the smallest of tidbits. Ultimately, when she couldn't be tempted by any of her favorite foods, we accepted the hard fact: she had little or no appetite.

Trying to be sensitive to her physical needs, we alternate visits and keep them brief; Daddy had confided that all she does is sleep these days. Angie and I spend every spare minute with her. Our hearts were slowly breaking as we came to grips with her decline.

"I know, honey, she's truly one of a kind," Angie somberly agreed. "Mia, it was so thoughtful of you to purchase that beautiful ceramic rose. She's going to love it."

"Hey Angie, has Mama ever shared anything with you about grafting her roses?" I asked.

"Hmm, not specifically, but I do seem to remember some vague reference. Maybe I just wasn't paying enough attention at the time. You know me, always the scatterbrain."

"Well, I stopped in for a quick visit one day last summer. It was a perfect day and not surprisingly, I found Mama busily at work in her garden. Up until that day, I guess I really never realized the type of skills Mama had developed; she basically taught herself some things that I personally would never attempt."

"What kind of skills? A garden is a garden: plant, weed, water, what else is there?"

"Well, it seemed pretty advanced to me, and I was intrigued by the process she was undertaking. She described it as grafting in. It was really amazing, Ange. In a nut shell, she learned how to blend the attributes of two rose plants into one using this process. The desired result of this process was that the newly created rose, if I can use that term, would be much stronger and healthier."

"I've read about it, but never realized she was experimenting with her beloved roses."

"It was apparent to me how much she loved doing what she was doing. But Angie, I had the distinct feeling that she was trying to say something to me, something deeper. Unfortunately, Daddy interrupted us, and I never pursued it again. I could kick myself now," Trina mused.

"Here, let me do it for you," Angie laughed.

"I remember she did say something like, 'I hope and pray your brother, sister, and you will come to learn the *lesson*' just as she had learned it, regarding grafting in. Mama also said that when we do learn the *lesson*, we will reap its *joys* and *benefits*," I continued, as the train slowed to a stop.

"So, do you have any clue what lesson it was that she learned?"

"Nope, beats me! But I'm going to pursue it with her. I am very curious about the joys and benefits she mentioned."

We carried our packages to the car and settled in for the ride home when Mia abruptly jolted us with a shout, "Hey, I have a great idea!"

"Well, out with it, girl," her mother chided.

"We all know how much Grandma loves her flower garden, right?" she responded.

We all nodded in unison. No arguments there.

"Let's set a date when our whole family can dig in, pardon the pun, and get her garden shipshape before summer. Grandpa hasn't done much yet this spring … It's kind of in shambles. What do you all think?" she asked.

"I think that is a brilliant idea, and I think you're brilliant. I'll be happy to organize lunch, you know, easy stuff," Angie responded.

"Fantastic! Sal and I will take care of the mulch. The boys will be a big help with this, and we'd better let Daddy know what we're planning. It would be fun to surprise Mama, but he should know."

"Right, agreed! Now I'm getting excited. I'm thinking this can't be very hard? Mama usually does the flower garden alone," Angie said.

"She's going to be thrilled. Mia, you're such a sweetie."

"Hey Sal, I need to grab some supplies for our work day at Mama's, so I'm heading over to the garden shop. Do you want to come?" I asked.

"Sure, sweetie, give me a minute. I'll let Buddy out and be right with you."

"So, how much mulch do you think we'll need for the flower garden?"

"I have no clue, but I'll ask one of the workers. This is going to be fun, and it's not really a very big job. I'm certain we can easily finish it up in one day."

"I think you're right, and I know it will mean the world to her. Oh good, it doesn't look very busy," I remarked as we pulled into the parking lot.

"Well it is pretty early in the season for most New Englanders to get serious about gardening. It's better if we tackle this project as soon as possible, your mom is so weak now ..." not finishing the sentence he gave Trina a sideways glance. I'm sorry, honey, that was thoughtless of me."

"That's okay, Sal, I'm not blind. It couldn't be more obvious that she's rapidly declining, but this will perk her up. I'm sure of it."

He put his arm around me as we walked toward the garden center. "Trina you do know that you don't have to tough this out alone. You know what I mean ... appear strong for the rest of the family. It's okay to give in to your emotions. I promise I'll be right here by your side. I love you."

"You're the best, Sal. And I love you too and just in case you haven't noticed, I've already cried buckets."

"That's good, actually healthy, I think. Doesn't it say somewhere in the Bible that He bottles our tears?"

"Wow, interesting you would mention that today, Sal. I was just reading that scripture this morning in my daily devotions. I believe it's from Psalm 56:8. 'You keep track of all my sorrows, You have collected all my tears in your bottle. You have recorded each one in your book.' I can't tell you how comforted I felt after reading that. Just knowing my sorrow and grief is in no way lost to Him; He knows and He cares."

"I'm glad to hear that, honey. We'll get through this, together."

"Hey, do you mind if I poke around in their outdoor tent? I'd like to take a peek at their new garden ornaments while you get the mulch, okay?"

"Sure take your time, we're in no hurry, and they usually have the best selection in our area."

He was right. What a great selection. My eyes fell on a group of beautiful stepping stones. I guessed each one was meant to be the focal point in a garden. I examined one particular stone that appeared to be embellished with hand painted yellow roses, but my breath caught as I took a closer look. The cursive text said, *Garden of Hope*. I couldn't believe what my eyes were seeing. It alone had that phrase … one of a kind.

Sal had apparently finished his own shopping and was now silently standing behind me. Needless to say he was more than a bit curious to find me crying in the garden shop tent, but when his focus shifted to the stepping stone I was holding he understood. Smiling, he said "Honey, she's going to love it!"

Like good little soldiers, every one of us reported for duty without complaint by nine o'clock on Saturday, including our dear Cindy. She had a great relationship with our mother, and they had grown to love one another. She often expressed her longing to have actually had a grandma just like her. But God truly works in mysterious ways. Over these past couple of years, Cindy had been present at so many family gatherings that she, in fact, did feel like one of the grandkids.

Daddy cheerfully greeted us at the kitchen door. "Buon giorno, good morning, good morning Agosti Landscaping Company," he said chuckling. "Mama is in the living room and mama mia, will she ever be surprised?"

Mama slowly walked into the kitchen, supporting herself on pieces of furniture as she came. Seeing the whole crew standing before her, she laughed and sat heavily in her chair. "And to what do I owe the honor of this early morning visit, children?" she said in her mockingly formal manner.

"Mama, we the Agosti Landscaping Company, has come to get your flower beds in tiptop condition. Summer is right around the corner, your garden badly needs our attention, and I don't mean to boast, but we are the best in town."

"The best *what* in town," Mama snickered.

"Angie brought her famous blueberry muffins and some luncheon stuff, so you have nothing to do on this glorious morning but sit and relax or you may just feel the need to supervise these amateurs as they do their thing. How does that sound? We will be sure to call you should we have any questions, but I think we can handle it from here," I stated.

Covering her face with her hands, she sniffled and laughed simultaneously. We stood awkwardly speechless for a few moments, but Jake quickly spurred the group on toward the task at hand while Daddy helped Mama back to her living room chair.

"Everyone, about face!" he barked, sounding like General Patton. "Forward march to the garden where tools and jobs will promptly be assigned," he said grinning, full of himself.

Angie and I stayed behind for a few minutes, giving Mama big hugs along with stacks of magazines to help her pass the time, when she wasn't snoozing that is.

"I'll be in later to get lunch on the table, so don't you do a thing. But I expect the kids will drift in and out all morning for muffins and juice," Angie reminded our mother.

"I'll bring you outside when the sun has sufficiently warmed the earth," I joked. "If you'd like, I'll have one of the boys set out your lounge chair so you can properly oversee this crazy group."

"I dearly love that crazy group," she responded with her weakened voice. "I'll just rest in here for a little while if that's okay. But pretty soon I will come out, if only to take my rightful seat on the throne," she joked.

It was only the end of April, but I could have sworn a beautiful butterfly flittered by me; it was my imagination or wishful thinking. As we dug into the task at hand, I couldn't help but revel in the sounds of laughter, singing, and good natured bantering all around me.

I love this family! I smiled to myself.

I just wish my bullheaded brother would deal with his issues once and for all. I am way, way beyond tired of his stubbornness, not to mention his hard heart. He's missing so very much and that alone is enough to grieve my heart.

Sadly, he's not the only one being hurt by his self-absorption: Ellie and the children have also inconsiderately been cut off, depriving them of the wonderful camaraderie we have always enjoyed together. That doesn't even begin to consider the toll on the rest of our family; the loss of their precious company is like a vacuum, never again to be filled.

Sal was right, it really didn't take long at all; the job was done in a jiffy. The volunteer work detail was supercharged, motivated by their love for this special woman. We finished up shortly after lunch break, and the time had arrived to bring her out and reveal our masterpiece. Angie and I supported her by each taking one of her elbows and slowly walking to her waiting lounge chair. It was a short walk, but still her breathing became labored; walking was no longer an easy task for her.

"Oh my! How beautiful!" she exclaimed. "So alive, so perfectly manicured! You did better than me. Many hands make light work my papa always said."

"He was right about that. This job was a piece of cake."

"What is that?" she asked as her eyes fixated on the stepping stone.

"Mama, as far as I can tell, it's a one-of-a-kind stepping stone," I said as I knelt and tipped it up for her to read.

She was overcome with emotion as she digested the words, "*Garden of Hope*. Oh how perfect! Where did you ever find such a thing? Look, Vincent, it even has beautiful yellow roses sculpted on it. I will cherish it all the days of my life," she smiled at each of us through tears. "Thank you, thank you my precious family. I will sit here every day, enjoying the warmth of the sun and think of your hard work and … your love."

The kids were extremely proud of themselves, especially Mia. They pointed out each of the jobs they completed as a group and then what their individual parts were in the overall project. I am convinced they would have worked their knuckles to the bone for their beloved grandma. She, in turn, affirmed even the tiniest part they may have played in blessing her with this wonderful gift.

Happy with our accomplishment, we simply stood before her without words but full of emotion. Our questioning eyes darted to one another, trying hard to maintain our smiling faces. Doubtless each were silently questioning exactly how many days she would have to enjoy the warmth of the sun in her Garden of Hope.

Chapter 22

Dr. Lowe cavalierly suggested we begin to get Mama's affairs in order.

Affairs in order! A harbinger of what's to come. The reality of that statement was like being hit head on by a Mack truck. None of us were deluded enough to deny the inevitability of what we were facing, however, not one of us was willing to let go either. We, like all families of cancer patients, were hoping against hope to witness a miracle in our very midst.

Painful as it was, Angie and I had frequently tossed around the need to discuss her ... final wishes, and we agreed the time had come and Daddy needed to spend a few minutes with us. We considered it to be a perfectly reasonable request, which is why we were flabbergasted at his explosive reaction. Reminding me of a three-year-old child, we witnessed him stamping his feet, huffing, and puffing as he agitatedly paced the floor like a caged animal. Bottom line, he wanted no involvement in what surely loomed heavy on the horizon, none whatsoever. When the dust of his child- ish rant had settled, he had managed to shift his responsibilities squarely in our laps. And so, by exasperating default, Angie and I would shoulder the lion's share of decision-making, leaving him totally out of the equation.

Joey's the oldest ... the son ... shouldn't he be the one to guide us through this process?

The very next night, I stopped by Joey's house unannounced, giving him no excuse whatsoever to avoid my visit. And to his credit, he didn't try to escape once I was there."

"Hey, Ellie, so good to see you," I said nonchalantly as we hugged.

"What a nice surprise," she responded with sincerity. "Joe is working in the basement. Let me get him for you."

"Terrific! Take your time, El, I'm in no hurry," I said as I plopped into my favorite armchair. I could hear muffled voices coming from the cellar stairs, but couldn't quite distinguish the actual words. I'm guessing the conversation was going something like, "now what the heck does she want?"

"Hey, Sis, what's up? Anything wrong? Mama okay?" he rapidly fired at me.

"No, nothing is *terribly* wrong, but Angie and I need your help."

"Oh yeah, what kind of help?" he said warily.

"Here's the deal, Joey, Daddy has relinquished his decision making responsibilities to us regarding ... Mama's last wishes. What I mean is ... he wants nothing to do with any of those details, leaving it all to us."

"Why am I not surprised?"

"Joe, we need you to be involved in this, I mean to be *with* us in this."

"You girls are perfectly capable of handling any problems or of making any decisions. You don't need me."

Fueled by my Sicilian temper, I yelled back, "Not on your life, Joe. No way! You are going to be part of this process, like it or not. Mama has *three* children," I yelled shoving three fingers in his face.

Much to my surprise, he raised both hands in mock surrender, whispering back, "Okay, okay, relax Trina! I give! Just tell me when and where you guys are meeting to discuss ... everything."

Well, that went well. I smiled as I jogged to my car.

Angie and I sipped ice tea while waiting for big brother to grace us with his presence. If the truth be known, even though I bulldozed him into coming, I couldn't deny that since this whole eruption, his presence made me somewhat uncomfortable; the tension in the air was palpable. It bothers me immensely that he continues to hold the family at arm's length. Sure, I am truly grateful for Joey's regular visits with Mama (whenever Daddy is out of the house), but that doesn't placate me one bit. I'm still holding on to any shred of hope for complete and total restoration between those two blockheads.

"So what do you think, Sis? What are we hoping to accomplish today?" Angie ventured.

"I don't know how to answer that. I guess for starters, we need to seriously consider the ramifications of her living will for one thing. Also, it would probably be wise to get her wishes down on paper … you know … funeral arrangements. I can hardly bring myself to think about this stuff." I said as my voice trailed off to a whisper.

Just then, Joey sauntered through the kitchen door after an almost indistinguishable knock. "Hey, I'm here," he said.

We both stood and warmly embraced our brother, already sniffling.

"Okay girls, there is *one* and only *one* ground rule for this meeting. No crying!" he said with that beautiful smile I've sorely missed.

"Sit down, you big oaf," Angie said as she playfully smacked the back of his head.

There it was, the Agosti love. No matter how splintered and damaged, it was still there.

I poured Joey a glass of iced tea asking, "No sugar, right?"

"That's right. You remember," smiling once again.

"How's Ellie?" I asked.

"She's really good. Her job is steady and she loves it," he quickly answered.

"What about Anthony and Sammy? I miss them so much," I responded.

"They're good too. You guys already know that Anthony and I work for the same company now, but he's in the North Andover garage. Sammy, of course, is still in school. He's bounced around a bit, but we think he's finally found his niche. He's at University of Massachusetts in Lowell studying electrical engineering," he answered.

"Wow, I didn't know that. Would it have killed you to keep us in the loop, Joe?" Angie responded indignantly. "Last time I checked, we were still a family," she said and quickly went to the sink attempting to conceal her wounded feelings.

Not wanting this meeting to get emotionally hijacked, I quickly interjected, "What about your job? Was it hard to make that change? I mean … never mind," I said clearing my throat and changing the subject.

"No, Sis, it really wasn't hard. It's a good fit for me."

"Good, good. I made some sandwiches so we can eat while looking over Mama and Daddy's paperwork. So, what do you say we get started? I'm betting none of us wants to be at this all day."

"Exactly what do we have to decide? Shouldn't Da … her husband … make all these decisions?" he said with an edge in his voice.

"Well, as I told you the other day, our dear old dad has delegated the decision making and responsibilities to us. He's really hurting and can't bring himself to …" she stopped, noticing an ugly glare creep across Joey's face.

"Guys, I feel like I'm walking on egg shells here. Can't we just get to what needs to be decided … please?" I blurted in frustration.

"Fine, I'm good with that," he agreed.

"Me too," Angie added.

"Excellent! First, I think we need to talk about her living will. It is *her* living will, which means she has already expressed and written down her wishes: what she wants and does not want if the times comes that she is unable to verbalize those desires. Ethically speaking, I do not think we should attempt to dissuade her from those stated wishes. But, I don't think we should be blindsided by them either. We need to know what it says and have ample time to digest it. Agreed?"

"Sure I agree, but what does it say? Do you know?" he asked.

"Yup, Daddy gave me a copy. It's right here … well it was right here," I said as I searched the manila folder in front of me.

"I remember seeing it, but I didn't actually read it," Angie added.

"Give me a minute and I'll find it, but in the meantime let's talk about … and I know this is upsetting, but we need to sit with her and with as much sensitivity as we can muster, find out if she does in fact have specific funeral plans. I recently read in one of my professional magazines that a surprising number of people highly value controlling or directing details of their funeral, and exactly how they might be honored during the actual funeral."

"Her pastor has been so faithful to visit regularly. I believe he will be invaluable when that time comes. Don't you think?" my sister asked.

"Yeah, I bumped into him a few times during my clandestine visits."

"Sure, he's terrific, but I wondered if we should also have some input?"

"Hmm, girls, in my humble opinion, I would encourage Pastor to sit with her in the comfort of her own home and work it through. Because of their close relationship she'll feel secure enough to express her desires with regard to favorite scripture readings, special music, that sort of thing. I would trust him to do whatever is appropriate and in accordance with her desires," he added.

"Ange? What do you think?"

"I'm totally cool with that. I don't see any need for us to take control when she is perfectly capable of deciding for herself."

"Okay then. I'll let Daddy know of my plans to arrange a meeting between Pastor and Mama. I'll urge Pastor to schedule it … as soon as possible, and I will stress to Daddy that he should be present."

"Good luck with that."

"Well, that wasn't so bad, was it?" Angie said tweaking Joey's ear.

After discussing several other less pressing items, Angie asked, "Is there anything else needing our attention as long as we are together?"

"I think that's about it. That was ... painless, don't you think? Guys, I'm sorry, but I can't seem to find the living will, but I bet it's at the house," I said.

"We're done here, so why don't we just drive over there now? No need to drag this out for several more days, and besides I don't have anything else planned for this afternoon," Angie said. "Kevin and Mia are there with her now." Turning her attention to Joe she said, "Daddy's friend picked him up early this morning; they are attending some kind of garage meeting in Haverhill."

Joey looked at us very cautiously, but in the end agreed to go, knowing our father would not be there.

When will this ever end?

"Angie, you can drive with me, then catch a ride home with the kids, okay? Joey, do you want to ride along with us as well?"

"No, I'll take my car. I'm not planning to stay long."

"Okay, okay, let's go," I said, shoving the leftovers in the refrigerator and grabbing my keys.

During the short drive to our parents' home, Angie commented that she too is beginning to believe this rift will never get resolved. We rode silently, both wondering if and how we should intervene.

The three of us walked into the kitchen only to find Mia with a frantic look on her face. She appeared to be hanging up the phone.

"Thank God, I'm glad you guys are here. I was just trying to reach your house again, Aunt Trina," she blurted out with a shaky voice.

"Why, what's wrong? Is Grandma okay?" Angie asked.

"She is now, but she had a seizure. Kevin and I didn't know what to do. It didn't seem to be a really bad one, but it was still scary."

"Oh honey, I'm sure it was," Angie said, pulling her daughter into a tight embrace. "Where is Kevin?"

"He's still upstairs with her and ..." her voice trailed off as the three of us were already sprinting up the stairs to check on Mama.

As we approached the second floor landing, our attention was diverted to the bathroom. Kevin was standing at the sink splashing cold water on his face, attempting to regain his composure, I assumed.

Without hesitation, Angie began to encourage her son, "It's okay, honey; we're here now. Why don't you go on down with Mia. We'll take it from here." He simply nodded and slowly scuffed down the stairs.

As we were about to enter Mama's bedroom we heard voices … sobs. We instantly knew Daddy was with her. I instinctively withdrew my hand from the doorknob as we all backed away.

"Joey, I'm sorry. I, we … didn't know he'd be here … honest. His friend must have dropped him off sooner than anticipated," I whispered as he protectively wrapped his arms around his body.

"I think Mia was trying to tell us that, but we didn't stay long enough to hear her out," Angie also whispered.

He simply nodded, looking like a little boy, torn between seeing his mother and facing his father.

Not knowing exactly what to do next, the three of us stood stock still outside the partially opened door, listening, yet not wanting to intrude. It was soon apparent this was a very, very different type of exchange between the two of them.

Daddy's voice was rising and lowering, dreadful sobs choking in his throat. At this point, curiosity prompted us to very quietly peek in through the cracked door. We were frozen, captivated by the scene unfolding before our eyes. Daddy was hovering over his beloved wife, weeping and hugging her in desperation, a forlorn man. Angie and I not willing to be found out, stifled our tears as we witnessed their private interaction. Finally, the indistinguishable words he'd mumbled into her hair while locked in their embrace, became crystal clear.

"Maria, I am so sorry. I am so sorry," he wailed. "I love you more than my own life. I never wanted to hurt you. Maria, I can't live without you," tears dropping from his swollen eyes onto her thinning hair.

"Vincent, hush, hush now. You will be all right. You have the kids and the grandchildren to think about, they need you."

Becoming very sober now, needing ... no ... demanding her full attention, he said, "Maria, please listen to me. You must hear me out. I cannot bear this any longer. There is something that I must tell you ... Oh God help me. I should have told you this so many years ago," he pleaded through great heart wrenching sobs. "I am not the man you think I am."

"Vincent ..."

"I need you to forgive me for something terrible, horrible. Please, Maria, forgive me ... I ... I ..."

"Vincent ... I forgave you many years ago. I loved you then, and I love you now. You *are* forgiven," she said weeping.

"What? You knew? How could you have known? You knew and you forgave me anyway?" he wept bitterly, drawing her up into a sweet embrace.

"Vincent, I don't want to waste what few hours I have left, talking about *that*," she softly said. "I want to dwell on the sweetness of our love and the beautiful family our love has created. But, please Vincent, try ... do whatever is in your power to make it right with Joey," she said.

As though rehearsed, we simultaneously withdrew from the door and tiptoed away. At the bottom of the stairs, Angie hugged Joey goodbye then went directly to her children. I half listened to her soft voice reassuring them that their grandmother was resting comfortably.

Silently mulling over what we had just witnessed, I walked my brother to the door, knowing he was ready to make a hasty exit.

"Trina, I have to get going so why don't you just stick a copy of the living will in the mail or drop it off at my house whenever it's good for you. I'll come back to visit Mama whenever ... well soon," he said with a hesitant smile.

"Joey, my head is reeling. I can hardly believe what we just witnessed. Life has way too many twists and turns lately," I said. "What do you think could possibly have been so bad to have caused Daddy to be ... well ... tormented with guilt all these years? Why would he, at this point of her life, so desperately need her forgiveness?" I ventured.

My brother stood there silently, but I could tell he was thrashing it around in his head, trying to decide whether or not to answer me.

With fear and trepidation I began, "Joey, whatever it was, it was big! But here's the thing, Mama apparently found it in her heart to forgive him," I said in a husky voice. "Can you please forgive Daddy for whatever hurt he's caused you?"

With stone cold eyes, he half hugged me, turned, and stomped to his car without a word.

Chapter 23

Later that week, I mailed Joey a copy of Mama's living will with a simple note stating, "Call if you have any questions." My sister and I put aside everything else in our lives and endeavored to make the end of our mother's life as pleasant and sweet as possible. We stepped up our visits, brought gifts, family pictures, food, whatever we felt prompted to bring that might bless her in these final days. I personally was astounded by her inward strength and grace. Although she now slept away most of the day, we kept our promise, managing to frequently get her out into her garden, which visibly refreshed her, if only temporarily.

Mia and Leah spent numerous hours assembling a wonderful scrapbook, which included hundreds of family pictures. In their naive innocence, they didn't hold back from including Joey or his family. Mama loved thumbing through it day after day, and she repeatedly told the stories that more fully explained those photographs. The girls were so proud to have brought such happiness into their grandmother's otherwise cheerless days.

I requested and was granted family leave, giving me the freedom to assist Daddy with Mama's care; he emphatically refused any outside assistance from home health agencies.

"She is my wife, and I will tend to her every need," we often heard him spouting.

Angie agreed to relieve me and fill in over the summer months, if necessary. But truthfully, I wanted Mama all to myself; she could never have been a burden to me. I wouldn't trade one precious second of time I was able to spend with my mother. It was life-giving for me.

During our quiet afternoons, she shared with me many of her personal joys as well as hidden fears, but never did she even hint of the secret that she had long ago forgiven. I didn't pry.

She even confided that Joey, Ellie, and the boys visited while Daddy was in Boston on garage business. He had visited many times during her sickness, and I respected and loved him for that.

How cruel it seemed, at this time of her life, to be deprived of her only son's company, I thought, while listening to her description of their snippets of time spent together.

One beautifully clear afternoon late in May, Mama and I were in the garden serenely taking in the warmth of the sun. "The spring sun always feels the best, doesn't it, Mama?"

"Indeed it does, sweetheart. Maybe it radiates the hope of things to come," she smiled.

The temperature was likened to a mid-June day, and it felt good. Mama abruptly pulled herself upright a bit more, "Look, Trina, look there at that rose. It's one of the roses I grafted, do you remember? Thank you, Lord," she uttered as if praying.

"I certainly do remember. It is undoubtedly going to be the most beautiful in your garden; it looks perfect to me."

She was smiling at that lovely rose when abruptly she said, "You won't forget what I told you?"

"What's that, Mama?"

"Remember, sweetheart, my most ardent prayer for my children is that each of you learn the lesson I have learned so well. And, honey, in doing so, you will reap the joys and many benefits that accompany being grafted in," she said in a hushed voice. "See how uniting the two have become one ... one even more beautiful rose."

"Mama, I'm so proud of you. You've become quite proficient as a master gardener," I joked while gently hugging her frail shoulder.

"Oh, no dear, there is only one Master Gardener. But He does use my poor arthritic hands to accomplish His beautiful design. I'm so grateful to have seen this exquisite flower coming into bloom. Now ... I wait for His promise," she smiled weakly at me.

We sat quietly for a while, admiring the miracle of that rose bush.

"Mama, what do you mean ... exactly ... that you wait for His promise?"

Her mind was million miles away, and she seemed to be getting uncomfortable; I was just about to suggest we head indoors when she asked, "Honey, could I have a glass of water please?"

"Mama, for you anything," I quipped. "Back in a second!"

As I poured water and dropped in a few ice cubes, I couldn't help but ponder her words, "Now I wait for His promise."

My Mama, what an incredibly mysterious woman!

Walking back into the garden, I couldn't tear my eyes away from that magnificent rose as I distractedly said, "Here you go, Mama," offering her the glass of ice cold water. "Mama?" now giving her my full attention.

Smiling to myself, I thought, *I cannot believe she fell asleep so quickly.*

Suddenly her hand dropped heavily to her side, "Mama? Mama!" I wailed ... knowing. "No, no, please Mama, don't leave us! I'm not ready to let you go." Dropping to my knees, I softly laid my head on her lap and cried like a child.

Grasping her hand, I couldn't help but think how fitting that she slipped away from me here in her garden—and into the hands of her Master Gardener.

I'm not sure exactly how much time had lapsed before I finally stood on shaky legs.

I wept, wondering, *how will this family ever function without her?*

Chapter 24 ⌇

Sobbing into Ellie's neck, Joey's remorse was palpable. "Honey, it has to be of some consolation that you ... we ... recently visited her," she whispered.

"Yeah, but it wasn't enough. It wasn't nearly enough. For her sake, I should have put aside my anger and sat with her every day. I knew this day was coming; I wasn't blind to it. What's wrong with me, Ellie?"

"Joe, listen to me, your father crushed something inside you and your mother was well aware of it. Only time overcomes that kind of devastation. I'm positive that your mother understood. She was a wonderful lady. I'm not suggesting that she accepted the division, but neither did she condemn you."

"So what am I supposed to do now?" he asked through tears. "It has been three years, and I still can't look at that man even though I've prayed and prayed. Ellie, I've asked the Lord to help me, to give me a spirit of forgiveness. For a short time, a bit of peace settles in me, then anger and fury take hold of me again. I'm beginning to wonder if I'm capable of forgiveness."

"Maybe in yourself you're not capable of forgiveness, but 'you can do all things through Him who strengthens you.' Honey, for now you just have to do what's right ...for Mama. We will attend the viewing, the funeral, and the mercy meal. You'll never forgive yourself if you don't. Deal with your relationship with Pops when this is all behind us, okay?"

"You're … you're right, but I'm … I don't know what I am," he said with exasperation. "My sisters don't know what happened, so they can't help but judge me, and I don't blame them."

"Wait a second! Your sisters and the rest of the family are not judging you. They don't understand the root of your anger or your inability to deal with it, but they've never been anything *but* accepting of you and our family. Where do you come off with this judging stuff? You are dead wrong there."

Retreating to the solitude of their living room, Joey sat heavily into his recliner feeling totally frustrated. Raking his hands through his thick, dark hair, his attention was grabbed by a beautiful family photograph proudly displayed on the mantle. *Those were happy times*, he thought to himself, and that revelation was a dagger to his heart. After submitting himself to a time of painfully honest introspection, he dragged himself back into the kitchen.

"Okay, honey, I guess I have to admit you're right."

"Of course I'm right," she smirked. "Aren't I always right?"

"El, promise me you'll stay close to me over these next couple of days. I'm going to really need your support."

"I promise, Joe. I promise I will always be there," she said as they embraced. "And Joe, I'm confident you have their support as well."

"How will I live without my Valentine? I don't want to get out of bed. I don't want to eat. What is the purpose of my life now?" Dad moaned through red-rimmed eyes.

"Listen Daddy, don't you think that we are all grieving? Do you think you're the only one who is hurting? But please hear me. Mama would definitely not want us to stop living our lives. During her worst days she never gave in to a pity party, she never isolated herself in a cocoon. She joyfully experienced every minute God gave her," I retorted. "Come on now. Let's honor her memory, all of us!"

"You're right, Trina," Angie chimed in looking directly at Daddy. "No doubt, she's left an immense void in this family, one that is impossible to be filled, but I believe part of her lives on in each one of us. She deposited something of herself, in a unique and special way, into each person she loved. I'm choosing to cling to those wonderful memories—memories we've made together."

Jake chucked his wife under the chin, "Well said, sweetheart, and I for one, am extremely proud to have known her. I loved that she referred to Sal and me as *sons*. That revealed her accepting heart."

"I agree, Jake. It always touched something within me whenever she introduced me as *one of her sons*," Sal added. "She was one of a kind."

"Okay, I get it. You are all correct, but you will have to help me get through these next few days," Daddy said. "The world is not very beautiful to me today, but for my Valentine … I will try to go on … to live."

"Come on guys, we'd better get to the funeral home. Joey and his family are meeting us in the main parlor," I said.

With that, Daddy turned abruptly to face his daughter, "Wait, he's coming to your mother's viewing?"

"Of course he's coming to *our* mother's viewing, Daddy," I responded indignantly.

"For three years he can't find his way to his mother. Now she's gone and suddenly he wants to be the dutiful son," Daddy angrily replied. "Why didn't he love her enough … respect her enough to visit her when she was alive? What kind of son doesn't hold his mother's hand when she's wasting away with that ugly disease?" he yelled.

"Daddy, calm down," Angie went to him.

"Daddy, listen to me. There is something you should know," I cut in trying to keep my calmest social worker demeanor. "He *did* visit her quite regularly, as a matter of fact. He, Ellie and the boys visited her all the while she was undergoing chemo, here at the house while you were working at the garage or at different meetings," I said quietly.

"What … what! She never told me. You never told me. Am I a big, bad ogre that my own family sneaks around behind my back?" He was livid.

"No, no Daddy you're not. And I don't know why Mama didn't tell you. Maybe you should ask your son. I'm … I'm tired of being in the middle of this mess … that's what! You two need to get this straightened out. Whatever *this* is," I said, abruptly leaving the room. I needed to freshen up, and I desperately needed to feel the peace of the Lord before heading off to Mama's viewing.

"Did you see Daddy's eyes?" Angie asked Jake. "They were like saucers. I bet he couldn't believe Trina's response to his comments."

I was just about ready to leave when I heard Daddy's muted voice. I tiptoed toward the sound, not wanting to intrude. He wiped his face and neck with his handkerchief as he slowly lifted his eyes to the ceiling. I shouldn't have but I listened to his quiet prayer, "Oh God, please … don't let my family come apart. Forgive me of my failures and my rotten attitude."

Unusual as it is, Sal and I were the first to arrive at the funeral home; I needed to get out of that house before I dissolved into tears. Besides, those extra minutes afforded me ample time to tie up loose ends with the undertaker before settling in next to the dreaded casket.

Angie and I tried to talk Daddy into cremation with a memorial service, but he wouldn't hear of it. He said Mama left this part up to him, and he stood firm for the traditional way of doing things.

After that little confrontation back at the house, staring into the haggard face of my once beautiful mother was almost more than I could bear. Sal was glued to my side, ever the faithful and gallant husband. When he nudged me, I became cognizant of or maybe felt my brother's presence. I threw myself into Joey's arms and bawled like a two-year-old. Soon I was being enveloped by Ellie, Anthony, Sammy, and my brother. It was a soggy mess until we broke apart like monkey bread, sweet and sticky.

"Joey, I'm so, so glad you're here," I blubbered. "Everyone will be really happy to see you," I tried to reassure him.

"I doubt everyone, but thanks, Sis. You're the best."

"Just a heads up … he knows you've been visiting. So, you don't have to be concerned with hiding anything."

"Okay, but I doubt we'll have much to say to one another."

"Joey, Mama would have wanted … I mean she prayed for restoration between you and …" and with that the rest of the family walked into the funeral parlor.

Admittedly, after initial greetings of hugs and kisses were exchanged, save one, what I can only describe as awkwardness hung heavily in the air. Daddy found his place near the casket and kept his eyes down or on his beloved wife.

Soon, Ellie sidled up to him, giving a big hug, which to his credit, he returned without hesitation. This simple gesture opened the door for Anthony and Sammy to follow suit. Still, number one son stayed aloof.

Friends, relatives, and her church family came in droves, simply because they loved my mother. These gentle souls relayed countless stories of her boundless kindness. They told of meals she prepared for them, money freely given to them, and time she unselfishly shared with them. For much of the night, I pondered the details of every single expression of the love she so lavishly extended. None of this was lost on my sister or my brother. I watched Joey's facial expression as one of her church friends recounted a story of Mama forgiving wrongs done to her. The stream of mourners was steady and although we were physically exhausted, we were spiritually uplifted and bolstered by these dear folks.

Each of us was blessed by the attendance of our own friends and coworkers; however, the show of support the kids received was impressive. Mia and Ricky never really did become a couple; nonetheless, they remained close, and he was the first of her many friends to enter the funeral home. He reminded me of a five star general as he marched directly to my niece and pulled her into a fierce embrace, soberly extending his heartfelt sympathies. Joey wasted no time as he sidestepped a few people in order to shake the boy's hand, thanking him for coming. It was plain that the two were genuinely fond of one another and respected one another.

"Mr. A., I again want to say thank you for your concern for me … but mostly for the forgiveness you extended to me. If it weren't for you, I may have ended up in some gang or worse … in jail. But, because of you, I'm in trade school and have already been offered a job when I graduate."

"I'm … I'm proud of you, Ricky," Joey said in a whisper. "You did it on your own, no need to thank me."

"Yeah, but if you hadn't given me a chance … well, thank you. And I'm sending you and your family invitations to my graduation. I'd be honored if you could attend."

It was a difficult night but a fulfilling night as well. We, the family of Maria Fantino Agosti, were thrilled and proud to discover an unsung part of her life through the accolades of these precious visitors who simply came to pay their respects.

She, of course, would never have boasted on herself, never. Hearing those accolades made me think of a multi-faceted diamond. As kind and caring as we *knew* our mother to be, we couldn't possibly have known every other facet of her person. Imagining this multi-faceted diamond caused her to shine even more brilliantly before my eyes.

Feeling the need to bridge the uncomfortable gap between me and my father, I invited him to come home with Sal and me when the viewing hours were concluded, but he declined as we expected.

And so as the night drew to a close, we sought solace in the security of our own homes, too physically depleted to think about tomorrow.

If a funeral could possibly be described as beautiful, then Mama's was indeed beautiful. For many years I have admired their tiny white church that sets picturesquely back on a gently sloping hill.

During the winter months it seems to all but disappear, becoming one with its surrounding and the snow covered landscape. Although most people would describe it as structurally small, the heart of that congregation is large—extremely large and extremely loving.

Today, that little white church on the hill was packed to capacity. Our jaws dropped, witnessing the steady procession of Mama's friends, family, and casual acquaintances as they respectfully passed the casket, bidding their personal farewells.

How could one woman have impacted all these lives?

Her pastor eulogized her life as a "life not wasted and a life of hope." He waxed eloquent, underscoring the love she had for her Lord and her desire to live in obedience to Him. He related to the attentive crowd how she glowed when bragging about her children and grandchildren. To my surprise, Pastor next spoke in great detail about her Garden of Hope. Naively, I had considered the garden just a family thing, but he became quite animated as he attempted to portray Mama's wonderfully healthy, robust roses.

Explaining that while she undoubtedly received great personal gratification from her garden accomplishments, she was much more focused on the life lessons learned in that garden.

"She had confided in me," he said in hushed tones, "that while experimenting with the process of grafting, her Lord and Savior taught her so much more—greater truths to live by. We talked together many, many times about her beloved garden. As a matter of fact, she planned to teach the ladies Bible study about the spiritual lessons she had learned in her garden. Unfortunately, that was not to be."

There it was again; those roses she grafted held a deeper message. Glancing sideways at me, it was evident that Angie had also caught the reference.

Joey and Daddy sat like book ends at opposite ends of the pews, but it was obvious both were touched by every endearing word spoken by this other man who faithfully walked beside her down every mile of this difficult journey.

The congregants of this lovely church graciously hosted the mercy meal for our family in the community room. I couldn't deny feeling humbled as these women who obviously loved Mama, quietly served her family.

It was then that it occurred to me how frequently she herself had served other families who had experienced loss. Observing these women move about, I felt ashamed for the many years I declined Mama's invitation to serve alongside of her. Sadly, I missed many opportunities to spend time with her—time I can never recapture.

While lingering over dessert and coffee, I noticed Joey shuffling behind me, moving toward Daddy. My eyes were fixed on my brother, attempting to read his facial expression.

In an almost inaudible voice, I heard the words, "Pop, let's take a walk." To his credit, my father did not hesitate and did not draw any unwanted attention as they walked together toward the parking lot.

Sal and I grabbed each other's hands, and I think he mumbled a quick prayer, but I couldn't be certain. My thoughts were preoccupied. Angie leaned over, whispering, "Is this good or bad?"

"Not sure. Should we join them?" I asked.

"Noooo, let them duke it out. I mean … talk it out," she said. "This has been brewing for three years. They need private time; I'm not going anywhere near those two knuckleheads. Besides, I … I'm having another cannoli!" Angie said with a broad smile, intentionally cutting through the tension, as only she can do.

"You're funny! But my curiosity is bound to get the best of me," I said, but remained seated. "Oh all right! Pass me the cannoli tray," I said, returning my sister's grin.

Ellie was smiling at us with that knowing expression she so often displayed. I responded to her by lifting my cannoli in a mock toast, which caused a ripple of laughter, releasing the heaviness that was beginning to build.

I couldn't resist. I shuffled to the screen door and watched Daddy and Joey in the parking lot. They walked in deafening silence. I thought it fitting that my brother broke that silence.

"Pop …" he haltingly started.

"Oh, now it's Pop? Your mother is gone and now you can call me Pop again," Daddy lashed.

Joey almost … almost turned and walked back to the church hall, but something unseen held his feet to the ground. They stood facing each other, three years of raw emotions hung between them like storm clouds.

Daddy took the lead saying, "I'm sorry. I shouldn't have said that. Trina told me you visited your mama regularly. Thank you for that."

Sheepishly, Joey began again, "Listen, Pops, I am still struggling with … you know, but the last time Ellie and I visited Mama, she pleaded with me to forgive you. Angie, Trina, and I were in the hall outside your bedroom door the day she had the seizure. We didn't mean to overhear, but we did. They don't have a clue, but I knew you were begging forgiveness for … *that*," he said, eyes filling with tears. "Honestly, I was blown away that … that … she knew all these years and she had already forgiven you. I couldn't believe my ears."

"Your Mama was an exceptional woman."

"Well, what I'm trying to say is … I'm trying to forgive you too. It may take a while, but I'm working on it. Okay? I haven't told anyone except Ellie, and I don't plan to uncover you to the rest of the family."

"Son, for that, I thank you. I'm so sorry to have put your mother and you through this, so very sorry. I only wish she was here. You are a good man, Joe. I … I love you, son." Daddy wept on Joey's shoulder and to my astonishment, my brother ever so slowly embraced his pop.

I quickly moved away from the door, taking my place next to Sal. Together, we watched with exhilaration as father and son returned to their family. Sal winked at me and smiled as he drew me close; the heaviness to which we'd become accustomed had finally lifted. The Agosti family no longer felt constrained to tiptoe around these two stubborn lugs. We spontaneously let loose with heartfelt embraces for both Daddy and Joey.

I could almost hear the chains—three years of bondage—smashing and falling to the floor. Freedom!

Mama was smiling down on her family, I just knew it. It seemed fitting that our entire family should leave this place and spend the remainder of the day in Mama's Garden of Hope.

And that is exactly what we did!

Chapter 25

I cannot honestly say that Daddy and Joey jumped right back into their old camaraderie. They did not. But I'm thankful for their steady, although slow progress toward the reconciliation that our Mama longed to witness.

Ellie and the boys frequently visited now, happy to be reconnected to the family. I probably annoy my brother to no end, but I feel compelled to remind him just how blessed he is to have that woman by his side. Through thick and thin Ellie has never wavered.

Our entire family remains completely in the dark as to the reason they fought, and I've accepted the fact we may never know.

I imagine getting up, getting dressed, and going to the garage every day gives Daddy purpose and a sense of continuity. However, his seventy years are telling; he now only manages to complete half of his scheduled repairs. I have to bolster my emotions in order to avoid getting sucked into his depression, yet I continue to drop by the garage whenever my schedule is light.

"Hey Daddy, what's up?" I asked walking into the garage.

"Hi, not much," he droned back lifelessly.

"I brought you a hoagie from Jim's and a piece of chocolate cake. Sal nearly tackled me when he saw the last piece going out the door," I said attempting to coax a smile.

"Thanks, Trina, but I'm not too hungry today. Save it for your husband."

"Daddy, listen to me," I firmly responded. "You have to eat! Mama has been gone for over a month. She wouldn't want you moping around like a sick puppy. Besides, you're getting skinny."

"I know, I know. Just leave it, honey. I'll nibble on it this afternoon."

Somewhat placated I started, "Angie and I would like to come over tonight or tomorrow night and … and … sort through some of Mama's things. We didn't think you'd want to go through her closet or …"

"Stop right there! I do not want your mother's things touched. Nothing will be removed, not yet! I feel … I don't know … comforted by having her personal items there with me," he said with glistening eyes.

"Okay, Dad, I understand. When you're ready, we'll be there so you don't have to do it alone. We just want to help you. Okay?"

"Yes, yes," he said more tenderly now. As we hugged, I could feel his bones through his coveralls.

He's shrinking away before our very eyes.

"Daddy, I'm planning to have family and a few friends over for our Fourth of July picnic. We haven't all been together since May when Mama passed. It's time. She always loved our picnics, right, Pop?"

"I don't feel up to a picnic, but you all have fun together. Have a hot dog for me."

"No! I won't take *no* for an answer. I can have Sal pick you up so you don't even have to drive."

"Little girl, I am perfectly capable of driving," he said with a half-smile.

"Okay then, come on over right after church. And don't bring a thing; we'll have gobs of food. You know we always have too much," I cheerfully responded. "We'll talk more about it when it gets closer."

"You are just like your Mama ... won't take no for an answer."

"Well, I'll take that as a supreme compliment."

"Yes, yes, it is."

Whew, that was like pulling teeth! Looking back over my shoulder as I started up my car, I caught a glimpse of my father with head in hands, weeping.

"Hi Mia, how is one of my favorite nieces?" I joked into the phone.

"Aunt Trina, you always say that, and it's not funny anymore. Besides one out of two isn't such a compliment," Mia responded in a rather haughty manner.

"Sorry, guess I didn't realize I was getting stale. But you and Leah will always be special to me, and you are my favorite nieces. Is your mom home?" I quickly said, anxious to change the subject.

"Mooommm, Aunt Trina's on the phone!" gets yelled into my eardrum, nearly shattering my glasses. It was somewhat muted, but I was able to hear Angie scolding Mia for hollering.

"I'm right here, for goodness sake, no need to wake the dead."

"Hi Sis! Are you totally deaf now?"

"Sheesh, what was that all about? She's not her usual chipper self," I responded.

"No, not by a long shot. Hey, you should try living with her."

"I'll pass for now."

"It's boy problems, yet again. She's being witchy today."

"I don't remember us being like that when we were teenagers. Do you?"

"Maybe not quite as bad as Mia, but we did have our moments ... But hey, look how good we turned out," she laughed.

"Well anyhow, the reason I'm calling is *yes* I did stop by to see Dad, and you are right, he is still in a major funk. I did my best, coaxing him into eating, but he will probably toss my hoagie into the trash when he gets home. He also declined my Fourth of July invitation, at least until I put the squeeze on him. I realize it's only a few weeks since Mama's passing, but he's not taking care of himself. He's losing weight."

"I know. We had Ellie and Joey over for dinner last night, and I tried to express our concern. He listened, looked a bit concerned, but didn't offer any suggestions. I noticed the looks between them at various times during our conversation. I doubt they will ever reveal the *dread* secret. But the good news is that they will be coming to your picnic. Yeah!" she blurted triumphantly.

"Great! Good job, Sis. That's the best news I've had in a long time."

"I thought so."

"Oh, and just so you are in the loop, Daddy most definitely does not want anything of Mama's sorted, cleaned, or even touched, at least for a while longer. He said that he finds comfort having her things around him. So, I didn't coerce him. I recognize the symptoms of depression, and he's got them for sure. But I feel it's premature to suggest counseling or medication. What do you think?"

"That's probably wise. He needs more time to heal, as do we. We just need to keep a close eye on him … well, we would anyhow. Personally, I can't do one thing in the kitchen or the garden without a Mama flashback. She was such a great mom and …"she broke off and into sniffling session.

"Same here! Simply picking up a utensil can trigger one of those flashbacks you're talking about."

"Do you think Joey is wrestling with this also?"

"I'm sure he is. You know I have spent years counseling clients and helping them get through the grief process, but it's not so easy when it's your own mama," I admitted. "So, it's pretty understandable what our dad must be experiencing."

"We'll get through this together, Trina, we all will," she said. I now detected a smile in her voice.

After drying our eyes, we set our sights on planning the picnic—the first one ever without Mama.

Chapter 26

"I'm glad you girls slept over last night, you were a big help to me and Uncle Sal," I said, chucking Leah under her chin.

"It was fun. Besides, you make the best popcorn, hands down," Leah laughed.

"Sure do! Aunt Trina, I'm sorry I was so … so … snotty on the phone last week. I really am," Mia whispered. "I don't know why I let Greg get to me like that. He can be so sarcastic, or he can be so sweet. I can't figure him out," she confided.

"Well, I accept your apology. As for Greg, I don't think he's good for you, but you're eighteen and quite capable of making good, sound decisions. Remember this, honey, you can't make them better. They are who they are, so pick one like your dad or Uncle Joey or my Sal. They are all loving and considerate men, and … they treat their wives with respect."

"Now that I think of it, his dad talks so nasty to his mother. I remember Grandpa saying 'watch them carefully in their home setting; that is how he will treat you some day.' Hmmm…he's history!" she said with a wide smile. "You're pretty smart, Aunt Trina."

"That was an easy decision. You must have been 99 percent there already. You just needed a nudge in the right direction," I said as we hugged each other.

"Oh, Aunt Trina, she's off to college this fall, she was really just looking for ways to clear the field," Leah blurted out.

"Actually, you're pretty much on target there, little sister. I plead guilty as charged."

"Huh, I knew it," Leah said smugly.

"Aunt Trina, I invited Cindy, if that's okay? Well, I guess I should have asked before I invited her, huh?"

"Cindy is always welcome here, you know that. Besides, a little birdie told me that she and Kevin are dating. Is that true?" I pressed.

"Yeah, it is. But they've only been out together twice. Once to Salisbury Beach and once they drove into Boston, I think," she confirmed.

"They make a nice couple, but they both have lots of school ahead of them. Hope they move slowly," I said.

"Cindy is determined to get her degree. She doesn't want to box herself in with limited options for the rest of her life ... like her mom. And you know Kevin is a self-proclaimed nerd. He will definitely finish school, no doubt about that."

"Good! Now, would you girls please grab the paper products from the laundry room? It would be a big help if you would start setting up the tables out back. Uncle Sal is already there getting the coolers and grill ready. I need to get going and finish up this potato salad."

"I thought my mom was bringing potato salad?"

"Nope, we rearranged the menu, a hundred times. She's bringing pasta salad and chocolate cake. Aunt Ellie is bringing deviled eggs, tossed salad, and peanut butter cookies."

"Okay, now you've got me drooling," Mia chuckled.

"I'm so glad Grandpa is coming today. He's been so ... out of it ... since Grandma died. I'm not judging him, it's just that he just seems so, I don't know ... lifeless. I miss her too, so much that I can't stop crying some times," Leah said.

"I know, honey," I reassured her with a hug. "We all feel lost without her, but maybe he'll perk up today. Just having you two around does it for me."

"I hope so."

Just then the kitchen door swung open and in walked the happy couple. "Hi Aunt Trina," smiled Kevin.

"Hi there, Mrs. Lamazo," Cindy sang out.

"Cindy, it's about time you called me Trina. You make me feel … well … old," I said with a laugh and a lick of the potato salad dressing.

"Humph," laughed Kevin. "You *are* getting there," he chortled lifting me in a big bear hug.

"Put me down. You are getting too big for your own britches. Besides, I'm only forty-five. That's young, very young," I giggled.

"Here, I brought potato salad," Cindy said as the girls shot a quick glance in my direction while hiding a knowing smirk.

"Thank you so much. That was very thoughtful of you. We all love potato salad."

"How is your mom, Cindy? You should have brought her along."

"She's doing very well, thanks. She and my dad are going for counseling. The goal is reconciliation, permanent reconciliation. Can you believe that he's still sober and this time he truly wants to be a family again?" she said smiling.

"I could not be happier for you … and for your mom," I said. "Miracles do happen."

"Yup, even though it took a broken jaw to get one," Kevin joked as he gently tickled my chin.

"Small price to pay for a reunified family," I said, "although, my jaw clicks occasionally, reminding me of my clicking chalkboard."

"I'm still so sorry about that Mrs., I mean Trina," Cindy said through sad eyes. "I wish that never happened to you."

"Tell me, honey, how does your dad feel about you dating my nephew? I mean Kevin did pummel him pretty good!"

"I asked him about that the day before Kevin and I drove into Boston. I was surprised at his response; he said he would have done the same thing if he were in Kevin's shoes. He assured me he's not harboring any hard feelings," Cindy said as she took Kevin's hand.

"That's good to …" just then I could hear Joey and his family in the back yard. "Oh, good big brother's family has arrived," I said walking toward the kitchen door.

"Hey guys, glad you're here," I yelled out.

I laughed as Anthony roughhoused with Buddy, glad to see that picture once again.

Joey and Sal were already interacting in their same old casual manner as though their relationship had never been breached. Ellie and Sammy carried food into the kitchen, giving sideways hugs as they searched for counter space for their goodies.

I gave Ellie the biggest hug ever, whispering in her ear how much I've missed this. She readily returned my affection.

I made a point of observing Joey and was grateful that he seemed relaxed, that is until my father came through the back gate. He stiffened ever so slightly, and his demeanor became a tad more reserved, still he was remarkably civil to Daddy. I was briefly distracted from the gathering so I didn't notice whether or not they hugged, but I was pleased these two were now willing to be in the same place at the same time.

The kids, helpful as always, busied themselves with chilling down the beverages and setting up folding tables, allowing our entire group the luxury of eating outside together. It was getting hot, but it was still a gorgeous day; not a cloud in the sky.

I laughed to myself hearing my sister's familiar singsong banter with Jake as they floated through the gate. Nothing keeps that girl down!

"Hey family, we have arrived! Let the party begin!" she bellowed after unloading her dishes onto the kitchen counter. And she is so right. The party simply cannot begin until my crazy sister makes her grand entrance. Mocking a Hollywood socialite, Angie makes her rounds planting exaggerated hugs and kisses on every single person, including a non-person, my Buddy.

It goes without saying that I was in my glory, watching my family happily interacting with one another. I have waited three long years for this scene to unfold. *Mama, I can see the smile on your face.* I felt a wellspring of joy rise up from deep within me as I studied each person and was overcome with gratitude.

"Okay, this grill master is ready! Trina, grab the hamburgers first, then I'll throw on the hot dogs," Sal announced.

"I'll get them Aunt Trina," Sammy offered. "I'm starving."

"Anthony, do you mind filling the potato chips bowls? Anything to stave off your hunger," I said.

"Sure, and I'll just have to sample a few … you know, quality control. It's my job," he said shyly.

After the first round of hamburgers was grilled, Sal asked for a blessing over our food, and within seconds the familiar Agosti free-for-all began. Arms were crisscrossing across the picnic table, reaching for pickles, potato salad, burgers, and anything else these boys managed to mound onto their plates.

The Agostis are back in town.

"Hey, leave some for the grownups," Angie chided the big boys with a gentle nudge to her son.

"And for us," Mia and Leah simultaneously shouted as they playfully pushed their cousins.

"Daddy, can I fix you a plate?" I asked.

"Nope, I'm good. I'll wait until everyone else gets theirs."

"Pops, you better grab it while you can. Have you noticed these appetites?" Jake snickered.

Everybody managed to get something to eat and quickly settled into easy, relaxed conversation. I tried not to hover over my father, but couldn't help but notice that he was picking at his food—pushing it around on his plate was more like it.

"I thought Donna and her family were coming?" Angie asked.

"They were, but Pete picked up some kind of viral infection. He's been out of commission for a few days," I answered. "Honestly, I'm kind of glad they couldn't make it … just this one time. I feel selfish, but I'm so happy to have the family all to myself."

"Trina, you are the least selfish person on the planet. Perfectly understandable after … you know … the fractured family thing," Angie laughed just as someone got her good with a squirt gun. "Hey, who was that? I'll get you … you dingbat," she snarled in the direction of the kids' table.

"You best believe her," Kevin said to Cindy. "She loves to get even."

"You got that right! Hey Ellie, come join us at the girls' table," Angie yelled. "Your hubby is happy to release you into our clutches, right big brother?"

"She's a big girl, completely free to do whatever she wants. I'm not her boss, but ... before you go, Ellie, grab me another hot dog," he said in his old playful manner, which caused a ripple of laughter. Even Daddy laughed.

With a big grin, Ellie blew a kiss across the yard toward her husband and settled down at the girls' table, leaving Joey to fetch his own hot dog.

"Girls, I'm so happy to be here back together. I was starting to worry those two stubborn mules would never resolve their differences, not that it's 100 percent resolved, but they are making progress. I've missed these times, being with all of you. Let me tell you, it was a *long* three years. And ... I miss Mama so much. She was like a second mother to me," she quietly said.

"I know, she sure was, and we've missed you too. Ellie, do you know what caused the fight? It must have been pretty significant ... I mean three years is a long time to hold a grudge," Angie ventured.

"Eh, I made a promise to my husband to keep their confidence. I cannot break that promise," she said, pink creeping into her cheeks.

"Of course. I'm sorry, I shouldn't have asked, and I won't ever ask again. I respect that ... we respect you for that, right, Trina?"

"Sure do. I'm just glad we're finally sitting at the same table again. So, when are we going on another girls' day out?" I playfully asked.

"I'm ready whenever you ..." Angie was interrupted by a crash coming from the kitchen.

"I'll check, Buddy probably knocked something over again," I said as I instinctively scanned the group looking for my father, not finding him.

Sal and I raced to the house, arriving at the kitchen door at exactly the same time. Terror gripped me as my brain tried to make sense of the image before me. My father's body was sprawled on the floor.

"Daddy!" I frantically screamed. "Daddy!" I screamed again to his motionless body.

Everyone instantly stumbled into the kitchen.

"What happened to Grandpa?" Leah cried.

"I'll get a wet washcloth," Jake sputtered. "Maybe the heat got to him."

"Call 911," Joey yelled to Anthony who was standing closest to the telephone. "His breathing is very shallow."

"Oh God, please! Daddy, open your eyes!" Angie cried out. Jake embraced his wife after he handed a cool washcloth to Joey.

Within minutes the ambulance arrived, the wailing sirens had diminished then abruptly were silenced. The EMTs did not waste one second on small talk but instantly and fully focused on their patient. Daddy had not stirred during their cursory examination.

"Come on, kids, move away, we need to give them plenty of room to check out Gramps," Sal shouted.

Both EMTs appeared to be quite young; nonetheless, they purposefully ministered to Daddy without faltering as though performing these same steps a hundred thousand times before.

Our eyes remained fixed, glued to these two men who were hunched over Daddy's motionless frame. Not wasting a second, as if rehearsed they gingerly lifted Daddy onto a litter and headed out the door.

"This can't be happening," I muttered as Sal pulled me closer.

Almost as an afterthought, one of the EMTs yelled back over his shoulder, "You can meet him at Lawrence General Hospital," and with that they were speeding down the road.

Standing rigid like robots, Cindy broke the silence, "Go … you all go. I'll clean up here and put everything away. I'll call my mom for a ride. Go, go," she yelled again. We thanked her profusely and flew out the door to our cars, speeding after the ambulance toward the General Hospital, which was only a few miles away.

Minutes later our entire family was gathered in the room designated for friends and families of emergency room patients ... waiting. Joey and I approached the desk, providing the clerk with their requested pertinent information. Joey asked if we could see either our father or a doctor. The triage nurse nodded and disappeared through a side door.

We waited, but no one came to us. Finally when Joey could take it no longer, he knocked on that same side door. Immediately a shy looking little nurse came out, quickly stating that the doctor was on his way to speak with the family ... our family.

"Thank you," he responded not meaning to sound quite so curt.

A few more agonizing minutes passed without the appearance of the promised doctor. Unexpectedly, from an entirely different door, we noticed an unfamiliar doctor approaching our group.

"Are you the family of Vincent Agosti?"

"Yes, yes, we are," I blurted out, pointing to Joey, Angie, and myself. "How is he doing? What happened to him? When can we see him?" I fired off a barrage of questions to this mild-mannered physician standing before us.

"I'm ... I'm ... very sorry to tell you that your father did not make it," he quietly said. "Actually, he had a massive heart attack and was likely gone within seconds. I'm very sorry."

"Nooo," I keened. "Not Daddy too! It can't be!"

"Oh my God!" Angie fell to her knees, sobbing relentlessly.

"Pops, no Pops! I've been such a fool. I'm so sorry, Pops," Joey joined our keening, covering his face with his shaky hands. The rest of the family rushed to us, fiercely embracing one another in feeble attempts to console.

We were all hysterical, every last one of us. Mama was gone and six weeks later—Daddy. How could this be?

When the physician left us, that same timid little nurse stepped forward offering to call the hospital chaplain, explaining we may benefit from such comfort. We thanked her, but declined, explaining that once home we'd call his pastor. Compassion sweeping across her face, she offered us coffee, water, or soda. She undoubtedly was attempting to calm our family enough to satisfy herself we were capable of driving home safely, which we did.

In a fog of grief and disbelief, we somehow managed to make it back to my house where Cindy was just finishing up in the kitchen. She dissolved into tears, not willing to believe Daddy was also ... gone. She clung to Kevin, hoping to be of some encouragement, to lend some moral support.

Wordlessly, we gathered in the living room, desperately trying to absorb this latest loss. Shocked didn't come close to adequately describe our emotions. We sat for at least an hour, each locked in our own emotional prisons. Silence hung in the air, except for the rippling undercurrent of sniffling and whimpering, not a word was heard.

Angie was the first to pierce through the blanket of stillness. "He's always been our rock, our patriarch," she sobbed. "I know he'd been slowing down, we all knew it, but this ... I can't wrap my brain around this. How can he be gone too? Did anyone know he had heart problems? Did he mention it to any of you?"

"I had no clue! Come to think of it, I cannot remember the last time he even had a doctor appointment. He'd been 100 percent focused on caring for Mama ... nothing else mattered to him," I said. "And anyone who knows ... knew Daddy, couldn't possibly deny that he was depressed. Taking care of himself was low on his list of priorities. I should have seen the signs. I'm a social worker for goodness sake. What's wrong with me?"

"Stop it Trina," Joey said. It's not your fault. If anything, the lion's share of blame should be dumped squarely on my shoulders. It was me ... me ... who selfishly buried him under mounds of stress," he responded as he burst into bitter tears.

"Okay, let's *all* stop right now. I can't stand listening to you two beating up on yourselves. The truth is ... none of us is to blame. He succumbed to a massive heart attack. End of story. We're not God. Only He has the power of life and death in His hands," Angie passionately pleaded. "Besides, do you think this kind of banter would please either one of them? Both Mama and Daddy would encourage us to move on and stick together as a family. Let's honor their memories by living right?" Angie's voice of reason was clear and commanding.

"You should have been a lawyer. You make a very compelling argument," smiling at my sister. "I think we should call his pastor now," I said as I walked to the telephone. Still, the room was thick with raw emotion.

When Daddy's pastor arrived, the kids excused themselves to the back yard, leaving us to make some difficult decisions, yet again. They were hurting as much, if not more than us, but obviously were already helping one another begin dealing with the newest massive hole in their own hearts. I overheard them consoling one another with such rare tenderness and compassion.

Isn't that what family is all about?

Chapter 27 ❦

It was not even nine o'clock yet, but it was already unbearably hot and humid. Thunderstorms were forecasted, but hopefully would hold off until after Daddy's funeral.

I stood before my front hallway mirror, startled by my own reflection. The forty-five-year old woman staring back at me looked exhausted … and just plain weary. The humidity did its evil task on my naturally curly hair, making it uncontrollably frizzy. My skin was shiny with perspiration. The undertaker assured me that a tent had been erected at the cemetery for our comfort. Whether it was appropriate or not, I chose a cornflower blue sundress. Though lightweight as a feather, it was still acceptably modest and hopefully as cool as possible on a day like today.

Sal slowly approached me from behind attempting to embrace my sticky body saying, "I think our window unit is about to quit. Let's hope the church is cool."

"It's okay, not much we can do about it now. Let's get going," I said as I grabbed my purse and ruffled Buddy's neck.

I was astonished to find most spaces already filled as we pulled into the church parking lot. I suppressed unbidden thoughts as we stepped into the church foyer. I found myself identifying with the frustrated character from *Groundhog Day*; this is all too incredulous, reliving a nightmare. For the second time in less than two months, we were greeted by familiar faces and sympathetic hugs.

Thank God for family and friends and … air conditioning!

The graveside, however, would offer no such comfort.

As previously planned, my siblings and I met in the anteroom before taking our reserved seats. We were somewhat prepared for Mama's passing, but I could not come to grips with the ugly truth that today we bury my father. Even though Daddy was seventy years old, he had always been physically fit, at least until recently.

Why didn't I see the signs?

I couldn't stop castigating myself. The somber music began, signaling our family to take their designated seats at the front of the church.

Déjà vu, I thought to myself as I clung to Sal's arm. The pastor knew my father well and so proffered a beautiful tribute honoring his life, as he had done with Mama. By comparison, this church service was short, but lacked in no other way, and all attendees were invited to the graveside service. The pastor lightheartedly announced that a tent was provided and he would keep his graveside comments brief due to the extreme heat.

The outdoor temperature had indeed soared during the brief church service. I was distracted by how many people were dripping with perspiration—clothing sticking to their glistening bodies, including my own.

Even before our family settled into assigned chairs under the graveside tent, Angie became overwrought by the cold reality of the open grave. Mia and Leah, like their mother, were beside themselves and inconsolable. Miraculously, I held it together, at least outwardly.

Guests clustered closely around us, simulating a steam bath. Pastor conducted the committal service, quoting several of Daddy's favorite scriptures.

While meditating on those holy words, I looked up and through the crowd noticed two people standing afar off under a large tree. They appeared to simply be watching. I couldn't make out either of their facial features, but the older one was certainly familiar and she was dabbing her eyes, crying.

Was it …? Could it be …?

I strained my eyes, while still feigning interest in the pastor's words. In between the perpetual movements of the gathered crowd, I was able to catch brief glimpses of the older woman who was tenderly enveloping the younger girl in her arms. The younger appeared to be in her teens.

I was determined, even in this setting, to finally approach this ghost-like woman. I grew more certain by the minute that this is the woman I have seen before. *I will head right over there at the close of this service.* I was in mourning, I was one with my family, but my mind was also racing with unanswered questions.

When the pastor concluded and the crowd, like the Red Sea, finally parted, I immediately stood and scanned the cemetery. They were gone. They must be distant relatives or maybe someone from Daddy's business, not wanting to intrude.

No! She is the woman! I've seen her several times before … I'm sure of it.

We had made previous arrangements to gather back at Joey's home after the funeral, concurring that two mercy meals were above and beyond what the small church should have to provide. Although they graciously offered, we declined, opting for the comfort and privacy of Joey and Ellie's home.

We ordered food from a local caterer and took comfort in each other's company. It was the perfect environment in which to let down—cry or laugh depending on the particular story being told. It was soothing to hear young and old share their precious memories of their dad or grandfather.

The caterer delivered our hot food and provided us with every imaginable disposable item, which meant not being bothered with dirty dishes. "Donna said we wouldn't be disappointed with this caterer. She's right, I thought the food was pretty good," I said.

"Yeah, but pretty good is not *excellent*, *delicious*, or *amazing*; nothing compares to an Agosti woman's cooking," Sal said.

"Huh, thanks for the compliment, Sal. But I think we all agree this was a good idea and worked out well for our family today," Angie said while tossing the dirty paper products. "I'll cut the dessert later. Let's relax for a while."

Sammy dug deep into the cedar chest, dragging out old photo albums, sparking a journey down memory lane. Before long the kids were pawing through stacks of old albums. It turned into an amazing and healing experience—*the Balm of Gilead to our souls.*

We laughed uproariously when Anthony produced a picture of Leah at Canobie Lake on the day she fell into the lake and was rescued by her hero, Uncle Joey. Now thirteen, I thought she'd be embarrassed, dissolving into tears but to my surprise, she laughed harder than anyone else while hugging her uncle.

"Yup," Jake said, "I remember it well. That was the day we celebrated the opening of the Agosti & Son Garage, wasn't it?"

Solemnly Joey answered, "Yes, yes it was. Pop and I were already working together, but never officially had a family celebration. It was a nice day," he said quietly.

"Yeah, it was a nice day until Donna and Jake's house burned down," I added. "But all is well that ends well. No one was hurt and their new home is gorgeous."

"Look guys ... look at Aunt Trina in that bathing suit. How old were you then?" Mia laughed.

"Quit laughing, let me see that," I commanded snatching the photo from her hands. "Oh, that was on our family vacation at Salisbury Beach. Let me think ... I was fourteen. And I'll have you know, I got my first kiss that week!" I smiled demurely.

Everyone, especially the kids, broke forth into mocking cat calls and loud whistling at this newest revelation.

"What? Who kissed my girl?" Sal piped in pretending to be shadow boxing.

"Joey's best friend Lenny kissed me by the bonfire. It was our last night of vacation, and I thought I was going to die. I was positively lovesick."

"Why that snake," Joey retorted. "He never told me that. If I'd known, I would have decked him for taking advantage of my little sister."

"That's good, I'm glad to hear he kept our little secret. Besides, it only happened once, and it was a long time before I met the love of my life," I said wrapping my arms around Sal's neck. "I got the best deal of my life with this guy."

"You better not forget it either," Sal laughed good-naturedly.

"These are great pictures," Ellie remarked. "Who was the talented photographer?"

"Me! I took them with my prized camera, as a matter of fact. I captured everything under the sun and used up every single roll of film, but I'm clueless how so many ended up in your albums," Angie said.

"Mama had duplicates, even triplicates. She thought we'd like to have a few. Look at this picture of you three little angels in front of your house. Speaking of the old homestead, you guys do realize you're facing some heavy duty decisions about the house and its contents. Lots and lots of memories there, and lots and lots of stuff," Ellie said.

"Oh groan ... I don't want to think about emptying the place," I said. "But you're right. It's got to be done sooner or later."

Mulling it over Angie said, "You know what, I think the sooner, the better. I'm not back to the grind until September so I have the time now. What do you think?"

"I guess we could *start* working on it, a little at a time. Ange, just pick a Saturday and I'll join you. Is that okay with you, Joey?"

"No problem. Week days are tough, but Ellie and I can be there most Saturdays or Sundays. Just let me know your plan; I'll pitch in and lend a hand. Anyhow, you all have house keys."

"I'm afraid we're facing a really time-consuming job. Maybe the kids can eventually be added to the labor force. Joey, did you know Daddy would not allow me or Angie to touch or sort any of Mama's things?"

"Nope, didn't know that. Not surprised."

"Angie, how about you and I get a jump on it next Saturday," I suggested.

"Okay, let's grab breakfast together then spend the day at this formidable task. The rest of you can join us whenever you're free."

While helping Ellie in the kitchen, I turned to Joey asking, "Did you happen to notice a couple of people standing far back at the cemetery ... watching us?"

"No, can't say as I did. Why, who were they?"

"That's just it! I'm not sure who they were, but I swear I know them, met them, or have seen them. When Pastor concluded the committal service, they were gone."

"Hmm, strange huh! Maybe they were garage vendors and didn't want to interrupt the family time."

"I thought about that. But, in my gut, I know it's more than that, Joey."

My big brother turned, now giving me his full attention. "What are you talking about?"

"Remember at the beach ... we were kids, and this girl kept watching us? She looked so hauntingly familiar." I waited for an answer and didn't get one. "Then years later, I saw her at the stadium. Remember the big Lawrence vs. Lowell game?"

"Oh wait, I vaguely remember you asking me if I knew her ... or someone, but I only caught a quick glimpse before she was gone."

"Exactly!"

"Sis, don't make a big deal out of this. I'm sure she just wanted to pay her respects. Check the guest book, maybe you'll find her signature," he suggested.

"Hey, great idea, big brother! Where is it?"

"The undertaker gave me a box with sympathy cards and death certificates. Maybe it's in there," he said. "I'll get it for you."

Turning to my sister-in-law I said, "Ellie, thank you so much; your home is like an oasis for us today. I mean … your hospitality has certainly created an atmosphere for us to unwind rather than a restaurant or some cold community hall."

She drew me into a huge embrace and planted a big sloppy kiss on my cheek saying, "Mi casa es su casa. Sweet sister, it is truly my pleasure to make our home your home, if only for a day."

"Here ya go, have at it," Joey said, shoving the box into my hands. I settled down into Joey's comfortable recliner and began riffling through the sympathy cards. Nothing! The book was buried on the bottom of the box, and I soon started searching it line by line. I didn't find any woman's name that stuck out, but there was one strange entry on the last page: LIM.

So … this elusive person was one of the last to enter the funeral parlor. Hmm, but I never laid eyes on her in the funeral parlor. And why, for goodness sake, would anyone only sign their initials? Definitely not normal!

"Hey, Joe, come here," I yelled across the room. "Look here, look at this line. Why would anyone print their initials? Any idea who LIM might be?"

His face went ashen as he stuttered, "No … no clue. Never met an LIM person," he said and quickly walked away.

"You okay? You look … kind of pukey."

"Gee thanks. I'm fine."

"Hey Angie, can you think of any old friends of Mom or Dad with these initials?" I said pointing to the guest book.

"Hmm, nope, no one comes to mind. Why do you ask?"

"Just wondering. Kind of odd that someone would sign only initials, don't you think? I mean, the purpose of a guest book is to make the grieving family aware of exactly who came to pay their respects. It seems like only common sense, doesn't it?"

"Yeah sure, but, Trina, you would not believe some of my ditzy older students. They don't follow or even know what proper etiquette dictates, so printing initials would be no big deal and it does not surprise me in the slightest. Over my teaching years it seems to have deteriorated from a lack of manners to a lack of common sense. I see it every day."

"Hmm, that's sad. Okay then if you say so."

Ellie graciously served dessert while we tackled the mundane tasks at hand. We agreed to divide responsibilities equitably among the three of us. Notifying various entities of his recent death, paying personal and garage bills all seemed like daunting tasks. We were well aware that many other loose ends would materialize with the passing of time, but this was at least a start and would eventually require more intestinal fortitude than we collectively possessed at the moment.

"Joey, any thoughts on what we should do about the garage? What I mean is, should I call his scheduled appointments?" I asked.

"Nah, I'll just put a note on the door for now. Pops regular customers have likely read about his death already. As a matter of fact several of his vendors, not to mention quite a few of his older customers, were at the funeral. They've been with him for as many years as he's operated that garage. Can we look at this again next week?" he said. "I'm kind of mentally depleted here; I really don't want to think about any of that now."

"Sure, I hear ya!"

We stayed together for most of the afternoon and evening, reminiscing and offering each other comfort and support.

"I think we need to get some sleep, guys," Angie said. "At least I do. How about we give Joey and Ellie back their home?"

"Agreed! Come on, Trina, you look beat," Sal was already walking to the door. "Besides, Buddy needs the yard."

Hugs and kisses were exchanged with promises to meet again at the homestead. I for one dreaded the task that lay before us—not the work but discarding of memories.

Chapter 28

"I don't know about you Angie, but I am dreading this project," I confessed to my sister over French toast and coffee.

"Me too. Bad enough that it feels ... weird ... going into that empty house, but digging through their stuff ... I don't know. On some level, I feel as though ... we're violating them."

"My sentiments exactly, but is there any way around it? At least we have the advantage of the house being in Joe's name. It was a good move for them to do that so many years ago. What do you think Joey will do with it?"

"I'm not positive, but I do remember they had discussed it at great length quite a few years ago. Joey and Daddy both expressed the desire to maintain it, keep it in the family, in the event any one of us was in need. Or if unforeseen circumstances dictated, sell it and split the proceeds three ways. I hope he manages to keep it in the family, don't you?"

"Yeah, I hope so too, but we all have nice homes so it's unlikely any of us would want to move, but it would be too weird and unsettling to just turn it over to a perfect stranger. I mean, it's ... home. I get goose bumps just thinking about it. I don't want to go down that road."

"Well, Anthony, Sammy, and Kevin are all in their twenties, and it might not be long before we hear wedding bells. But for now, Sis, let's get cracking. I'd like to get a good start on this today."

When Angie turned the key and we slowly walked into that cold, lifeless house, everything in me suppressed a desire to collapse into a heap onto the floor and cry. But I was quick to remind myself that this house *was* full of life and *continues* to hold many, many years of wonderful memories. I bolstered myself with that reality. *That is the Agosti legacy!*

"My first order of business is to water the garden. Orders from my husband," I cheerfully said.

"I'll start with any food items needing to be pitched. Then, I guess I'll focus on the kitchen in general," Angie said more as a question.

"Sounds like a plan. I'll be right back; the garden is calling to me. Then I think I should tackle the office, just in case there are any pressing bills that should be paid."

"Good thinking."

Jumping into our self-assigned tasks, we found ourselves frequently sidetracked. Each and every piece of memorabilia captured our attention, eating up far too much time. The day flew by, and it was already after one thirty and both of our stomachs were growling in harmony.

"How about I run down to the corner for a couple of subs?" Angie suggested. "I'm about ready to devour some of that moldy cheese I just tossed out. Want anything else?"

"Nope, that will do it. I saw some soda in the pantry."

Attempting to match my sister's organizational skills, I dragged a bunch of cardboard boxes in from the mud room. I had a plan: I would fill one box with bills and items needing immediate attention and use the second box for items simply needing to be filed. My third box, labeled miscellaneous, would likely fill up first. I was proud of myself, accomplishing a great deal for the time spent.

Just as I was about to congratulate myself with a big egotistical pat on the back, I accidently knocked a huge stack of papers off Daddy's desk.

Great job, Trina, pride goes before a fall!

I assumed the prayer position, on my hands and knees, and began retrieving the scattered paperwork, but something shiny underneath the desk drawer caught my eye.

What the heck is this? Hmm... Looking closer, I discovered a key taped to the bottom of the drawer. *Why would my father tape a key here? He probably wanted to be sure he had a spare for the desk,* I silently reasoned. *Wait ... this drawer doesn't have a keyhole. Then ... what does this tiny key unlock? This seems like odd behavior, even for Daddy.*

I put the key in my pocket and wandered around his office searching for a keyhole meant to accommodate the key burning up my jeans. Nothing here seemed to fit the bill. I decided to expand my search. I scoured their bedroom, spare rooms, and the living room. Nothing! Now this was going to drive me nuts. Daddy was a practical man. If he had a key, it was definitely meant to open something.

"I'm back. Let's eat before I drop," Angie said laughing as she spread the food on the kitchen table.

"Okay, I'm ready, let's eat. Ange, while you were gone I found a key, but it doesn't fit anything. Any ideas what it's for?"

"Where did you find it? How big ..."

"This big," I said as I held the tiny key inches from her face."

"Hmm, looks like a jewelry box key or maybe it fits a small piece of luggage? Does it have any printing on it?"

"Nope! And it's pretty old, see the rust. I'll keep searching. Maybe he taped it there years ago and forgot all about it, long since trashing whatever it opened."

"True. Hold on to it Trina. If it fits anything in the house, we will eventually find it."

We sat silently, eating and looking around this old house as though seeing it for the first time. "We all grew up here, Ange, yet now it feels so cold and ... empty," I said in a hushed voice.

"Tell me about it. So many warm and comforting memories though: the Christmas dinners Mama made, the graduation parties, not to mention all the birthday and anniversary celebrations."

"They were great parents, weren't they, sacrificing everything for their children? Daddy was adamant about educating his children. I can hear him now 'education is the key to Agosti success.' I hope we made him proud, Angie."

"There is no doubt in my mind he was proud of his kids and grandkids. Let's get moving, Sis. Jake and I are visiting some friends tonight. I'm getting rank; they'll appreciate me more if I take time to shower."

"Okay, let's give it a couple more hours and then pack it in for today."

"Sal, I can't believe I was awake most of the night dwelling on that silly little key. It's probably nothing, but something in my gut tells me I have to find the missing keyhole. Do you mind if I put in a few hours at the homestead after church?"

"Sure, I need to trim the shrubs out back anyhow. Tell you what ... take as much time as you need and when you get back we'll just grab a pizza."

"Great idea! My brother was thinking about working there for a couple of hours as well. Okay with you if I invite Joey and Ellie to join us for pizza?"

"Fine with me, I miss double dating with them."

Walking into the house alone once again jolted me with that familiar empty feeling.

I've got about an hour before Joey arrives; I might as well get right at it. Hmm, think I'll tackle the attic.

No one in our family liked the attic. I can't even remember the last time Mama went up there. She always joked that it gave her the creeps, and she would promptly produce an exaggerated shiver following that statement. I'm guessing those creaky stairs haven't gotten any better over the years. *Sheesh, must be a spider convention going on up here. Eww, I hate those webby things in my hair.* This was not the most comfortable attic I've ever been in; I was hardly able to stand upright. *Good thing it's cool today, but still I'd better get these windows open … Ah, fresh air.*

Sorting through the attic promised to be relatively easy. No one ever wanted to trek up here with their stuff so there shouldn't be too much junk to plow through. *Okay, let's see what we have here: books in this box, old clothes in this box, oh, one of my prom dresses and … and … what have we here?*

I picked up a small intricately carved cedar box, possibly a jewelry box. *I never saw this jewelry box. It's too pretty to forget.* I carefully turned it over, inspected it. *Hmm, locked … where is that key?*

I ran downstairs, grabbed my purse off the kitchen table, and darted back up to the attic in record time. Impatiently, I fumbled with my purse trying to remember where I stashed it.

Ah, here we are.

I wished Angie was with me, this was like a treasure hunt, and I felt like a kid again. I smiled to myself recalling the excitement generated during treasure hunts that had been sponsored by area churches.

I sunk into a broken down old cane-seat chair and gingerly placed the box on my lap. Savoring the moment, I conjured up thoughts of a child's anticipation, claiming his long awaited treasure. I inserted the rusty old key and gently turned it. Click!

My smile changed to a questioning scowl. *What is all this stuff?*

I casually began thumbing through the box when a bolt of lightning hit my heart, and my eyes simultaneously fell on a picture of a young girl. She looked to be approximately three years old. I could not turn away, captured by her face for what seemed like an eternity. Returning to my search revealed another picture of that same girl, but older now ... high school graduation. Those eyes ... her emerald green eyes held me.

I know this face! The beach, the stadium! This is the girl. I could feel myself getting lightheaded, confusion was suffocating me. *Who is this girl?*

I hurriedly stuffed everything back in the box, grabbed my purse, and quickly ran down the stairs for a glass of cold water. Hyperventilating, I sat at the kitchen table vaguely aware that I was spinning out of control.

Somewhat calmed, I returned to the box like a moth to a flame. I slowly reopened the box and proceeded to methodically lay out every single item on the kitchen table. I could only stare in disbelief. I knew in my heart what it all meant, but refused to let my head accept the facts that were mocking me from the table.

As best as I could, I arranged every item in chronological order. Birthday cards to Daddy from Lily, grade school pictures of Lily, high school graduation pictures of Lily, even college pictures of Daddy and Lily together.

She was familiar to me even as a teenager because ... She has our ... her ... Daddy's emerald green eyes. *She alone has his eyes.*

Overcome by nausea, I ran into the bathroom and was sick! What do I do with this information? *He wasn't the man I thought he was ... we thought he was. How could I ever remember him in the same adoring way ... ever again? How did he manage to keep her a secret?*

I forced myself to return to the kitchen table and as I pulled out my chair, the kitchen door swung open. "Hey, Trina, I'm a little late, but I had ... what is all this stuff?" he said looking down at my discoveries.

Through great sobs I said, "Joey, yesterday I found a key taped under Daddy's desk. It didn't seem to fit anything. That is until ... I just started to clean the attic and found this box. Maybe I shouldn't have, but I opened it and ... and I'm so sorry to have to tell you about this, but I ..."

"Trina, stop right there," his eyes glued to the photographs, "I know about his other daughter," he said through gritted teeth.

"What!" I screamed as my hands flew to my mouth. "You knew? How did you know? When? My God, Joey!"

"Sit down. You might as well know everything now that they're both gone," he said with wide eyes.

"I'm listening," I replied, blowing my nose with shaky hands.

"Remember when Pops had that bad flu back when I worked at the garage? Well, it began that week. He began to stubbornly reject some of my ideas, claiming we weren't financially ready to expand. I vehemently disagreed. It was an ongoing battle between us. So, I decided to prove my point and take advantage of the situation. While both he and Mia were sick and I was alone in the garage, I went searching for paperwork, receipts, anything I could use to create a solidly projected budget, which I was confident would prove our solvency. He was a black and white kind of guy, so my assumption was he'd be forced to acknowledge our solid position if it was presented to him in black and white."

"Go on."

"Well, a big chunk of paperwork was missing, which I naturally assumed he'd misfiled somewhere. I found his key to the small office closet and began tearing into years of paperwork. What I found, Trina, was a lot more than office stuff. I discovered a personal checkbook, its register recorded cash deposits that were methodically made directly into this secret checking account from garage profits."

"By secret, I assume you mean that only his name was on it?"

"Yes! So, I scrutinized the entries and found a disturbing pattern. He was sending monthly checks to someone with the initials BI, who I later discovered was Lily's mother, Brenda Iveson. He continued this pattern, which of course meant that he was sup-porting Lily for eighteen years. The checks did continue after that, but it appeared to be only for special occasions like birthdays, graduations, and Christmas."

"My God, Joey, you're not describing the dad we all knew and admired. Is this the reason … I mean the source of …?"

"Yes! I sat on the information for quite a while before finding the courage to confront him, but things had already turned strained, at least on my part. To his credit, he readily confessed everything to me, swearing it only happened once and for what it's worth, I did believe him. But I lost it; I went ballistic. Trina, I actually physically attacked our father. I could have killed him."

"Joe, wait, wait …" I pleaded running again to the bathroom to be sick.

When I returned, I found my brother shuffling through the pictures and mementos on the table.

"Incredible! She is a dead ringer for Dad. He could never deny that she was his own, not with those eyes," he said as he pulled me into a comforting hug. "You okay?"

"I don't know. No … I'm not okay. My world has been seriously rocked. Our perfect family has been … I don't know … permanently tainted. At least my perception of our family has forever changed."

"I hear ya."

"Joey! Good Lord … she was at Dad's funeral. Remember, I mentioned that I'd seen that familiar woman again, but this time she was accompanied by a young girl. They purposely stood away from everyone at the cemetery."

"Yup and the guest book with the LIM entry … that must be her. She's probably married by now. I'm guessing you're right, Trina, she was probably there as a matter of fact, I'd bet on it."

"Please continue, Joe, I need to know everything."

"Well, as you well know, I couldn't bring myself to forgive him for all those years … three miserable long years. I felt such rage just looking at his face. I'm ashamed to admit that. Honestly, if we're being truthful here I didn't come close to forgiving him, that is, until I learned that our Mama knew all along and she, by God's grace, found the strength to forgive him."

"So, do you think Mama knew about Lily as well?"

"Think back, Trina. Remember the day we overhead him sobbing over her bed, pleading for forgiveness? She said she knew and had already forgiven him. I believe that she forgave him for his infidelity with Brenda, but I also feel deep inside me … that she somehow knew about Lily. We had an amazing mother."

"I remember his anguish that day; it was gut-wrenching. I also remember asking you what could possibly have been so awful to cause his desperate pleadings … pleadings for her forgiveness. You just looked at me and walked away, never uttering a word, never even hinting you knew."

"I'm sorry about that, but you have to understand that I promised I would not uncover his sin. With the exception of Ellie, I have honored that promise because I didn't want to hurt Mama. I had no clue at that time that she had long ago forgiven him, and apparently neither did he. I have wasted three years nursing this bitterness and rage inside of me."

"But still, I am so grateful that you made it right with Daddy before he left this planet. Mama would have been proud of you and thankful that you yielded to the Lord's prompting."

"The reality of her ability to forgive such a grievous wound and then hearing her words repeated through her pastor … well it all hit me like a ton of bricks."

"We have to tell Angie … right away. I don't know how she's going to handle all of this. Can you and Ellie come over tonight, that is if Angie and Jake are also free? We, just the adults have to weed through this mess."

"Sure. You're right. We'll get through this, Sis, we will."

"Sal was planning to pick up pizza anyhow, so come for dinner around six, and I'll call Angie."

Dropping this bomb on my husband left him emotionally devastated. As far back as our dating years, Sal placed Daddy on a pedestal. His own father was no prize and certainly was not the kind of man he chose to emulate. He found that wonderful role model in Daddy, but that persona was dashed in one painful moment. We feebly attempted to bolster one another, recognizing that an even more painful evening lay before us.

"So tell me, what's the big news flash?" Angie said as she and Jake shuffled through the door.

"Hi guys. It can wait until Joey and Ellie get here. They should be here any minute."

"Sure. No problem. So, did you get much accomplished today?"

"I wouldn't exactly say that, but … at least we got a bit of a start, and we don't have any deadlines looming over us."

"You're right. Hey, let me set the table. I hope the pizza is from Napoli's, yummy."

"Of course it is. Their dough is a very close second to Mama's recipe. I love making it, but I just didn't have enough time today."

"I hear ya! I'm making it less and less these days. I just can't seem to stay ahead of everything, and I'm not even back to school yet."

"Give me a break … you're the most organized person I know."

"Oh … let me grab the door for Sal. And look what the cat dragged in behind him. Hi guys," Angie laughed, planting a big kiss on Joey's cheek while holding the door open.

"Ellie, if I have lipstick on my cheek, it's from my crazy sister," Joey immediately averted his eyes at the realization of what he'd just said.

"Sit everyone, the pizza is hot and bubbly although not quite as good as Trina's pizza," Sal winked.

I poured iced tea then sidled up next to Angie while Sal slid slices of pizza onto each plate.

"Did you ever notice that we rarely get together without food being center stage?" Angie laughed.

"Are you complaining?" Sal joked.

"Uh uh, no way, I love that about us."

Shortly after devouring two large boxes of pizza, Joey and I instinctively made eye contact, which I took as the signal to begin our conversation.

"Don't bother with the dishes, Angie, I'll get them later. Let's go into the living room," I casually said while waiting for them to move in that direction.

Suddenly, it became noticeably quiet ... *The calm before the proverbial storm.* I didn't immediately bring out the box, but prior to their arrival had set it within easy reach.

"Where do we start, Joe?" I looked to him for moral support. This wasn't going to be easy. Angie, by far the most emotional sibling, idolized her daddy!

"Just spit it out, we're family here, remember," Angie said, looking between Joey and me with peaked curiosity.

With fear and trepidation, Joe stepped up to the plate and initiated the dialogue. Clearing his throat several times he began, systematically laying out the whole story as it had occurred in the garage. My eyes were fixed on my sister, waiting for her reaction. I myself was welling up even though hearing it for the second time, so I struggled to get a fix on how she was assimilating this awful news.

Without any warning she shot out of her chair and began screaming at him, "No, you're lying! I don't believe one word of what you're telling us. It's not true! No!" Jake immediately jumped up and held her in a tight embrace not unlike a straightjacket. "Honey, why would Joe and Trina lie? Calm down, let's hear him out," he said in a hushed tone, stroking her hair back.

We gave her several minutes to blow her nose and compose herself, but she was angry ... and hurt. *Please God, don't allow our family to sustain another fracture.*

"Angie, I had the same reaction this afternoon. But, but … I found this in the attic," I said, placing the box on the coffee table. "Remember the key that was taped to the bottom of the desk drawer? It fits this box," I softly said, desperately trying to diffuse this potentially volatile situation. "When you're ready, we'll open it."

She sat motionless, seeming to be mesmerized by the beautiful box placed before her. Quite abruptly she looked up and said, "I've seen this box before. I distinctly remember it … when I was … maybe thirteen." We sat stock still, giving her wide berth to describe her flashback.

"I remember running up to the attic carrying some old books Mama asked me to store there; she absolutely refused to go there herself. I didn't realize it but Daddy was there, and he was holding that box. It was so pretty. I asked him what it was and he brushed me off. I just turned away and ran downstairs again, never giving it a second thought. I hated going up there too," she quietly said. Then, quite coldly, she commanded, "Open it."

The six of us spent an hour or more going through the contents of the box, again setting every item in chronological order that seemed to make the most sense. Angie sobbed mournfully; she was now forced to acknowledge that Lily did in fact exist.

After sensing the weight of this ugly truth had settled a bit, I continued, telling them about Lily's appearance at the beach so very many years ago during our family vacation. I furthered explained that I'd also caught sight of her several years later during a high school football game. But the clincher was the revelation she had attended Daddy's funeral, which was unquestionably the biggest shock of all. I went on to explain that although I didn't know exactly who she was at that time, I tried to speak with her, but she vanished from my sight.

"Her eyes … her eyes were exactly like his, so now in retrospect, I understand why she looked so familiar," I said reflectively.

Angie was profoundly affected by the realization that Mama found the inner strength to forgive this man. We didn't doubt their love for one another, but some things test the limits, even of love.

We groped for answers to our innumerable questions. By the end of the night we were floundering, truly at a loss as to what to do next or how to proceed. The big question that continued to be raised was whether the grandchildren should be told? We were emotionally spent and bone weary by the day's end, so we concluded that wisdom dictated we say nothing, at least not yet. First, we ourselves sorely needed time to absorb the truth and any implications of this revelation, if that were even possible.

We agreed to meet together once again, but this time at the homestead following the reading of Daddy's will. None of us anticipated any surprises; Attorney Baylor indicated it was a necessary formality and our presence, while not required, would be greatly appreciated.

It was clear, at least to me, that my sister was going to need lots of love and support in the days and weeks to come. I couldn't help but wonder if her kids would sense something had radically affected their mom's normally sunny disposition. I promised myself to stay close to her, and to the rest of our wounded family.

We agreed to get together again right after our meeting with Daddy's lawyer. Hopefully, an additional week would allow us to begin the healing process, or at least get our raw emotions under control. Hopefully.

Chapter 29 ❧

I spoke with my siblings daily during the next week, hashing and rehashing the repercussions of our discovery; mostly we extended care and support, each locked in our own private pain. Apparently the kids, caught up in their own lives, never noticed any change in Angie's demeanor or never bothered to question it if they had become aware.

Attorney Baylor has been the family lawyer for years. Really, I can't remember any of us ever using anyone else. I've been guilty throughout our easy relationship of teasing him, labeling him the Agosti consigliere. He could accurately be described as a laid back kind of guy, never revealing his personal opinions; he simply responded to my jabs with his good natured smile. *He's aging well. I guess I would too if I spent a month in the tropics every winter.* I assumed we were fortunate to get an audience with him in August, since he also owns a palatial home on Martha's Vineyard and spends an inordinate amount of time there, basking in the sunshine. *Ah, the good life.*

My attention was pulled to the thick, well-worn file folder on his rich mahogany desk.

After politely waiting for us to be seated, he began, "First of all, let me again offer my condolences to each of you, his children, and to you his in-law children. He loved each of you and would frequently boast to me at how well you've turned out."

We all gave the appropriate nod of thanks in acknowledgment of his kind words.

"I'm sure you are aware that your mother had a living will drawn up; although she never felt the need for a last will and testament."

To which we again nodded in agreement.

"Would anyone like coffee or something cold before we begin?" he politely asked. We all declined.

"Several years ago your father conveyed to me that his children were in agreement with his decision to transfer the house to Joseph; I believe that was in 1990. I advised your parents to take that action in order to avoid losing the house in the event either needed placement in a long term care facility. He stated to me that he fully trusted Joseph to make appropriate decisions regarding either selling and dividing the proceeds or passing the home onto a family member. It is, however, Joseph's choice alone. Trina, Angie do you understand this statement?"

"Yes, we've talked about this as a family numerous times; we agreed with Daddy's decision then and we're still in agreement," I responded as Angie nodded.

"Wonderful. Now, regarding the contents of the home and their personal possessions, he simply asked that you work together amicably, dispersing items as you three deem appropriate. I understand that Joe has allowed you to begin this process and that is fine."

"We've only touched the surface," Angie said. "It's going to be a long process, but we'll do it … together," which prompted his smile of approval.

Looking down and without hesitation he continued, "The garage and all of the equipment comprised under the business name of Agosti & Son Garage, according to his express wishes, states it to be left to Joey and Anthony and shall continue operation under the name of Agosti & Son Garage. If for any reason this is not agreeable or acceptable to one or either of you Agosti boys, then it shall be sold and proceeds divided among all living grandchildren. If or when the business closes, the proceeds will be divided equally among all living grandchildren," he explained as he looked up with questioning eyes. "Trina and Sal, I understand that you do not have any children," he said looking for some reaction from one or both of us.

"No, no we don't, but I think that's terrific," I quickly said. "Sal, what are your thoughts?"

Sal took my hand and nodded, "Sure, I'm fine with Pop's desires as stated."

Turning to my sister I asked, "Angie, do you agree with that?"

"I do. I'm fine with that decision as well," she confirmed.

"Well, I'm happy that you kids concur with to your dad's wishes," he said with a warm smile. "Then again, it would not do much good to contest it. They are, after all, his wishes."

"So … if that's everything, then thank you, *consigliere*," I joked.

"You are all welcome, but hold on, we're not quite done. I have a rather delicate item I am obligated to disclose," he said in a hushed tone. "Several years ago your father informed me of a … a … relationship he had with a particular individual. That relationship, brief as it was, produced a baby girl," he said while intently studying each of our faces, no doubt waiting for an outburst. "I am obligated to locate and present that individual with an envelope left in my care. It is marked *confidential* and is only for that person."

We looked at one another, somewhat surprised, but not shocked. Our father believed in caring for his children; we were somehow cognizant he would not exclude her!

"Attorney Baylor, I have to inform you that after Daddy's funeral we found pictures and greeting cards, which he'd hidden from the family. It didn't take a rocket scientist to piece the puzzle together," I confessed.

"So you know he had a daughter from another woman?" he asked flatly.

"Yes, yes … we know *now* that he did. In all honesty, we are still reeling from that discovery, but I'm personally not surprised that he would want to leave her a note or feel obligated to bequeath her something."

"Well, he didn't have much, very little as a matter of fact. But he did, as a gesture, leave her a couple of small certificates of deposit … insignificant really," he informed us.

"I guess I'm not surprised either," Joey mumbled while running his hands through his thick hair.

"Thank you for everything," I said as Attorney Baylor stood signaling the finality of our meeting. We awkwardly conversed for a few minutes longer before actually leaving the office.

"I am sure this has been extremely painful for your family. You do indeed have my deepest sympathies," he said with a genuine smile. "Please don't hesitate to call me should you need anything, anything at all."

As previously decided, we drove from Attorney Baylor's office directly to the homestead. "Let's sit in the living room. We need a plan—some kind of agreed upon strategy," Angie said. "Joey, do you think we should tell the kids that somewhere out there," she said waving her hand in a broad sweeping motion, "they have another aunt and we have a sister?"

"Half-sister," Joey sharply retorted. "What do you think he wrote in that letter?"

"I haven't the foggiest, but I for one, would like to meet her," I said.

"What? You have to be kidding?" Joey quickly shot back.

"I'm dead serious. Aren't you the least bit curious about her? What kind of relationship they had? Where she lives? What she thinks of our family?" I went on and on.

"Not really," he firmly said.

Jake jumped in thoughtfully, "This is what I think … No! … This is what I know: Secrets eventually unravel. I've been wrestling with this all week, night and day, and I believe we need to break it to the kids … but very, very gently."

"I'm with Jake on this one," Sal chimed in. "Those kids of yours aren't stupid. They will, at some point, pick up on the slightest hint of secrecy, and what if one day she decides to knock on the door. What then?"

"Well, let me just say as the remaining *in-law* of this group, I agree," Ellie added. "Somehow, somewhere it will come out. I don't want the kids resenting or losing trust in us because we made a conscious decision to bury something this big from them. With that said, I full well realize it will not be easy and we should be prepared for some fallout."

"Joey, Angie what are you both thinking?" I asked.

"Guys, I'm really torn on this. Our kids had Daddy on a pedestal. This will devastate them," Angie said thoughtfully. "I just know it."

"Tell me about it, I practiced 'idol worship' for a whole lot longer than any of them," Joey said almost in a whisper.

I stood quietly at the window admiring Mama's beautiful garden, waiting for Joey and Angie to talk this through to resolution. Once again, the very essence of Mama's heart gripped me. "Hey guys, as I stand here taking in the beauty of her precious garden, I'm reminded of the fact that she found the strength and the grace to forgive him. After all, *she* was the offended party in all of this. There is no doubt, his image has been forever tarnished in our eyes, but who of us sitting in this room is perfect. After all, there is only *One* who is perfect. I can't help but wonder if we failed him. What I mean is … were we guilty of elevating our earthly father to that same place reserved only for our heavenly Father? I hope not. Sure, your kids loved and respected their grandpa, but I don't think this will cripple or permanently damage them. I truly believe they will be more accepting than you think."

Angie and Joey looked at each other and then to their spouses. They both nodded in agreement. "You're right," they said almost in unison.

Later, we ate together in the same old relaxed atmosphere that I so loved. But the forbidden topic burned within me and having the nature of a pit bull I could not let it go. I would not let it go.

"Anyone for dessert?" I called out. Not one declined, which was good. It's much easier to persuade this crew when they are sugared up. "Hey guys, I want to back up a bit," I sheepishly ventured as I slowly pushed my lemon tart around my plate.

"Here it comes," Joey blurted sarcastically. "I knew you wouldn't give up on this. Trina, how can you even think about meeting this girl … woman?"

"And why not," I shouted. "She has our father's blood. Her mother is dead; she's out of the picture. *His* daughter has done nothing wrong, except to be born. And … and she's part of this family, whether you want to acknowledge her or not," my voice escalated and Sal reached for my hand, attempting to stifle the Mt. Vesuvius eruption that was threatening to blow.

My little outburst brought the room to complete silence; it seems I alone possess a rare talent for changing the atmosphere from congenial to disagreeable. But, I foolishly persisted to make my case when my brother rudely cut me off.

"You know what Trina? I don't *want* to acknowledge her as part of this family. I just don't! In my head I can rationalize that she has a connection, and she bears no guilt in this, but I can't get my heart to embrace her as an Agosti."

My frustration with my brother became so exacerbated, I felt compelled to escape to the peace and tranquility of the garden. I would not sneak around behind his back in order to reach out to Lily, but I couldn't shake the feeling our mama would have encouraged us to embrace her. I sat on the garden bench for a very long time, relishing the beauty of the place while reflecting on so many conversations with my mama.

That's it! Without warning something akin to an electric shock surged through me, Mama's words echoing in my brain. *Trina, my prayer is that you, your brother and sister will come to learn the very same lesson I have learned from this beautiful process of grafting in; and from that lesson, you will reap its resulting joys and benefits. Was this what she was trying to tell me? She knew about Lily and desired that she be joined to this family … so that we would become one more beautiful, stronger family.*

For years Mama lived with the man she loved, knowing he had a relationship that resulted in a child.

How did she find out?

Maybe, just maybe, she also found the key that unlocked Daddy's secret. But she kept it to herself … and she eventually forgave him.

I quietly returned to my siblings, who were discussing the future of this house.

"Trina, Joey has decided to keep the house indefinitely until it's needed by one of the grandkids. Isn't that wonderful? It doesn't matter which one, I'm just happy it will stay in the Agosti family," Angie said with a broad grin.

"That is good news. And I will be happy to pitch in and help with the garden upkeep," I said. "Speaking of the garden, would you all please join me for a minute? I'd like to share something I just discovered … out there in her garden."

"I can understand why Mama loved this garden," Angie said wistfully as we made our way out back. "It's a beautiful and serene setting."

"Yes, yes it is, and I'll tell you why it is. Angie, remember I told you Mama was trying to convey something to me about the lesson she learned from the process called grafting in?"

"Sure I do. Her pastor even referenced it during her memorial service. Remember, she had plans to teach about grafting to her ladies' Bible study and exactly what she had learned right here in her garden."

"I have no clue what that means," Joey said.

Jake and Sal looked at each other then shrugged in agreement with my brother.

"I really don't know much about gardening, but doesn't it mean that two separate but similar plants are somehow joined together?" Ellie added.

"Exactly! Before Mama became so weak, she spent countless hours out here. She especially loved her roses. What do you see when you look at these fully bloomed roses?"

"They are strong and healthy looking. The colors are vibrant," Sal commented.

"These look to be a different type from those over there. As a matter of fact, these look way healthier ... more robust than those by the fence," Joey said as he carefully studied them.

"Bingo! Mama was trying to teach us the same lesson she had learned when two become one. She was hinting at the many resulting joys and benefits we would enjoy by taking Lily into our family," I paused waiting for the obvious objection. When none came, I proceeded, "We will all be stronger, healthier and more ... well ... beautiful for allowing her to be grafted into our family. I have no doubt that Mama had a strong desire to see that happen. She forgave Daddy, but for whatever reason, chose not to uncover his sin."

The garden, now silent except for the sound of birds flitting from birdhouse to birdbath, seemed to take on a glow. My eyes fell on the Garden of Hope stepping stone, which also appeared to be bathed in light.

After what seemed like an eternity of silence during which time I could only assume that my brother was going through all kinds of mental gymnastics, wrestling with his emotions, he finally looked up and firmly stated, "Okay, for crying out loud, you win!"

"You're the best brother I have," I said, giving him a giant bear hug. "I'm not sure I'll even be able to find her on my own. I may have to wait until our consigliere tracks her down."

"I have her telephone number," Joey whispered.

"You what? Why didn't you tell us? Never mind! How did you get her number? Never mind!" I said again, mockingly waving him away. "You're just full of surprises aren't you, big brother?"

"Yeah, guess I should have given it to Attorney Baylor, huh."

"Joe, does this mean you have spoken to her?" Ellie asked.

"No, I haven't. I called the number several times … I froze when I heard her voice, and … hung up the phone. It was right after I discovered … her. She may have moved by now, different phone number, who knows."

"Well guys, after you tell the kids and the dust settles, however long that takes, then I will give her a call. Everyone agreed?"

It seemed only fitting that I cut some of these beautiful roses, sending each of us home with a gorgeous bouquet of Mama's flowers, including her prized roses.

What a poignant reminder!

Chapter 30

"Good morning, Trina," Attorney Baylor's voice boomed too early in the day.

"Oh hello, how are you today?" I sleepily responded.

"I just called to let you know that supplying me with that number certainly made my job quite easy. I don't know where you obtained it, but thank you for Lily's telephone number."

"Actually, Joey found it at Daddy's garage, but he had no way of knowing whether or not it was her current number."

"Well, fortunately for me, it was indeed her current number. She informed me that your dad called and regularly visited. Does that surprise you?"

"No, it actually does not. He was faithfully involved in the lives of his children. He had a strong sense of obligation, so … no, it doesn't surprise me in the least."

"You may be interested to know that she seems like a lovely person and has eagerly agreed to meet with you, Trina. Actually, she seemed to be extremely anxious to get together. Shall I arrange it?"

"No, that's quite all right. You've already gone above and beyond for our family, and I'm confident I speak on behalf of my siblings when I say thank you for your kindness. I'll call her when we are ready. Oh, one more thing before I let you go … the envelope Daddy directed you to deliver … are you able to now tell us …"

"I'm really not at liberty to divulge that information. It is, after all, her decision whether or not to share its contents," he replied in his best lawyer voice. "And Trina, you and your siblings are indeed welcome; I have always held your father in the highest esteem. He was a good man, regardless of … Again, don't hesitate to contact me with any further questions."

Humph, thanks for nothing.

I find it interesting that his admiration for Daddy hadn't been altered by his … indiscretion.

I have no doubt that he wanted me to understand this and communicate it to my siblings.

"Please, Angie, I want you by my side, at least for the first meeting," I pleaded into the phone. "I can't do this alone."

"Okay, but let's do it before the end of the month. Teachers' in-service days are coming up quickly; you know how my life spins out of control from that point."

"I know, I know. Sal and I are on vacation next week. I'm sure he'd be fine with me taking off for a few hours. I'll call her and get right back to you after I've confirmed a time and date. By the way, Joey refuses to come."

"Wow, news flash," she laughed back to me. "I'm shocked beyond belief."

"Hello?"

"Hello, is this Lily Iveson?"

"This is Lily, but it's Mazzona now. Is this … Trina?"

"Yes, it is. I figured you would be expecting my call."

"I was hoping and praying you would call. I'm very happy to hear from you. I can only imagine how difficult this is for you …

and your family. I'm so sorry about your dad … our dad, and of course your mom."

"Thank you, Lily, I appreciate that. I understand Attorney Baylor already told you we would like to set up a meeting … somewhere? Actually, meeting sounds too stiff, too formal; we'd just like … for us to get better acquainted."

"Sure, I'd love that too. You're welcome to come to my home. I live in Lowell—have all my life. It's quiet and we would definitely have some privacy."

"That sounds terrific. My sister Angie is planning to be with me if that's okay with you."

"It certainly is. Is Monday at noon good for you? Lunch?"

"That is so kind of you. Yes that sounds wonderful. Can I bring anything … dessert?"

"I should decline, but I do love Tripoli's bakery … anything from there is delicious and would be appreciated."

After a few lingering moments of pleasantries, I scribbled down her address, directions, and cheerfully ended our dialogue.

Hmm, loves Tripoli's. Must be in the genes.

Within seconds of that conversation, I was jabbering with my sister. I retold the gist of our conversation, attempting to convey the warmth emanating from Lily's voice. Admittedly, we were nervous, excited, and wary all at the same time; the prospect of meeting our *sister* would soon become a reality. In my heart, I just knew Mama would have been pleased and proud of us for reaching out to Lily. Now more than ever I was convinced we were doing exactly the right thing.

I confessed to Angie the following Monday as we drove to Lowell, "I'm a wreck! This feels like a dream … you know what I mean … not real."

"Oh it's real!" Angie chortled. "I only wish Joey were with us."

"Me too! Maybe he'll change his mind. He's so bullheaded."

We found her home as easily as if we'd been visiting for years. It was a modest ranch home on a small, well groomed lot, surrounded by swaying white pines. The neighborhood around her development was familiar to me since I had conducted so many home visits on my job over the years.

I immediately smiled at the window boxes overflowing with vibrant colored petunias. The front door was painted a welcoming dark red with a lovely floral wreath hanging over the brass knocker. Before we got out of the car, we grabbed hands and uttered a quick but settling prayer, petitioning the Lord for a visit that would bear fruit—good and healthy fruit.

"This is so pretty, isn't it?" I whispered to Angie as I raised my hand to begin knocking. Before my knuckles made contact, the door swung open wide. There stood our beautiful, and I mean beautiful, sister. She nervously smiled, glancing between Ange and me.

"Come in, please come in," she said softly. "I have been so anxious for your arrival and ... a bit nervous."

"Well that makes three of us, Lily. Honestly, we have been a bit antsy too," I said as I awkwardly stepped closer attempting to draw her into a hug. Tears were trickling down her perfect olive complexion; she seemed to melt into my embrace.

"Please forgive my tears; I'm just so ecstatic to meet you ... to be with you," she confessed.

Angie and I smiled at each other, needing no further confirmation that this visit was indeed the right decision.

Handing Lily the familiar Tripoli Bakery box, I whispered, "Hope you like their cheese cannolis?"

"Are you kidding? Who doesn't love their cannolis? My husband and I make frequent Sunday morning bakery runs ... just for these gems," she said holding up the box.

"Wow, that's amazing, I'm surprised we never bumped into each other."

Lily directed us into the living room, which was simply and tastefully decorated. For a few awkward moments we sat without speaking. My eyes were immediately drawn to a photo on the mantle—Lily and Daddy on her graduation day. She followed my eyes, saying, "I hope that is not offensive to either of you."

"No Lily, not in the least. We were still reeling from Mama's death and then Daddy ... please try to understand, learning about you came as a big ... very big shock, to say the least. That is a beautiful picture, and you are his mirror image."

"I know. I have my daddy's eyes!"

"Indeed you do."

"Your home is lovely," Angie said, casually looking around. "How long have you lived here?"

Delaying her answer she responded, "Why don't we talk in the dining room over lunch, everything is ready?" already moving toward the dining room.

Taking a few minutes to pour ice water and settle down she began, "Well, to answer your question, Angie, I was raised in a two bedroom apartment ... just Mom and me for years. I was twenty when she died. Like your mom, she also had breast cancer."

"I'm so sorry, Lily," Angie said.

"Thank you. It was a huge blow, losing my best friend. Anyhow, I continued living in that apartment alone until I finished college. I attended Lowell State Teachers College, which is where I met my husband, Gino. We eloped right after graduation; no big wedding ceremony, no reception—just the two of us.

"We were financially strapped, but my husband is a whiz with money. I still don't know how we pulled it off, but we bought this place and had our daughter a couple of years later. I got ovarian cancer, which meant a hysterectomy, which also meant no more children. But she's nineteen and is the joy of our lives."

"Wow, we didn't know you had a daughter," I said glancing at Angie for her reaction to this news flash. She lowered her head and I couldn't quite read what she might be feeling. "I'm assuming Daddy was ... thrilled ... that you had a daughter?"

"Oh yes, and he surely loved her. It wasn't easy for Daddy ... our dad. As I got older I became more aware just how conflicted he felt, having his primary family and then *us*. He carried heavy guilt and more than his share of stress."

"I'm sure of that."

"Yet, he managed to visit with us whenever he could. I always knew; however, that you all were his first priority. I'm not suggesting I didn't feel loved because he certainly expressed his love for me and my daughter in hundreds of ways."

"That sounds like our daddy. He was a demonstrative guy, always hugging and kissing."

"Growing up, my mother made it very clear to me; he was a good man who made one big mistake and we in no way should interfere or purposely hurt the unity of his family."

"She sounds like an amazing woman, your mom," Angie said wistfully. "I don't know if I would have been as charitable … given the same situation."

"She sure was. She never married and never maintained romantic relationships with anyone, including with Daddy … none whatsoever. She was a good mom and couldn't possibly have been more involved in my life. And, for what it's worth to you both, she also was truly repentant for what they had done, but she repeatedly affirmed me, saying she wasn't sorry that I was born."

"Lily, I'm sure I remember seeing you on a few different occasions. You've haunted me for many years; it was because of your eyes … you just looked so hauntingly familiar. But I had no idea you were my … sister."

"Sister! What a beautiful word!" she said thoughtfully. "It was pure irony that I happened to be at the beach when your car, which I immediately recognized, pulled into the Polly's Villa driveway. I was staying with a friend in the cottage behind you. Curiosity got the best of me and I started sneaking around trying to get glimpses of his family. He hadn't mentioned and I had no clue you were together on a family vacation. We were at the same place, at the same time, purely by happenstance."

"Isn't that the strangest coincidence?" Angie said.

"I'm really ashamed to admit this, but I came very close to stalking your family that week. I hungered to be part of his life and his happy family; I was pitiful. I don't know with any certainty if Daddy saw me that week, but somehow my mom found out and pleaded with me to stay away. 'Please sweetheart, don't destroy his family' she would say. And so, for many years I made no attempt whatsoever to intrude, but I never stopped craving the closeness your family seemed to enjoy. Truthfully, I felt cheated."

"I admire your self-control; I don't think I could have stayed away. Your love for our father and his family is as natural as breathing," I said. "Don't be ashamed of that."

"That's very understanding and … kind of you to say that, but believe me I came dangerously close to marching right up to your front door more times than I'm able to count."

"But you never did. That took a lot of discipline … and respect!"

"Lily, tell me about the next time … at the football game."

"Well, many years later I was at the Lowell vs. Lawrence football game, again quite by accident, when we locked eyes. Our daughter had been begging Gino and me to drive her, along with a bunch of her friends, to the big game. She and her friends attended Lowell High and were psyched about this much touted rivalry game. When I spotted you, I knew immediately who you all were. I had to get away. The desire to be part of your family came back with a vengeance. I was ashamed of myself, after all I was a happily married woman with a beautiful child, and I was pining away with a blinding desire for something out of my grasp. It made no sense."

"It makes perfect sense to me," I said as we continued our easy exchange.

"May I ask, what about your brother? How does Joey feel about a new sister? I'm aware that he and Dad had a heavy-duty falling out. I never knew what they argued about; he didn't talk much about Joey these past few years. But I knew … in my gut that it was about my mom or me … I just knew it."

"I won't lie to you, Lily; this whole thing has overwhelmed him. He's the one who uncovered the secret, and it ate him up until he finally confronted Daddy. They had a terrible fight … Bottom line … they didn't speak for three years. Three long years!"

"That's awful. I'm so sorry."

"Thank God they reconciled just before Daddy's heart attack. I doubt Joey could have lived with himself, guilt ridden for the rest of his life. I'm not saying things were hunky dory between them, but they were civil to one another. But make no mistake, Joey loved Daddy; they had an enviable father-son relationship up until that day. Actually, I was hoping he'd come with us today. I believe he just needs time to absorb all of this."

"I understand," she softly replied. "Angie, Trina, please tell me about your mother. She has intrigued me for so many years; she is the most significant piece of this whole puzzle. I should … I don't know … resent her, since she possessed what I coveted all of my life. But, I actually had great respect and affection for her, although we'd never met. Dad spoke of her in such glowing terms. It was always my sweetheart, my darling, the love of my life, my precious Valentine; I desperately wanted to meet this captivating woman."

"Well, after all their years together, they were still deeply in love, so I'm not the least bit surprised he would refer to her in that way … glowing terms, that is," Angie quietly explained.

Lily took this in, revealing very little change in her facial expression. The single tear that slipped from her eye was not lost on my sister or me.

Attempting to paint a clearer picture of our mom, I continued, "She was a wonderful, unselfish and loving woman. I think it's safe to say she will forever be missed by our family. She could succinctly yet accurately be described as the heart of the Agosti family, and I for one am so grateful for her example of a godly woman. I can only attempt to emulate Mama. Lily, were you aware that she knew about you?"

With that, Lily's head snapped up. "No, I did not know that. Wait … but Daddy never let on that she … knew?"

"It's complicated," I said. "Apparently, she'd known about him and your mom for a very long time but kept it to herself. We can only assume she went through a long painful struggle, trying to find the inner strength to forgive this man who had … broken their vows."

"I can well imagine."

"If she hadn't eventually come to that place of forgiveness and reconciliation, there is no possible way she could have continued on living such a wonderful, peace filled life," I continued. "We don't have written proof that she knew you existed, but during the months prior to her death she attempted, in her own way, to hint at your existence. I'm guessing that her biggest fear was that the truth of your existence would destroy our family."

"I'm speechless," Lily said. "She must have agonized over me, yet she ... forgave him. Amazing!"

"If you knew Mama, you'd understand that she didn't hold onto hurts or wounds. She was a forgiving woman, and after all, *you* were innocent in all of this," I reasoned.

"Lily ... do you think, in light of the past, that it's possible for us to build a relationship?" Angie asked with a confident smile.

"You have no idea what those words mean to me; it's like my elusive dream has finally come true. When I think back over those years of my youth, I silently agonized in my loneliness, feeling so hollow and incomplete. I almost lost hope that I'd ever be accepted by his ... your family."

I could not take my eyes off this beautiful woman before me, trying hard to imagine ... to empathize with her that as a child, as a teenager, and now as a woman and mother, she never quite felt complete. I felt incredibly sad for the reality of her past life. *Oh Lord, how it must grieve you to watch the devastation caused by one ugly and selfish sin, its black tentacles reaching out to destroy its victims.*

"But, what about your own relationships ... I mean, with your brother? I don't want to come between you three."

"He'll come around, Lily, I'm sure of it. Let me just tell you, he is a great guy and more like a big teddy bear than this fake portrayal of a tough guy."

"That's right. My children idolize ... no ... not idolize him, but respect him. In the past ... before all of the histrionics, he was the natural leader of our family—smart, loving, and compassionate. He would do anything—anything at all—for his family."

"I have a great idea. Why don't you come to the homestead for lunch next week? We'll muster the rest of the troops; I'm sure they'd love to meet you. I'll prepare them," I said with a confident smile.

"I'd ... I'd love it," she said staring at me with those amazing green eyes ... Daddy's eyes. "But do you think it's too soon? What I mean is ... do you think your family is ready for this next step?"

"The sooner the better, I always say," Angie grinned.

"Umm, this is scary. I'm a bit nervous ... I'm going to need some moral support. Is it okay if my hubby and daughter come along?"

"Sure, let's make it a cookout for next Saturday. Will that work for you?"

"Yes, yes it will. Oh, Hope is going to love meeting everyone."

"What did you say? Your daughter's name is ... Hope?"

"Uh-huh, sure is!"

Chapter 31

Angie and I drove home in a complete stupor. We were in utter disbelief, repeating over and over ... "Her name is Hope! What are the chances of that?"

"I'm without words ... dumbfounded, Ange. How do you think this whole thing fits together? I mean Mama's Garden of Hope and Daddy's granddaughter Hope?"

"I'm thinking that God put this whole thing together a long time ago. Hope is nineteen years old. Mama probably didn't know that Lily had a daughter ... or did she?" Angie said.

"My brain hurts! We need to grasp what God is revealing to us, if anything. Here's what we do know: over forty years ago Daddy had a daughter with another woman, and as far as we know he kept that secret all these years."

"Check!"

"However, Mama somehow found out about the whole mess, probably from the monthly outgoing checks. Remember, she helped out in the garage for a couple of years. Maybe ... just maybe, when Daddy was out of the shop, she stumbled onto his personal check-book, just like Joey did. She was no dummy; she could have easily pieced together the whole scenario."

"That is a very good assumption, Trina. I had forgotten about those years she worked with Daddy. It was so long ago."

"So, she uncovered Lily's existence and over time, after much prayer, she privately forgave his sinful betrayal, which included the child resulting from that betrayal."

"Check!"

"But she didn't know … couldn't have known about Hope. There were no references of her in the checkbook or in the jewelry box, none whatsoever."

"Right, right," Angie said impatiently. "What are you getting at?"

"Well, the life lesson Mama learned was clearly… forgiveness. Because she forgave, she was able to accept Lily. Eventually, she began to fervently pray that she would be grafted into our family. Angie, how could that acceptance not include Daddy's granddaughter? The two separate plants, or families, are beautiful in their own way, but blending creates *one* stronger, healthier plant, or in this case … family. What do you think?" I asked.

"Bingo! I think that is exactly what she intended. Now, will Joey accept this lesson of grafting in, which includes another granddaughter named Hope? Let's head over there right now and lay this out for him and Ellie. If he doesn't agree, he can stay home on Saturday. What more can we say to him?" Angie declared.

"Hi Ellie, hope you don't mind us dropping by unannounced," I said as she opened the door wide to us.

"Oh come on, you guys are welcome anytime. You don't need an engraved invitation. Hold on a second, I'll yell for your brother," she said heading for the back yard.

Minutes later, Joey and the boys trundled in with welcoming smiles. "Hey girls, glad you stopped by … really. I was going to call you later to find out about your visit. I almost came, but chickened out at the last moment."

Ange and I looked at one another, truly shocked by his accepting response. "Really?" I said through a questioning smile.

"*No*, not really!" he snorted. "I'm just messing with you. What's up?"

"You're a stinker," I retorted with a shove. "For your information *King Joseph*, we had a nice visit and she is truly a lovely person. Can we take a few minutes to share our conversation?" I respectfully asked.

"Why do I have the feeling you'll share whether or not I agree?" Joey snickered.

"You got that right," Angie laughed.

"Hold on, hold on! I don't want to miss one word," Ellie shouted as she busied herself pouring iced tea for everyone. The boys quietly stood in the background, also waiting patiently to hear the details of our visit with their newly found aunt.

Ellie took a seat next to her husband, and I cautiously began. After sharing the meat of our conversation, I paused, studying his face for some kind of reaction. To my surprise, he seemed genuinely interested and engaged. Feeling safe to proceed, I attempted to convey the depth of Lily's heartfelt desire to be part of our family, which caused him to shift in his seat.

"Joey, please keep this foremost in your thinking ... she did nothing wrong. She couldn't control the circumstances of her conception or birth into this world."

"Yeah, I know that. I'm trying, I'm honestly trying," he said.

"Well, if you're sincerely trying, then I must tell you that you're in luck. What I mean to say is that you have another opportunity to meet her. We've invited her to the homestead for a cookout next Saturday."

"You what? You are kidding me, right?"

"No you knucklehead, I am not kidding. Joe, listen to me, she is happily married and has a daughter. We invited them to come along to meet the family."

After endless silence, even from the boys, I decided to forge ahead. What could I lose? "Joey, her daughter ... Pop's granddaughter ... her name is Hope!"

Joey fixed his gaze on me and in that instant, I knew *he got it.* With his head slumped forward I heard him mumble, "Garden of Hope."

"Whoa, we have another cousin?" Sammy excitedly asked.

I smiled at those two young men and smiled, "Yes, yes you do."

"Joey, can't you see that Mama was subtly hinting, and sometimes not so subtly, that we accept Lily, and how could we not accept her daughter … you know the grafting thing!" I pressed.

"So, that said, will you all come to the cookout?" Angie sweetly asked.

"Yes, we'll be there," Ellie excitedly jumped in answering for her husband. "Right, Joe?"

"All right, all right, talk about being ganged up on! We'll be there," he gave in flashing that smile I so dearly loved.

He didn't like it one bit, but we three girls were on him in an instant, smothering him with kisses and hugs, and it felt good.

Chapter 32

Saturday was one of the most beautiful days of the summer. There wasn't a cloud in the sky; the temperature and humidity were comfortable. And I was behaving like a child waiting for the carnival to come to town, and Sal couldn't resist teasing me.

I had the highest of hopes for this day, for this family. My loving husband made every attempt imaginable to emotionally prepare me in the event that all might not go as well as I was anticipating.

"You must force yourself to consider ... the Joey factor," he warned, trying to keep my feet firmly planted on the ground. He was deathly afraid my bubble would burst, raining disappointment and frustration down on my carefully planned parade.

Angie, Ellie, and I, without complaint, prepared food enough for a small army. This was going to be fun, I was sure of it—I think.

We had systematically been working on the old homestead, so fortunately didn't need to expend much time cleaning in preparation for our cookout. Sal and Jake, bless their souls, worked at weeding the garden, showcasing it exactly as Mama had always done.

I had communicated with Lily a few of times throughout the week and was keenly aware she had mixed feelings: both joy and trepidation. Trying to assure her those feelings were perfectly normal and everything would be fine, I found that I was bolstering myself as much as my newly found sister.

Angie gave one final pep talk to the kids, reminding them that Lily had done nothing but be born. "So guys, we need to accept her without reservation," she exhorted her brood. They all nodded like robots, which left me wondering if a time bomb was about to detonate.

Leah voluntarily cut and arranged armfuls of yellow daisies for the outdoor tables. God bless that kid! I have never known another thirteen-year-old to be more thoughtful.

"So how old is Grandpa's *other* granddaughter?" Mia asked rather acerbically.

"She's nineteen. Just about a year older than you, honey," I cheerfully answered trying to convey an upbeat tempo.

Joey's family hadn't arrived yet, which was my cue to start worrying. "They said they'd be here to help out by noon," I whined to Sal. The words were no sooner out of my mouth when I heard their car pulling into the driveway. Sal gave me that cocky, I told you so grin, which never failed to irritate me.

My brother's family sauntered into the house then marched directly into the back yard. They appeared rather sullen by first impressions, but not necessarily glum. I felt like the village idiot floating around attempting to make everyone happy. *Trina, this is either going to work or explode, and you can't do one thing about it. Relax!*

And so, miraculously, I did—sort of.

The clock held my attention as I absentmindedly fussed with food; I found myself willing the hands to strike one o'clock. My families' voices were muted, indistinguishable to me as I allowed my imagination to run wild.

Abruptly, I was yanked back to planet earth by the loudest doorbell chime I'd ever heard emanating from Mama's front door, or so it seemed. Sal yelled, "I'll get it," but at the speed of light, I was right by his side, not wanting to miss one precious second of this initial greeting.

"Welcome, Lily. Please come in," I said, sounding to myself like the proverbial spider to the fly. "Everyone is out back, but please come in, come in."

Oh there I go again. Relax!

"I'm Sal, Trina's other half," he said warmly extending his hand.

"Nice to meet you, Sal, and this is my husband Gino Mazzona and our daughter Hope," she said with enviable composure.

I watched the exchange of greetings and hand shaking that followed with interest, completely astonished at their perfect aplomb.

For goodness sake, girl, get a grip on yourself. You're the only one here breaking into a cold sweat.

"Wow," Sal loudly proclaimed, "you both have Vincent's eyes ... beautiful emerald green eyes ... Unbelievable."

"Are you ready to meet the rest of the mob? No, not mob ... the clan ... I mean the family," I sputtered nervously, feebly attempting lightheartedness. "In all fairness, you are hereby warned that we're a rather wacky group," I laughed.

"Trina, I have been ready for years. I just hope I don't disappoint you all."

"Don't be silly. You couldn't. Come on," I said, sounding more like myself.

"Hey everyone," I announced as we entered the garden from the kitchen door. "Let me introduce Lily, Gino, and Hope. "I'm not going to say everyone's name ... they will never remember, so please introduce yourselves at your leisure."

"At your leisure ...aren't we getting formal," Kevin mocked me with a big grin and a shoulder shove. He was first to stand front and center before our new kin. "I'm Kevin, and I might add, the most important person you will meet today. Come on, Hope, I'll connect you with the cousins."

"Cool," Hope said with a broad smile and great relief as she followed my nephew to the awaiting group of cousins.

Leave it to Kevin to break the ice and get the party rolling.

Still, Lily seemed a bit reticent to blindly jump into this group. I had an inkling that Joey was the big hurdle she wanted to overcome today.

Egad, now this is something that has never happened, ever. The whole family is tongue tied and gawking at our guests like they were Martians. This is going well.

Finally, Angie lunged forward pulling Lily into a warm embrace. "I … we want you to feel welcome. Please, come and sit with me. I'd like to introduce you to my family."

Good start! Come on, Joey, just acknowledge her, will you? I don't expect you to become best buds, just acknowledge her.

"You already met Kevin, he's twenty years old," Ange began her spiel. "Mia, the one in the red T-shirt, is eighteen, and here we have Leah. She's my baby, right, honey?"

"I'm thirteen, and I'm not a baby," Leah said sidling up to Angie.

Angie planted a sloppy, wet kiss on her cheek, which Leah promptly wiped off with the back of her hand. "Mommm, yuck!"

"And here we have my husband Jake … Jake Trayer. He teaches at Lawrence High and is *theee* best hubby in the world," Angie snickered. "Honestly, if any of my teachers looked like him when I went there, I would have stayed in high school as long as possible," she teased.

Jake rolled his eyes at Angie's comments, but promptly extended his hand in a welcoming handshake.

I could see Lily's shoulders visibly relax in response to Angie and her family's affable manner.

I stiffened slightly when I heard Lily say, "Well, Angie, I have to respectfully disagree with you. My husband is *theee* best hubby in the world!" Hearing a gentle ripple of laughter at the picnic table prompted me to relax and join in the laughter.

"As long as we gals are boasting on husbands, I have to cast my vote for this guy right here," I said, winking at Sal. "He patiently puts up with an awful lot from me."

"Amen to that!" he said.

"Hey, I'll negate that vote if you're not careful," I tittered.

When those introductions concluded, that familiar awkward silence began to creep in once again. But this time it was broken by Ellie's cheerful voice. "Hi Lily, Gino … I'm Ellie, and I'm married to that handsome lug over there. Joey, come on over here," she almost commanded. His reluctance to stand was not lost on me, but to his credit, he dutifully meandered over to his wife.

Without being prompted, Joey held out his hand, first to Gino then to Lily. "Yup, I'm her other half," he quietly said, "but definitely not the better half."

Ellie continued, "We have two terrific sons. Anthony is twenty-three … there in the Red Sox shirt. Sammy is twenty-one. Oh, he's in a Red Sox shirt also. No secret that we are all Sox fans."

"And Celtics! And Patriots!" Joey vehemently added.

"Well, we have that in common," Lily laughed toward Joey.

Hope scooted up next to her mom, saying in a stage whisper, "Too bad these guys are my cousins. They are all sooo cute!"

Success! The iceberg was officially shattered with that last comment as we spontaneously broke into laughter. The familiar bantering that I love so much was now well under way. What was I so worried about? This is the Agosti family I know and love.

"Hot dogs and hamburgers are ready. Come and get 'em," Sal shouted to the group.

The younger set stampeded, shoving their plates to his chest, completely discarding their table manners. *Yup, voracious appetites trump table manners.*

Voices were now temporarily hushed and only because of mounded plates and healthy appetites. It was satisfying to observe the kids as well as adults in animated conversations as though they were old friends.

Sal and I had agreed earlier that we should bring the keepsake box out after dinner. No sense pussy footing around or postponing the inevitable. Later, after a pleasant meal and as the cannolis and cappuccino pie were being served, I discreetly placed the box on the picnic table, which at first went unnoticed.

Joey abruptly nudged me, "What's up with that?"

"Sal and I think we should be as open and transparent today as possible. Do you agree?"

After a very, very long pause, he looked at me with glistening eyes saying, "Trina, you're a good social worker and a good sister;

I trust your decision." I grabbed him, burying my wet eyes in his neck, "Thanks, Joey. I love you." That was all the affirmation I needed to forge ahead.

"Lily, we've truly enjoyed having your family here today ... with our family. I'm going to speak for my sister and my brother now," nodding at them with a smile. "We want to be honest with you. As you know, until very recently we had no idea you existed, but we have determined to work through our roller coaster emotions, together if possible."

"I can only imagine how this has affected each of you. I have to continually remind myself that I was raised with full knowledge of all of you," she gently responded. "I must have been a monumental shock to you."

With that very sensitive comment, I slid the box closer to Lily and said, "My father ... our father kept this keepsake box hidden from us. He was guilt ridden, of that we are certain. Anyhow, we want you to have it. It is clear evidence ... you were loved."

"May I ...?" Lily said as she slowly pulled the box toward herself. When she opened the box, she immediately recognized the stack of envelopes that were tied together with an old frayed ribbon and marked with her return address. "I was always very careful to send mail only to his post office box, just as my mother had instructed," she said as she lovingly clutched the envelopes.

Not wanting her to feel any pressure, we allowed her a few minutes to thumb through the cards, pictures and notes. It was an unsettling moment for my siblings and me. Personally, I worried we might be invading her privacy. Without words or warning, she wept uncontrollably over the mementos.

Maybe this wasn't such a good idea.

Gino put his comforting arms around his wife, and we respectfully waited until she was composed enough to speak.

"This box, these memories ... they are precious to me. It is so kind of you to pass them along to me; I will treasure them. He was my hero you know. I loved him very much, yet something was always missing in our relationship. I lived my life, day in and day out, with this void deep within me that I could never fill. My only desire was to be accepted and brought into his family ... this family."

"Lily," Joey's deep voice surprised us all. "I want to tell you about our Mama."

"Yes, please. I know he loved her very deeply," she said looking at him intently with those arresting eyes ... Daddy's eyes.

"I last thing I want to do is lie, so I'm going to tell it like it is or ... was," his voice breaking. "When I found out about his infidelity, I was enraged. I was in total disbelief that this man, my hero, could have wounded my mother so profoundly, so deeply."

"I understand."

"But she ... somehow ... found out about your mother and then you. She never admitted to him that she knew anything ... at all. I don't know why, but knowing Mama, my best guess is that she was preserving his dignity. Who knows? But here's the thing, Lily ... she forgave him, which to this day still blows me away. Things could have been so different if only he found the courage to confess; I believe she would have openly embraced you. That's the kind of mama we had."

"You and your family have truly been blessed by your mama's strong character," she replied.

"Yes, yes we have. I've struggled with the weight of this burden for over three years. Sadly, I've come to the realization that I have wasted precious time: precious time that could have been better spent with her ... and with him. And so ... I want to do something on her behalf, something that would honor our Mama."

"Joey," I started "please don't beat yourself up about ..."

"Hold on a second, Trina. I need to finish, and I'm not going to pretend this is easy for me. But here goes," he cleared his throat and fixed his eyes directly on her penetrating green eyes. "Lily, today ... I want to accept you into the Agosti family or as mama would say ... graft you into the family."

I have never been more proud of my big brother than I was at that moment; he stepped forward and drew Lily into a deep hug, both of them openly weeping. By now the kids had formed an outer circle around us, intent on hearing every word. They knew our families were now forever blended.

"Lily, my mother loved this garden. She spent countless hours out here cultivating her beloved roses," I explained. "Over the years she became quite the gardener, honing her skills until she mastered the process of grafting one rose plant into another. Apparently, through trial and error, she learned that two separate rose bushes had the potential to become *one* beautiful, stronger and healthier rose bush."

Lily took in every word, while fixing her eyes on one particularly beautiful yellow rose bush.

"In the months prior to her death, Mama was continually alluding to a deep truth she learned while grafting her roses; it was far greater than simply joining two plants. In retrospect, one simple fact has become crystal clear and we now understand that her greatest desire was that her children also learn that same truth. And Lily, we finally got it!"

"What ... got what?" Lily asked.

"We believe her heart's desire was for us to extend forgiveness, should that be necessary, and to be emotionally and spiritually healed. In doing so, we would be free ... free to accept you into our family ... becoming one bigger, stronger family," I proudly proclaimed.

"Look Mom, look at that stepping stone," Hope nudged her.

"Oh how absolutely perfect ... I see it ... Garden of Hope."

"We just thought it so ironic, that years before your Hope was born, Mama named this place her Garden of Hope. She walked and lived in hope. I'd like to read this passage she highlighted in her Bible, if it's okay?"

"Certainly, please do."

"Romans 12:12 says, Rejoice in our confident hope. Be patient in trouble, and keep on praying."

For a while, everyone sat reverently digesting the scope of those few words our mama loved and lived by. "She also wrote these powerful words in the margin of her Bible, 'I must forgive! Then and only then shall bitterness be rooted out. I will be free and empowered to walk in the *hope* that the future holds,'" I continued.

"It sounds to me that your mama had a deep and abiding spiritual life. It's obvious what she penned were not trite or empty words," Lily responded.

"You got that right."

"Lily, I have a question," I ventured. "You and Gino have been blessed with a beautiful, daughter; I'm sort of curious why ... how you happened to name her Hope?"

"Well, it's really quite simple; I'm sort of an open book. As I have said, all of my life I hungered to be part of a real family ... his family. That deep desire never left me, even after I fell in love and married this wonderful guy. More than a year later, when I found out I was pregnant, hope sprung up in me like a spring flower bursting forth. My disposition changed from moody to hopeful. Gino and I, like all expectant couples, were tossing around both boy and girl names, but I knew in my heart I was going to have a girl, didn't I, Hon?"

"Sweetie, you were more than confident; I never saw anything like it," her husband agreed.

"I'm so grateful he was in agreement because at her birth, I declared her name to be Hope. It was my personal, maybe even secret way of reminding myself, every single day, every time I spoke her name, that I would someday become part of his family."

"Mom, you are the most hopeful and positive person I know— so full of hope," her daughter chimed in.

Smiling at her daughter she said, "I guess I never let go of that desire; I hoped for all good things and my heavenly Father heard both my spoken and unspoken prayers. And see how He's answered my prayers."

"Wow, that truly leaves me speechless," I said.

"Wait ... Stop the presses ... Historic moment ... Trina is speechless. I have to write this down since it will never happen again," Angie joked.

Pushing her away with a gentle nudge I snickered, "Funny, very funny."

After the wave of well-meaning laughter dissipated she continued, "After our father died, I was contacted by your family lawyer, and he gave me a letter that Dad had written. May I read it to you all?"

Serious minded again, we all nodded, anxious to hear the contents of this personal and private letter. I am quite certain my brother would have inquired about it before the end of the day had she not volunteered to share it.

She scanned everyone's eyes then began softly and quite shakily:

My dear Lily,

It is the night of your high school graduation, and I feel compelled to put pen to paper. If you are reading this letter, then you are dealing with my passing, since I have instructed my lawyer and old family friend to pass this to you in confidence.

Because of the delicate nature of our relationship, I wanted to write this letter so that you would always walk in the confidence of my love for you. I first want to say that I have always been aware of your longing to belong, to fit into a loving family. I am so very sorry that you have been deprived of brothers, sisters, and an ever present father. Your mom, however, has done an excellent job of raising you. I am very proud of you and amazed at the woman you are becoming right before my very eyes.

I have honestly tried to spend time with you without robbing the rest of my family. I won't lie to you, they are my very life. But Lily, you are just as important to me and if I could, I would have shielded you from the hurt you often felt.

Someday, you will meet and marry a very fortunate young man. I can only hope and pray that he will bring you the happiness you rightly deserve.

Please forgive me for lacking the courage to confess my infidelity to my wife. God knows how many times I tried. I cannot bear to hurt the woman I love and honestly fear losing. She is a good woman, a wonderful woman, and would have likely grown to love you.

I pray you maintain that special sweetness and gentleness I see in you. Please know that I love you and am so very sorry for any pain I have caused you.

Your loving dad

A sweet hush fell over the room as she finished reading the letter. While I never wanted this situation to occur, I suddenly began to feel something akin to my old admiration for my father welling up in me once again. Acutely aware that his sin was far reaching, still he desperately desired that Lily bore no guilt or shame. He loved this other daughter in the same way he loved us and wanted assurance that when his time came to leave this earth, she would rest in that love, as do his other three children.

With tears streaming down Joey's face, he lifted his head and smiled at Lily, then Hope. "After Pops confessed to me, I'm ashamed to admit that I became bitter and self-absorbed. I refused to give one single thought to what your life must have been like. Our Mama, on the other hand, refused to give bitterness a stronghold in her life. She had every right to wallow in self-pity, but she did not. Lily, can you find it in your heart to forgive me for my bitter attitude?"

Without missing a beat, Lily quickly walked to Joey and drew him once again into a warm embrace. "There is nothing to forgive. I truly understand how you must have felt. I never wanted to hurt you or your sisters. All I ever desired was to be accepted into this wonderful family," she said.

"And so you have received your heart's desire," Joey responded with a wide grin.

There was not one dry eye in our now stronger, healthier Agosti family as we moved about the garden, hugging and welcoming our new sister and her family.

I reminded myself that by God's grace, my mother found the strength to extend forgiveness rather than wallow in self-pity or be consumed with bitterness. Her desire to walk in obedience to God's Word set her free to live an abundant life—a life worth living.

As my eyes fell upon the *Garden of Hope* stepping stone, I whispered, "Mama ... your prayers have been answered. Your children have finally learned that lesson you so fervently prayed we would learn. And Mama ... I am confident we have already begun to reap the blessings of the abundant joy you spoke of ... joy that will continue to grow and blossom throughout our lifetimes."

Epilogue

The passing of our parents certainly left a void in our family—one that was impossible to fill. However, we have moved forward in a manner that would have made them proud. My head spins at the realization of all that has occurred over the last three years.

"Vincent, hold still a second," I smiled down at this precocious little three-year-old. "Let me fix your collar; we don't want to be late for the wedding. Sweetheart, do you know that today is a very special day ... and *you* are my very special guy," I said sweeping him into a big bear hug, just like Papa used to do with his own children.

"Trina, are you ever going to be ready? You do realize the wedding will start on time, with or without us," Sal chided me as he tickled our son.

"Sal, I still cannot believe this little boy is ours. I have known so many children in the social service system who transitioned from foster care to adoption, but this ... this child is our very own miracle."

"Yes, yes he is! We are indeed blessed. Now, little Mama, we'd better get going."

I could hardly contain my anticipation as Sammy ushered our little family to a reserved pew at the front of this lovely church.

"This is so cool, huh, Aunt Trina?" Sammy whispered before leaving us in order to seat the remaining guests.

"Yes, Sammy, this is totally cool."

Within minutes, I turned to catch Anthony escorting Jake and Angie to their reserved seats. Teary eyed but elated, she shot me that knowing raised eyebrow accompanied by a wink. Running from store to store with her was obviously worth the time and effort; there sat the most beautiful mother of the groom I have ever seen. She looked young enough to be a bride herself, thanks to her ever happy disposition and Lady Clairol.

Shortly after they were seated, the music changed, signaling the start of the wedding procession. I quickly reached for my camera and focused on our beautiful Leah, gracefully tossing rose petals on the carpet, as she stayed a few steps ahead of her sister. Mia, also absolutely stunning, held herself like royalty. Are these young women the same toddlers I babysat so many times? At sixteen and twenty-one they have blossomed into cover girl beauties—absolutely breathtaking.

My throat caught at the very first note of the familiar bridal march. Oh, how I wish Mama and Daddy could be here today, but I take consolation knowing they are witnesses to this blessed event from their place in heaven.

Naturally all eyes were fixed on the approaching bride. Cindy slowly began her walk on the pure white satin runner while clinging to her father's arm. Ted could not have been more proud of his little girl, and we could not have been more proud of Ted. Looking beautifully angelic, Cindy nervously smiled at the guests now standing in her honor until she found Kevin's face, only then did she relax. Stepping forward, he took her hand and brought it to his lips—such a sweet and meaningful gesture.

Once they were in their designated spots, all eyes turned to the second bride at the back of the church.

Gino tenderly kissed his daughter's cheek, wrapped her hand in the crook of his elbow, and together they slowly walked down the aisle where she would meet her very own prince charming. Hope was gorgeous, her emerald green eyes glistening with tears of joy. Ricky's mouth dropped, completely caught up in the vision of loveliness that was slowly approaching him. Mesmerized by her beauty, he took Kevin's lead and also reached for his bride's hand, bringing her to his side.

These two couples, so in love, soberly stood before the pastor as he asked God for His blessing on their lives and proceeded to unite them in holy matrimony before friends and family.

Today we are enjoying the joys and blessings that flowed from your act of forgiveness. Thank you, Mama.

Joey has matured in so many wonderful ways over the past three years, not the least being spiritually. He found no rest until yielding to Pops wishes stated in his last will and testament. Ellie was in total agreement that he should leave his job and take over the garage once again. We watched as he rebuilt Agosti & Son Garage back to its former level of prosperity. Eventually, Anthony was brought on board as any one of us could have safely predicted.

Ricky had been coming around the garage, but he no longer visited with Mia. He was totally smitten with Hope, who often helped out on the counter. Our family grew to love and respect Ricky and needless to say, Hope was head over heels in love with this handsome young man.

Not long after their engagement, Joey surprised Ricky by offering a position to this now skilled mechanic. He quickly became a huge asset to the business as it continued to grow by leaps and bounds. It was back to its former glory.

The day before this beautiful wedding, Joey hung a freshly painted sign for all to see: Agosti & *Sons* Garage. Ricky was swept into our crazy clan, just as we had embraced Lily and her family years before.

The double wedding ceremony was God-honoring and we were completely supportive of these two young couples. Of course a double wedding called for a double reception, and it was everything we hoped it would be and more. In keeping with the Italian way of celebrating, food and fun were the order of the day. Did I mention food?

My heart overflowed with gladness as I scanned this group, amazed at what God had done in each of their lives in just three short years.

Ted and Lana danced together, laughing and exchanging words of endearment. Their marriage, well on its way to health and stability, was nothing short of astounding. He proved himself to be serious about his family's reunification by offering himself to the pastor's regular tutelage—a miracle in our midst.

Over the years, Ricky's mom repeatedly attempted to locate her husband, to no avail. Sadly, this abandoned young man was not likely to enjoy a father-son relationship. However, Joey had obviously become his surrogate dad; his godly example of a family man strongly impressed Ricky. Because of this role model, he is much more likely now to become a wonderful husband and hopefully someday, a wonderful father.

Always the life of the party, Angie quickly initiated the conga, weaving the dancers around the tables or anyone unlucky enough to stand in her way. Jake and Angie were in rare form on this happy occasion. Watching the two of them strut their stuff on the dance floor sent ripples of laughter throughout the crowd. They were lost in the cha-cha, the twist, and eventually even the chicken dance.

Gino and Lily, a bit more sedate, yet they never missed an opportunity to trip the light fantastic on the dance floor. Lily's beautiful eyes rarely left her daughter's radiant face; she was so proud of her daughter. She told me just before the wedding that she never, in a million years, dreamed her many years of prayers would be answered in such a magnificent way. Our God is a big God and does nothing in a small way.

Sal and I each took one of Vincent's tiny hands and danced in a circle with him, which totally delighted the little guy. Instantly, I flashed back to a time when Mama and Daddy danced with each of their children in exactly the same way. We would no more break with this tradition than we could the tradition of serving plates and plates of amazing Italian cookies at a wedding reception.

Not long after the much talked about double wedding, life returned to status quo for everyone. Well, almost everyone. Being a stay-at-home mom now allows me the privilege of more fully serving in our church, just as Mama had done. Doting on our new son, however, continues to give me the biggest thrill of my life; he is inquisitive, loving and oh so precious to Sal and me. I cannot contain my laughter as he daily scampers with Buddy throughout the house. They have become the best of friends.

Kevin was offered, and accepted, an amazing position fresh out of college. The financial remuneration was considerably more than he ever expected, and all of his hard work has paid off for this young couple. Cindy, to her parents' delight, continues to work toward her own college degree while waitressing part time at our favorite restaurant. The two of them have their heads on straight and will do just fine.

Hope changed her major at Lowell State, feeling that the Lord was calling her into the field of social work. I was flattered and happy for her, confident it was a perfect fit for her personality. It would, however, be some time before she actually had her degree in hand. Because Ricky and Hope were a bit tight, financially speaking, my wonderful brother did not hesitate to offer the homestead for as long as they needed or wanted to live there. Everyone was in total agreement.

"Come here, sweetheart, let's get you dressed. What do you say we go for a drive?" I cajoled my little boy. "Why don't we pop in for a visit to see Hope? Would you like that?"

As though on automatic pilot, my car turned into the driveway of the old homestead, just as it had a thousand times before.

After repeatedly ringing the doorbell, Vincent and I toddled around to the back yard in search of Hope.

We found her crouched down on her knees, weeding the garden, exactly as our Mama had so often done.

"Hey, there you are! Vincent and I came for a quick visit, and I brought biscotti … fresh out of the oven."

"Oh man, I'll never lose any weight being part of this family. Wow, do they ever smell scrumptious, Will you share the recipe?"

"It's Mama's recipe, and I certainly will share it with you. So, how is the new bride?"

"Oh, Trina, I'm terrific. I love being married to Ricky, and I love living here and being part of this amazing family."

"Well, sweetheart, we love you too and are delighted this place makes you so happy."

"It does, it really does. I especially love this garden; it is so tranquil out here—like being in another world. But it's more than that; it's peace-giving. What I'm trying to say is … I don't know … I get a special feeling whenever I'm in this garden. This is where I come to meet with God, to seek God."

"Hearing that would have made my Mama very happy. I believe the same was true for her."

"Really, now that is amazing."

"Mama, cookie?" Vincent reached into the well-worn biscotti tin and pulled out one for each of his pudgy little hands. "Mmm," he grinned up at us with powdered sugar all over his beautiful little face.

I smiled at this sweet young bride and said, "Never in a million years, Hope, would I have guessed that this garden Mama loved so much would one day become your very own garden? Her Garden of Hope was in the heart of God from the very beginning."

What an awesome God we serve!

Contact Information

To order additional copies of this book, please visit
www.redemption-press.com.
Also available on Amazon.com and BarnesandNoble.com
Or by calling toll free 1 (844) 273-3336.